Help Me, Rhonda

Book 3 in the
Northwoods Adventures Series

By Amy A. Corron

Copyright 2006 by Amy A. Corron

Help Me, Rhonda
by Amy A. Corron

Printed in the United States of America

ISBN 1-59781-757-0

All rights reserved solely by the author. The author guarantees all contents are original and do not infringe upon the legal rights of any other person or work. No part of this book may be reproduced in any form without the permission of the author. The views expressed in this book are not necessarily those of the publisher.

Unless otherwise indicated, Bible quotations are taken from the New King James version of the Bible. Copyright © 1982 by Thomas Nelson, Inc.

Contact the author through
www.northwoodsnovels.com

www.xulonpress.com

This book is a work of fiction. Although Atlanta, Michigan is a very real place (located half-way between Gaylord and Alpena), I have taken much creative license with the setting for the sake of the story. All the characters portrayed in this novel are figments of my imagination. Any resemblance to real people, living or dead, is merely a coincidence.

This book is dedicated to my nephew, Brett Hannum, formerly of the United States Army, 75th Ranger Regiment. And to my nephew, Petty Officer 1st Class Justin Johnston of the United States Navy, my niece, SPC 4 Casey Shehu of the United States Army and in loving memory of my "nephew-in-law," PFC Juan Garza of the United States Marines, who made the ultimate sacrifice for his country on April 8, 2003, during Operation Iraqi Freedom. And to all of those who are currently serving, or who have ever served, in the United States military. You are my heroes! May God bless and keep you all.

A special Thank You to my nephew, Sgt. Gary Cole, Jr., of the Evart, Michigan police department, and to my nephew, Brett Hannum, formerly of the US Army. Their expertise and input were essential in helping me "keep it real."

CHAPTER ONE

Spring was in the air. Rhonda Weaver rolled down the window of her 4x4 pickup truck and stuck her head out, breathing deeply of the damp morning air. It always took a little longer for spring to raise her sleepy head in the woods of northern Michigan. But now the earth was finally shedding her mantle of snow, and a faint shadow of green could be seen in open patches of ground. After months of hibernation, Rhonda couldn't drink in enough of the fresh air with its promise of warmth and new birth.

"Behold, I make all things new," Rhonda murmured the words from the Book of Revelation as she took a deep breath. God was making good on His promise. The deadness of winter was passing away. Spring was bringing forth new life.

In no real hurry on this Saturday morning, Rhonda drove slowly down the rutted dirt road, heading toward Atlanta and her job at the Spot of

Tea Shop. She was supposed to be there at nine, but since getting married last November Rhonda's boss, Emma, was no stickler for punctuality. Emma was too blissfully happy being Mrs. Tyler McGillis to care if Rhonda was a few minutes late. Considering Emma's own romantic heart, Rhonda was sure her boss would understand her need to soak up a little bit of spring's promise.

As she passed the Cooper farm, Rhonda automatically glanced toward the farmhouse, making sure all was in order. She slammed on the brakes. A gleaming pickup truck was parked in the driveway. Who would be visiting? she wondered. The Cooper place had been empty since Carl and Deanne Cooper had been killed in a tragic car accident two years before. Their oldest son had left for the army years ago and hadn't been heard from since. A younger son, Rhonda's childhood playmate and sweetheart, had been murdered when Rhonda was a freshman in high school.

Her truck idled in the middle of the road as her blue eyes examined the vehicle with Georgia plates. The front door of the house stood ajar and the drapes that had been tightly closed for more than two years were pulled aside, inviting the morning sun into the living room. In a split-second decision, Rhonda turned the wheel of her truck and pulled into the drive. Though the Weaver and Cooper farmsteads were separated by nearly a mile of fields and woodlands, the Weavers took their job as neighbor seriously. Rhonda felt it her sworn duty to investigate this uninvited guest.

She pulled up next to a sparkling, cadet blue Dodge truck that put her battered, mud-covered 4x4 to shame. At least her tires were bigger, she thought smugly as she opened her door and slid to the ground. Slamming the door, she looked around. As she took a step toward the front porch that extended across the front of the cozy, stone farmhouse, a man with a drawn pistol materialized from around the corner. Rhonda gulped. The barrel of the gun was pointed directly at her chest.

"Who are you and what do you want?" the stranger asked, approaching her stealthily. The hand that held the gun was alarmingly steady. Though he was of medium height, his arms bulged with muscle and the black t-shirt he wore stretched across a broad chest and shoulders.

Rhonda gathered courage she didn't feel and sent up a brief prayer.

"Okay Lord, help me out here," she muttered under her breath. "I think I should be asking you that question, mister," she said with more bravado than bravery.

The man stopped ten feet in front of her. Grey eyes, as cold and hard as tempered steel, never wavered from her.

"Since I have the firepower, I think that gives me the upper hand in the interrogation department."

His hair was black as pitch, cropped close to his scalp on the sides, a little longer on top. The hatred in his eyes kept Rhonda rooted to the spot.

"I'm Rhonda Weaver, from the next farm over." She gestured with her head in the general direction of her home. "No one lives in this house anymore. When I saw the truck and the front door open, I figured I'd better check it out."

The pistol was lowered. The man clicked on the safety and tucked the gun in the waistband of his jeans.

"Someone lives here now," he said. "I'm Wes Cooper."

"Wes?" Rhonda's voice squeaked with disbelief. "I never would have recognized you! I thought you were in the army."

"Was. I just got out." He moved forward and Rhonda was pinned once again, not by the gun but by the gunmetal grey eyes. "Little Rhonda Weaver, huh? I never would have recognized you, either."

"Well, you've been gone a long time. I've grown up some since then."

"Some." His eyes raked her up and down, measuring her diminutive size as a cynical smile turned up a corner of his hard mouth. "You use a step ladder to get up in that truck?"

"I manage just fine, thank you." Rhonda's red-headed temper began to rise and she drew herself up to the full extent of her five-foot frame. "You always greet your neighbors with a pistol in your hand?"

"Yep, till I know what's what."

Rhonda raised an eyebrow but let the comment slide.

"How come no one knew you were coming home?" she asked instead.

"No one to tell, remember." The ice was back in his eyes and had seeped into his voice.

Help Me, Rhonda

"I'm sorry about your parents," Rhonda said with sincere sympathy. But how could she convey that sympathy to the virtual stranger in front of her? "You could have called us. We could have at least aired the house out for you…"

"Given me a welcome home party?" Wes interrupted. "Maybe a parade? I've heard some soldiers coming home from Iraq have gotten those." Sarcasm dripped from every word.

"You were in Iraq?" Rhonda's heart nearly stopped at the troubling thought. Of course he would have been, she should have known. Why had the thought never occurred to her in all the years since Wes had disappeared to join the service? "We didn't know. If we had, we would have given you a parade. Maybe we still will."

"I've been lots of places a pretty girl like you would never want to see," Wes said, fishing a pack of cigarettes from his t-shirt pocket. He shook one out and placed it between his lips, digging in his front jeans pocket for a lighter. "And we both know no one in this town is going to give Wes Cooper a parade for coming home alive."

The compliment to her looks might have made Rhonda blush if it hadn't been for the distasteful cigarette dangling from the chiseled lips that spoke it.

"You would think if God spared you from getting killed by the enemy then you would have enough sense to not jeopardize your health with those stinky cancer sticks," she complained, waving smoke away from her face.

"God," Wes snorted, taking a deep drag on the cigarette. "The only person who gets credit for me being here today is me. I'm alive because I'm very good at killing people."

"Wes, what a terrible thing to say!" The cold admission had Rhonda admonishing as she temporarily forgot about the cigarette and the dangerous piece of metal tucked away in his waistband. "Your parents raised you better than that."

"And what did it get them?" he asked, taking a menacing step forward. Rhonda shrank back and Wes stopped. "I've got work to do."

Work! Rhonda glanced down at her watch, blanching. Oh man, was she late now!

"Yeah, me too. I was on my way into town when I saw your truck." Nerves suddenly overtook her former bluster and she began to ramble. "You remember Emma Dawson? She owns a teashop in town now and just got married last fall. She's Emma McGillis now. Lots of things have changed around here. Nate Sweeney is getting married in June. You should come into town and see everyone. You can find just about everybody at the Spot of Tea."

"I can just picture that," Wes said with derision. "Wes Cooper walking into a fancy teashop and greeting the residents of Atlanta like he was a normal, upstanding citizen." He took a drag on his cigarette, a wry smile twisting his lips. "I don't think that's going to happen. We both know the people around here would only welcome me back if I came home in a casket."

"You're wrong about that, Wes," Rhonda argued, her heart breaking at the bleakness in his eyes. She couldn't help but remember the boy he had once been, before circumstances had thrown them both a curve ball. Wes had left Atlanta a shunned and rejected kid and had returned a cold and bitter man.

"No one wanted you to get killed," she continued. "Like I said, a lot of things have changed since you've been gone. I hope you'll give us all a chance to prove it." With that she walked to her truck, throwing one last look at him before climbing into the cab. "Hope to see you around."

Getting in, she slammed the door and backed the truck around. Heading down the driveway, she couldn't resist glancing in the rearview mirror for one last look at the man with the pistol in his belt.

"Fat chance of that," Wes muttered, squinting through the rooster tail of dust the departing pickup left hanging over his driveway. He took a final drag on his cigarette before tossing it to the ground, grinding the butt under the heel of his boot. He really should quit. If he could just come up with one good reason to kick the habit.

Turning, Wes strode back around the corner of the sturdy farmhouse, built by his grandfather from native rock dug out of the surrounding fields. His eyes glanced up to the second story windows and took in the neat, white trim. Even after sitting empty for two years, the house was still in tip-top shape. Of course, his father wouldn't have left it any other way.

Wes felt the familiar stab of pain at the thought of his parents and all the empty years that hung suspended between them, a bridge he could not cross. He shook his head to clear the thought. Nothing he could do about it now. He headed toward the hip-roofed barn situated far behind the house, its once red paint faded to a soft rust.

Rhonda Weaver, all grown up. Well, sort of, Wes snorted. Of all the people to run into on his first day home, he never would have dreamed it would be her. Wes stopped outside the huge double doors of the barn and searched the clear, blue sky.

"You been keeping an eye on her, Bri?" he asked, looking up. "She's grown into a pretty, little thing; red hair, freckles and all."

The memory of his brother seared as it always did. Time did not heal all wounds. Curling his hand around the door frame, Wes felt the rough wood cut into his flesh, welcomed the physical pain that pushed away the emotional hurt. He remembered well his brother's devotion to the little red-headed girl next door. Now here she was, vibrant and alive while Brian had returned; ashes to ashes, dust to dust.

A welcome home parade! What a laugh. Only Wes didn't really find the humor in it. The bitter bile rose in his throat as he remembered how quickly the town had turned on him after his brother's murder. Burying the painful memories back in the deep recesses of his mind, Wes instead turned his eyes to the surrounding farm fields. Dark furrows turned their brows up to the warming sun. Rhonda's father must have been over to plow. Wes realized he would have to go over and talk to Mr. Weaver about the lease agreement on the land. His land.

Fishing into his pocket, Wes withdrew a white envelope, unfolded it and withdrew the sheet of paper from inside. His eyes quickly scanned the anonymous letter, the fourth such missive he had received since his parents' death. Someone wanted his property, badly. Wes raised his eyes from the paper to once again stare out over the fertile fields just waiting for seed. What did this land hold that someone else was so desperate to get their hands on?

Refolding the letter, Wes slid it back into his pocket and turned to enter the barn. He had work to do, plans for the future of this farm that he had to get started on. For years, all Wes had wanted was to return to his home in peace. Dreams of coming home to work the land were about all that had kept him sane as he slogged through jungles, up mountains and across deserts.

He checked the pistol at his waist. Rhonda Weaver was wrong. Some things didn't change and Wes knew there was at least one person out there who wasn't going to be happy that he had returned to Atlanta alive.

The silver bell over the front door of the Spot of Tea tinkled as Rhonda pulled it open and hurried inside. Four heads swiveled her way. Emma and Tyler sat at a table near the door along with Nate Sweeney and Penelope Scott.

"Well, it's about time you showed up," Emma complained with a smile. "Nate here was just about to call out a search party." Emma motioned toward the sheriff's deputy.

"I'm sorry I'm so late," Rhonda apologized, sliding to a stop at the end of the foursome's table. "But you aren't going to believe who I ran into."

"Like, literally? I hope you didn't hurt them with that truck of yours," Penny said, pushing her long, blond hair back over her shoulder.

"No, not literally." Rhonda waved away the joke. "You aren't going to believe it. Guess."

"But you just said we wouldn't believe who it was, so how can we guess?" Tyler wanted to know.

"You wouldn't be able to guess anyway, Tyler," Rhonda explained. "You don't know him. And neither do you, Penny. But Emma does, and so does Nate."

"Okay then." Nate took a sip of coffee and draped an arm over the back of Penny's chair. "Don't leave us in suspense. Who did you run into?"

"Wes Cooper." Rhonda was satisfied with their reaction as Emma and Nate both stared at her in shocked surprise.

"You're kidding," Emma finally said.

"Wes Cooper? Are you sure?" Nate asked. "He's been gone nearly ten years."

"Well, he's home now. Must have arrived last night or early this morning. I talked to him on my way here." Rhonda purposely left out the fact that Wes had greeted her at gunpoint. As a Montmorency County Sheriff's officer, Sergeant Nate Sweeney would not be too thrilled with that piece of information.

"Well, well, well. So the prodigal son has returned," Nate said, turning a spoon over and over on the tabletop. "Whoever would have believed it?"

"Why now?" Emma asked, still trying to digest the news.

"Because he just got out of the army," Rhonda explained.

"Who is Wes Cooper?" Tyler asked.

"And why is his coming home such a big deal?" Penny wanted to know.

"It's a long, sad story," Emma said, shaking her head. "He's a local boy. Well, not a boy anymore."

No, Rhonda thought, imagining Wes in his tight black t-shirt holding a gun on her. He definitely wasn't a boy anymore.

"I think he was at least a year ahead of me in school," Emma was saying. "Funny how people get frozen in time. He must be nearly 30 now."

"His brother, Brian, was murdered," Nate took up the story, sliding a compassionate look Rhonda's way. "About ten years ago. The case was never solved. A few months after it happened, Wes took off and joined the army. No one ever heard from him again. His parents were killed in a car wreck a couple of winters ago and he didn't even come home for the funeral. It was never proven, but Wes was considered the prime suspect in his brother's murder. His running away after it happened just added more weight to people's suspicions. Of course, this was several years before I joined the force, but I've seen the file. It's still an open case."

"Well, he's home now," Rhonda said, trying to dispel the memory of the man with cold grey eyes and a gun in his hand. "He said he's been to Iraq, and a lot of other horrible places. He's served our country. I think that earns him the benefit of the doubt."

Rhonda turned and headed into the kitchen where she tied an apron around her slender waist. When she came back into the dining room, she noticed Blake Dalton sitting at a table sipping coffee. Rhonda and Blake had been dating since Emma and Tyler's wedding the previous November. He had taken to stopping in at the Spot of Tea in the mornings before starting work at the Amaco station just down the street.

"Well, hey Blake, I didn't see you sitting there," she said, approaching him.

"That's okay, baby," Blake put an arm around her waist and pulled her possessively to his side. "I understand you were a little distracted when you came in. I couldn't help but overhear the news about Wes Cooper. That's really something, ain't it?"

"Sure threw me for a loop," Rhonda agreed, draping an arm over his shoulders covered in a dark blue work shirt. She pulled a white-blond curl back from Blake's forehead and gave it a teasing tug as she looked into his warm, brown eyes. "It will give the town plenty to talk about, that's for sure."

"That's for sure." Blake nodded and smiled. "I just hope it doesn't start a ruckus, him coming back after all these years. People around here have long memories. Yep, I sure hope it doesn't start a ruckus."

CHAPTER TWO

Wes jumped down from the seat of the tractor he had been tuning up and brushed a wrist over his brow, avoiding his grease-stained hands. Funny how things came back to you, he thought. It was as if he hadn't been gone for ten years. Like riding a bike, he hadn't forgotten the peculiar quirks of his father's old John Deere. Pulling a rag from his back pocket, Wes wiped at the grease on his hands as he strolled to the barn door. A grumble from his stomach told him it was time to take a lunch break.

The back door of the farmhouse led into a glassed-in mud room. Work coats, covered with a fine layer of dust, still hung from pegs along one wall. Without thinking, Wes reached for a cap hanging from one of the pegs. His dad's hat, with his father's sweat still staining the band. He turned the bill around in his hands and stared at the seed company logo on the front. Like a whale breaching for air, memories long buried came rushing to the surface. Wes felt the sting of tears and swallowed hard. He hung the hat back in its place and turned to push open the door into the kitchen.

Thoughts of hunger had fled. Instead, Wes found himself prowling the house that had been home to his family for three generations. The rooms echoed with a sad emptiness. The furniture, still covered with white sheets, sat like hulking ghosts, the only inhabitants of the home that once rang with laughter and promise.

His hand trailed along the banister as he climbed the narrow stairs to the bedrooms on the second floor. Pushing open the door to Brian's old room, Wes found himself holding his breath, unsure what he would see. A shrine to his dead brother, the favored son? An odd mixture of relief and resentment filled him as his eyes took in the neatly made day-bed, the sewing machine sitting on a table under the dormer window, shelves filled with an assortment of unfamiliar books and brick-a-brack. What had happened to all of Brian's things?

Pulling the door closed, Wes walked the short distance down the hall to his own room. Heart beating with an unusual dread, he turned the ancient iron knob and pushed the door wide. He stood on the threshold, stunned. It was as if he had entered a time warp. The room was exactly as he remembered. The green and white checked quilt still covered the bed. His football trophies and 4-H ribbons still lined the shelves that ran around the perimeter of the room near the ceiling. Wes took a hesitant step farther into the room, looking around in wonder. Every piece of his former life was still in place, frozen in time, as if his parents had been waiting all those years for his return. And he had never come back.

The emotions clawed their way up from deep inside him, making Wes want to throw himself across the bed and weep. Instead, he forced them down with steel-like resolve and walked to the dormer window. His old guitar leaned against the corner and he picked it up, blowing away two years of dust from the polished wood. Without conscious thought, he cradled the instrument in his arms and strummed a few familiar chords.

The memories welled again, forcing Wes to close his eyes and lean his head against the cool glass of the window. Maybe coming home wasn't such a good idea after all. There were too many ghosts here. Wes was beginning to think there was no place on earth where he could find peace from the memories that haunted him. Thousands of miles across the globe hadn't been far enough. Why had he been foolish enough to think he could face the apparitions in his own back yard?

"So, what do you really think about Wes Cooper being back in town?" Rhonda asked Emma as the two cleaned up from the day's business. Rhonda carefully washed the antique cups and saucers while Emma took an inventory of ingredients on the kitchen shelves.

"I'm not sure what to think," Emma admitted. She finished counting tea bags before scribbling the total on her notepad.

"Blake's worried it could cause a ruckus. He says people around here have long memories."

"Well, that's all too true," Emma agreed. "His coming back to town will dig up a lot of things that some people would say were best left buried."

"Like Brian?" Rhonda asked, eyes wide.

"Like Brian. Oh, I don't mean literally," Emma explained, seeing the troubled look in her friend's eyes. " I don't think they'll exhume the body or anything. But figuratively. It will bring the whole thing back up again, have people talking and wondering and probably pointing fingers. I would say a ruckus is a mild description of what Wes Cooper's return to Atlanta could cause."

"Do you think he did it? Killed Brian, I mean?" Rhonda nearly choked on the question.

Emma shrugged and leaned back against the counter. "I don't know." Her dark brows drew together in thought. "Obviously there wasn't enough evidence to prove that he did, or he would have been arrested. I would think you would know better than me, anyway. You knew Wes a lot better than I did, being neighbors. Plus you and Brian were pretty much inseparable back then."

Rhonda stared down into the sudsy water in the deep, stainless steel sink and blinked back tears.

"Brian was my best friend," she whispered. Lifting her hands from the dishwater, she wiped them on her apron and turned around. "His murder caused a lot of hurt and confusion. I could never figure out what he had done that was so horrible that God would strike him down like that. You know, back then, with six kids to raise, my parents used the fear of God to keep us in line. For years, when I thought who was responsible for Brian's death, I always thought it was God's fault."

Rhonda crossed her arms protectively over her chest, trying to contain the painful memories from long ago. She leaned a hip against the edge of the sink.

"I think my parents tried to protect me from the rumors about Wes, but I heard them. In a town as small as Atlanta, it was impossible not to. I think that caused even more confusion for me, the rumors, the whispers. It would have been easier had my parents just sat down and discussed the whole thing and got it all out in the open. I'm not blaming them," she emphasized, looking at Emma across the room. "I'm just saying, for a 15 year old, well, that's a hard enough time in a girl's life as it is. Brian's murder and everything that surrounded it, just made things harder for me in a lot of ways, you know?"

Emma nodded, as if she did know.

"Anyway, I didn't know Wes all that well. He was four years older than me, three years older than Brian. It was Brian I was always tagging after. If there was a chore the two boys were doing together, Wes tolerated me, called me 'kid' all the time, rarely by my name. He had this mystique for a teenage girl. I always thought he was the handsomer of the two, but Brian was the more caring and sensitive one. Wes was responsible, a hard worker; Brian was the dreamer. I always thought their parents spoiled Brian a little more than they did Wes, but Brian made it easy to spoil him, always coming into the kitchen with flowers he'd picked in the garden, or a baby kitten to show his mom. She would fill a plate with cookies and shoo us back outside, never bothering to ask if Brian had done the chores she originally sent him out to do."

Rhonda turned and plunged her hands into the cooling water. She turned on the hot tap and swished her dishrag around, feeling the emotions swirling inside her. It all had been a long time ago, but talking about it brought it all back as if it had happened only yesterday. Turning off the water, she sniffed and went back to her dishwashing.

"I grew up believing Brian was my soul mate. I never wondered 'who will I marry?' I just always assumed it would be Brian. Looking back now, I don't even know if I was really *in* love with him, I just loved him. Always. When he died, it left this huge, gaping hole in my life. I tried not to think too much about who killed him. But I never believed it was Wes."

Rhonda carefully rinsed the delicate china and set it in the dish drainer, her mind lingering on another time and place.

"It's true there wasn't a lot of love lost between them, the older Wes got. When we hit our teen years, Wes had less patience for Brian's antics. And as he took on more of the farm responsibilities, he seemed to resent his parents' favoritism of Brian more. But murder?" Rhonda shook her head, making her curly, red ponytail sway. "No, I don't think Wes hated Brian enough to murder him."

"Jealousy and resentment, that's enough motive for some people," Emma said.

Rhonda thought of Wes' declaration that morning, that he was very good at killing people. Had his expertise started with his brother? The thought sent pain knifing straight through her, just like the knife that had plunged into Brian's chest. Blake had been right, Wes Cooper coming home was creating a ruckus, and it was starting in Rhonda's own heart.

Wes strode across the lower pasture, crushing tender shoots of green grass under his boots. As if they had a will of their own, his feet had carried him down the stairs and across the field to the edge of the cedar swamp. The trail was still discernable through the bracken and undergrowth, worn deep into the ground by his and Brian's feet over the course of so many years. Wes remembered well how, as young boys, they had pretended it was an Indian trail, traveled by moccasin-wearing braves searching for game. The trail had been their door to high adventure. For Brian, it had ended with the biggest adventure of his life.

Pushing aside the overgrown branches that reached out to tug at his face and arms, Wes picked his way down the trail until it broke out into a clearing, a murky pond just a few yards away. Tree stumps rose from the surface of the water and at the far end an abandoned beaver lodge rose like the shaggy hump of a camel.

Wes stopped, his grey eyes scanning his surroundings out of habit, his ears alert to the flutter of birds' wings in the bramble. How little had changed in ten years. The undergrowth crowded in a little closer to the trail, the trees reached their seeking arms a little farther out over the surface of the water. But for the most part, nothing had changed.

In the center of the clearing, just a few feet from the pond's shore, was the tree. It was much taller and broader now, the oak beneath which Brian had died.

Looking down at his hands, Wes could still see his brother's blood staining his skin, could still feel its sticky warmth. Absently, he rubbed his thumb over his forefinger, lost in memory. He distinctly remembered the smell of death, the smell of blood soaking into the earth. It had been seared into his brain that day. Wes lifted his hands in front of his face, seeing Brian's blood there. His had been the first, but it wasn't the last.

His gut twisting with grief and guilt, Wes dropped his hands and turned his face to the sky. A different memory assailed him. A Bible story from his distant youth, of Cain and Able. What had God said to Cain? "The voice of your brother's blood cries out to Me from the ground." Would it forever be the same for him? Would Brian's blood cry out from the ground, staining him with guilt forever?

Wes finally realized the truth. He would find no peace here, or anywhere else, until the truth of his brother's murder came to light.

CHAPTER THREE

Rhoda trailed Penny, Nate, Emma and Tyler out of church, into the weak warmth of the April sun. She had fallen in love with the church, the congregation and Pastor Bennett during Emma and Tyler's wedding festivities. It had taken time for her parents to accept her decision to attend another church. They were good, hard-working, God-fearing folk, and they had raised their children well. Eventually they saw that Rhoda was growing and thriving spiritually and embraced the change. It was here that Rhoda had finally been able to stop blaming God for Brian's death and had learned about her loving Savior.

"I thought Blake might come this morning," Emma observed, turning her steady, hazel gaze on Rhonda.

Rhonda tensed. She knew this was coming. Blake's irregular church attendance was a sore spot with Emma. Rhonda wasn't happy with it either, but she was not Blake's keeper. She knew what the Bible said about being "unequally yoked," but it wasn't like Blake was a heathen. And they weren't married yet, or even engaged.

"He probably got called into work. They're short of service people and Blake's the best mechanic they've got," Rhonda automatically made the excuse.

"Hmmm," was all Emma would say, obviously not swallowing the explanation. "Well, anyway, since you're on your own, why don't you join us for lunch? Nate and Penny are coming home with me and Tyler. I've got a ham in the crock pot. There's plenty if you want to come."

Rhonda looked at the two couples, feeling like the odd-man-out.

"Come on, Rhonda," Penny encouraged. "What else are you going to do?"

"Fold laundry?"

"Oh, that's sounds like a hoot," Penny snorted. "Wouldn't you rather come with us and listen to Nate and Tyler regale us with their harrowing tales of crime and rescue?"

"Gee, put like that, how can I possibly refuse?" Rhonda laughed and headed toward her truck. She really did appreciate the friendship the two couples offered, and they always tried so hard to include her. But Rhonda couldn't help but wonder, if Blake had come to church, would the invitation to lunch still been issued?

A short time later they were all seated around Emma and Tyler's dining table, enjoying a wonderful Sunday dinner of ham, scalloped potatoes, salad and crusty rolls. True to Penny's word, Nate and Tyler were entertaining the women with a story of a recent incident where both the sheriff's department and the fire and rescue squad had been called upon.

"So, Nate and Lydia and me and Caleb walk up to the door real slowly," Tyler explained. "And what do we hear? A woman screaming, 'I'm gonna kill you, I'm gonna kill you,' so Nate and Lydia immediately draw their weapons, and me and Caleb get as far behind them as we can get!"

"I swear this is one for the record books," Nate said, shaking his dark head, his blue eyes twinkling with merriment.

"The neighbors are all standing on the sidewalk, staring," Tyler continued. "Nate pounds on the door and yells, 'Police, open up!' The woman starts screaming 'go away, nobody's home, go away. I'm going to kill you.' Caleb and I turn to the neighbors, asking them who is in the house, and they all just shrug and shake their heads and tell us as far as they know, it's old Mrs. Garfield and she always has to yell because Mr. Garfield is stone deaf, but they've never heard her threaten to kill him before."

Tyler took a bite of his dinner and chewed, still grinning. When he had swallowed, he took up the story once more.

"Nate calls for backup and when they arrive, here's all these cops storming the door of this pathetic little house. Nate's yelling 'put the gun down' as he charges through the door and when they get inside, what do they see?" Tyler's green eyes sparkled with laughter as he looked at Nate.

"What? What did you see?" Rhonda asked Nate, intrigued.

"A big, blue parrot."

Rhonda quickly covered her mouth with a napkin before half-chewed food could go flying across the table.

"A parrot?" She laughed, choking. She quickly took a sip of iced tea.

"Yep, a parrot. He was sitting up on top of the curtain rod, going up and down, screaming fit to kill. Mr. and Mrs. Garfield were nowhere to be found. Seems they had gone over to Alpena to shop. The parrot had belonged to Mrs. Garfield's sister in Flint, who is right now sitting in jail for shooting her husband. I guess the previous owner used to scream at her husband all the time that she was going to kill him, until finally one day she made good on the threat. The parrot was just mimicking what he had heard." Nate shook his head and turned his attention back to his meal.

"Unbelievable," Rhonda said, giggling. "I can just imagine a bunch of cops storming a house and all that's inside is a parrot. Did you cuff his little wings together? Read him his rights?"

"I told you it was one for the record books."

Rhonda continued giggling. "I'm so glad Penny talked me into coming. She's right, hearing that story was much more entertaining that folding laundry!"

"Well, I sort of had an ulterior motive for wanting you to come to lunch with us," Penny admitted.

All eyes, including Rhonda's, turned Penny's way.

"It's only a couple of months until the wedding, and as you guys know, Nate has made arrangements to move my mother here."

Penny's mother was the victim of a massive stroke and currently resided at an assisted living facility in Detroit.

"Nate and I wanted to talk it over with Rhonda and see if she might possibly be interested in earning some extra money by helping with my mother's care."

"But I'm not a nurse," Rhonda said, laying a hand on her chest. "I don't know anything about taking care of a stroke patient."

"You wouldn't really have to know anything," Penny explained. "She'll have a visiting nurse come in each day to care for her medical needs. I was thinking more of someone I could call on to keep her company, if I'm working and Nate's on nights, that sort of thing. It would be something you could work around your schedule at the Spot of Tea, since Emma doesn't normally need you full-time. You've got a couple of months to think it over. Will you at least consider it?"

"Of course I will," Rhonda agreed instantly.

"There's only one problem," Emma cut in.

"What problem?" Penny asked, turning her golden gaze on Emma. Rhonda, too, looked at her boss, questioning.

"I'm going to be needing Rhonda at the shop more. I hadn't gotten a chance to talk it over with her, but I was preparing to offer her a full-time position." Emma and Tyler exchanged a loving glance

Help Me, Rhonda

across the table as a soft smile turned up Emma's lips. "You see, the reason we asked all of you to lunch was to make an announcement. Tyler and I are going to have a baby."

"A baby!" Rhonda squealed and jumped from her chair, throwing her napkin on her plate. She rushed around the table to throw her arms around Emma from behind. "That's the greatest news I've heard in awhile! Congratulations!" Emma chuckled and gave Rhonda a one-armed hug. Rhonda promptly went to Tyler and gave him a kiss on his scarred cheek. "A baby. You're going to be a dad. Isn't that the coolest thing?"

"Yeah, I have to admit, I think it's pretty cool," Tyler said, his eyes resting tenderly on his wife.

Rhonda took her seat as Penny and Nate got up to give the happy couple their congratulations. Excited babbling rang in the small dining room. A baby! Rhonda stared down at the remnants of her salad and tried to quell the longing that had sprung up in her heart. Her gaze strayed to the four people who had found love and happiness and a tiny seed of jealousy put forth a seeking root, trying to take hold. She shook her head and crushed the feeling. She loved all of them, she wouldn't deny them their happiness for the world.

"Well, that still leaves us with our dilemma then," Penny said as she resumed her seat.

"What about Mrs. Brisby?" Rhonda asked, referring to the owner of the cottage Penny rented. "She was a teacher for years. She has tons of patience, and she's a widow. She might be interested."

"That's a great idea, Rhonda," Penny said, grateful for the suggestion. "I can't believe I hadn't thought of it. I'll ask her first thing tomorrow."

The Briley Township cemetery lay just outside Atlanta proper, on a stretch of flat meadowland interspersed with pine trees and bordered by a high, white, iron picket fence. Wes turned into the drive and drove slowly toward the rear of the cemetery as if it hadn't been a decade since he had last been there. He stopped at the familiar spot and turned off the ignition, sitting quietly for several moments.

It was peaceful here, calm. A few small flags fluttered over the graves of past veterans. When it came his time, would there be anyone to place a flag on his grave? Wes doubted it.

Slowly, Wes got out of the truck and made his way across the bed of pine needles to the granite headstones. He squatted down, mindlessly plucking away a few weeds that had sprung up at the base of the marker. He figured they would be here, buried next to Brian, their beloved son.

Sitting on the ground, Wes leaned back on his arms and stared up at the pale blue sky, fighting the thickness in his throat. A sudden breeze came up, making the pine trees sigh and sway. A chill was in the wind, but Wes didn't feel it. His body had been schooled long ago to pay no attention to temperature or discomfort. Swallowing hard, he finally forced himself to look at the names engraved on the black granite.

"Hey Mom, Dad," the words fought their way past the lump in his throat. "I'm sorry I wasn't here to say goodbye. I was over there in Afghanistan, fighting the Taliban. Couldn't just hop a plane and fly home. Of course, by time the news reached me where I was, it was too late. You wouldn't believe the places I've been. Your boy has seen more than his fair share of war, I can tell you that. Seems like I've been doing nothing but fighting one battle after another for ten years or more now. I'm beginning to wonder if it will ever end."

Wes sat forward, folding his legs Indian-style. He dashed a tear from his cheek as the cold north wind bore down.

"It all started with Brian here." He patted the grass over his brother's grave. "And it seems it's not going to end 'till I wind up in the ground with you all. Maybe then I'd have some peace. Some blessed peace."

He laughed, a bitter, harsh sound.

"Guess that won't happen either, since you guys are living in glory, singing the hallelujah chorus, and we all know I'm headed straight for hell. A man can't kill as many people as I have and then go striding up to the pearly gates, expecting to be let in. No, I guess I'm stuck here, fighting this thing out to the bitter end. I just wish I understood what's going on. None of it makes any sense."

Early that morning, Wes had been awakened by the sound of the barn door slamming. He had gotten up to find the door wide open, the wind blowing it back against the side of the barn. He knew for a fact he had secured the door before heading in for the night. Upon investigation, he had found the tools on the workbench moved, rearranged to form two simple words.

Leave now.

Someone was already up to no good. Chiseled lips turned up in a mocking smile. Wes didn't believe in ghosts, and the four letters he had received in the past two years erased all thoughts of mischievous spirits from his mind. No, someone real, someone of flesh and blood, was hoping to scare Wes Cooper into leaving Atlanta. Whoever it was, they had no idea who they were messing with. Wes had seen and done too much in the past ten years to scare easily. A creaking barn door and a silly warning weren't going to do it. He was a soldier, highly trained, a fighting force of one. And he was ready to fight for his home and his happiness.

Dark was just beginning to fall when the doorbell of the Weaver home pealed out a long, bonging note. Rhonda's little sister, Becca, came careening down the stairs just as Rhonda rushed from the sunken family room toward the door.

"I'll get it," Rhonda informed Becca, tugging on her sister's ponytail. "It's probably Blake."

The fifteen-year-old stuck out her tongue in a childish gesture of sibling rivalry.

"Fine. I was just going for some ice cream," she said, turning toward the huge, inviting kitchen at the back of the house.

Rhonda swung the front door open, a ready smile on her lips. The smile froze in place when she saw Wes standing on the front porch. He was wearing a faded denim jacket that stretched near to bursting over his wide shoulders, a black t-shirt just visible underneath. His eyes still held the cool distance of the day before.

"Wes, hi, I wasn't expecting you," Rhonda found her voice and held the door wide. "Please, come in."

She gestured for him to enter and Wes took a cautious step into the foyer, his eyes scanning his surroundings. As he stood next to her, Rhonda couldn't help but notice what a perfect height he was, not too tall, she didn't have to crane her neck to look into his eyes. Her heart tripped oddly in her chest.

"Is your dad home? I came by to talk to him about the land lease."

His voice was deep and husky. Rhonda found it attractive. Probably from smoking too many cigarettes, she reminded herself.

"It depends. Are you packing heat?" she asked.

Wes cocked an eyebrow at her. Rhonda held her ground, her blue eyes never leaving his cool, grey ones.

"Maybe, maybe not. That's for me to know. You can try to find out if you want to take that chance." Wes' eyes gleamed wickedly as he offered the challenge. Rhonda merely stared back, crossing her arms defiantly over her chest. Finally, Wes stuffed his hands into the front pockets of his jeans. "Look, you don't have to worry, I'm not here to do any harm to your dad. I just want to sort out the land use agreement."

"Fine," Rhonda finally shrugged and turned. "He's back in the kitchen, come on."

She could barely hear his soft footfalls on the hardwood floor as she led the way, but Rhonda was all too aware of his presence close behind her.

"Dad, there's someone here to see you," Rhonda announced as she entered the kitchen. Her father looked up from the accounting books that were spread across the scarred work table. "You remember Wes Cooper?"

"Of course! Wes, good to see you, son," David Weaver got up from the table and pumped Wes' hand. "Rhonda told us you were back. I was real happy to hear it, real happy. Terrible tragedy, what happened to your parents. Terrible. You have our deepest sympathy."

"Thank you, sir." His tone had changed from cocky to respectful in the space of a heartbeat.

"Have a seat." David pulled a chair out from the table and resumed his own. "Rhonda, get us some coffee, will you?"

"Sure." Rhonda watched the exchange between her father and Wes with interest, then turned toward the coffee pot on the counter. Becca stood with the freezer door open, staring open-mouthed at their guest. The doorbell pealed again. "Sheesh, suddenly we're Grand Central Station," Rhonda muttered, heading toward the door.

"I'll get it," Becca shoved the freezer closed and took off toward the front door, leaving Rhonda shaking her head as she poured two cups of coffee.

"Mr. Weaver, I wanted to talk to you about the lease agreement on my farmland," Wes said as Rhonda carried the cups to the table.

Help Me, Rhonda

"Okay," David answered, pushing his books aside.

Rhonda placed the coffee on the table, trying to think what excuse she could use to linger in the kitchen. Her curiosity was definitely aroused by their gun-slinging neighbor.

"Hey Ronnie, someone's here for you," Becca said in a singsong voice as she re-entered the kitchen. Rhonda turned to see Blake close on Becca's heels.

"Blake!" she exclaimed in surprise. Just a few minutes ago, hadn't she expected it to be Blake at the door? How was it that Wes Cooper's unexpected arrival had thrown all thoughts of Blake clear out of her head?

"Hi sugar," Blake draped an arm over Rhonda's shoulders and planted a kiss on her hair. "I missed you today, thought we might go get a piece of pie or something." Blake raised his head and looked at Wes, going still. "Wes, heard you were back." He didn't move forward to extend his hand.

Wes looked from Blake to Rhonda, his eyes shuttered.

"News always did travel fast in this town," was his only reply.

"Just let me slip on my shoes and a jacket and we'll go," Rhonda said, squeezing Blake's arm. There was a sudden tension in the room that she couldn't explain and made her uncomfortable. And why did it bother her, having Wes see her and Blake together?

In minutes Blake was escorting her out the door to his classic Mustang parked behind Wes' pickup.

"What did Wes want?" Blake questioned as soon

as Rhonda had buckled her seat belt.

"Oh, he just wanted to talk to Daddy about the land lease. You know Daddy's been farming the land since the Coopers were killed. I suppose now Wes will want the rights back."

"I don't know why anyone would want to break their back farming," Blake observed, turning the key in the ignition.

The car's powerful engine roared to life. Blake was inordinately proud of his car. He revved the engine a couple of times before putting it in reverse, backing out of the drive and squealing down the road toward town.

"It's a good way of life, Blake," Rhonda argued. "It's all my family has ever known."

"I know that, baby," Blake reached for her hand and kissed the back of it. "It's one thing for your daddy. But Wes, he's been gone ten years now, obviously he's seen a lot of the world. Why would he want to come back to Atlanta and work in the hot sun all day, fight the elements every season and barely scrape by?"

Rhonda looked across the front seat, her eyes seeing, somehow for the very first time, Blake's girlish curls, his elfin face with its pointed chin, the brown eyes that always seemed to be sparkling with some sort of mischief. Blake was always ready for a good time. Why did she find herself comparing his light hair to Wes Coopers dark, Blake's thin lips to Wes's full and chiseled mouth? She shook her head, trying to dispel the image of Wes Cooper's wide shoulders filling the doorway. She had no business thinking about him. She didn't *want* to think about him.

"I don't know why he came back." Rhonda finally gave a shrug. "He hasn't felt the need to confide in me, and considering the chip he's carrying on his shoulder, he probably won't. Maybe he won't stay. Give it a year and he'll probably be ready to sell out and move away."

"You're probably right," Blake said, smiling devilishly at Rhonda. "And in the meantime he'll be eating his heart out with jealousy, seeing that I've got the prettiest girl in Atlanta."

"I'm not the prettiest girl in Atlanta," Rhonda protested. "I think that honor goes to Penny." Mentioning Penny reminded Rhonda of that morning's announcement, and Blake's absence from church. "I missed you at church this morning."

"I'm sorry, sugar," Blake answered, his eyes steadily on the dirt road beyond the car's headlights. "I promised my old man I'd help him tune up the engines of those old ATV's he wants to sell."

Rhonda didn't argue that Blake could very well have done that after church. Arguing with him did absolutely no good. He'd just turn those puppy dog eyes on her and sweet talk his way out of her bad graces.

"Well, you missed the exciting announcement. Emma's going to have a baby! Isn't that great?" She turned sideways in her seat and clutched Blake's free hand with both of hers.

"A baby, huh? Tyler sure made quick work of that, didn't he?" Blake flashed her a flirtatious look and winked. "Lucky guy."

Rhonda wasn't quite sure how to respond to the

comment.

"They're so happy. I, I envy them a little," she finally admitted.

"Don't I make you happy, sugar?" Blake asked, frowning. "Don't we have a good time together?"

"Of course we do," Rhonda said, suddenly unable, and unwilling, to explain her deepest feelings to Blake. He wouldn't understand. All he cared about was having fun. And they did have fun together. It was just that Rhonda wanted more than a good time. But how could she explain that to Blake? And did she want the "more" with him? Unable to answer her own questions, she changed the subject.

"Anyway, it will be good for me, too. Emma said she'll need a lot more help around the shop and she's offering me a full-time job."

"That's great, baby, great," Blake said, pulling into the parking lot of the diner. "Now let's go get some pie, I'm starved."

CHAPTER FOUR

Moving about the confines of his parents' bedroom, Wes trailed his fingers over the heavy maroon comforter on the dark four-poster bed. He didn't recognize the bedspread, or the matching drapes hanging at the window. The wallpaper was new. But the crocheted dresser scarf was the same one Wes remembered. He touched a finger to the starched white threads before lifting a framed photo from its spot on the dresser top. It was a picture of himself and Brian, taken at Wes' graduation ceremony. The boys were side-by-side, Wes in his cap and gown. Even in the photo, the emotional distance between the two was evident.

Replacing the photo to its spot, Wes pulled open the top center dresser drawer. The words "Holy Bible" glared up at him in gold from a worn leather cover. He lifted the Bible from the drawer and held it in his hands. How long had it been since he had read the Word of God? As he fanned the pages, a piece of yellowed paper drifted to the floor. He stooped to pick it up. Laying the Bible on the dresser, Wes unfolded the brittle paper and stared down.

His mother's handwriting covered the page. It was a prayer, or a list of prayers, all for him.

God, keep Wes safe. Lord, be with Wes wherever he is. Jesus, protect our son and bring him home to us. Father, watch over Wes, be his strength and his shield...

On and on it went, the familiar, slanting penmanship covering the page front and back. Resisting the urge to crumple the paper in his hand, Wes instead forced himself to carefully re-fold it and place it back where he had found it. He set the Bible back in its place and firmly closed the drawer. His mother had continued to pray for him, even after everything he had done. But was there Anyone to hear those prayers and answer? Wes doubted it.

Moving to the window, Wes held aside the drapes and stared out at the dark farmyard. He dismissed thoughts of his mother's prayers and instead turned his attention to more pressing matters. The incident from the night before had caused Wes to consider his sleeping arrangements. His old room upstairs looked out on the front yard and the road, too far away from the barn and other outbuildings, should his nighttime visitor make another appearance. His parents' downstairs room looked out on the barn and was only a few steps from the kitchen and the back door.

Turning, Wes moved to the closet and opened the bi-fold door. His mother's clothing still hung with precision on the rod. Opening the opposite door revealed his father's suits and flannel shirts hung with the same fanatical neatness that Wes himself had inherited. He lifted the sleeve of a black and red checked shirt and held it to his nose. The essence of his father still lingered.

Wes closed the closet, thankful that his aunts and uncles had honored his wishes and had not fallen upon the farmhouse like a swarm of hungry locusts. He had always known that eventually he would return to Atlanta, to his home, and when he did so, he had wanted it to be intact, the way he had remembered it. Someday soon he would call the family and ask if there were things they wanted. The clothes would have to be taken care of, he had no use for his mother's blouses or his father's Sunday suits. But for today, he wanted things to remain the same. He could pretend, if only for awhile, that life went on as usual.

Wes supposed that some people would find it creepy, the thought of him sleeping in his parents' room, with the dead couple's clothing hanging a few feet away. But Wes had slept in far creepier places. He had slept in caves and ditches and even once in a blown out mud hut with a dead body. Those places had been filled with real danger, things that nightmares were made of. Here there were only memories.

With one last patrol through the house to make sure all was secure for the night, Wes went back to the bedroom and exchanged his jeans for a pair of worn grey sweat pants. If his previous night's visitor did return, Wes had no intention of running him down in his underwear. Folding the comforter down to the end of the bed, Wes slid between the sheets and pounded the pillows into a shape that suited him.

Laying back, an image of Rhonda Weaver popped into his head, standing there challenging him, asking if he was packing heat. And what had he been thinking, asking her if she wanted to find out? Wes' heart kicked at the thought of Rhonda patting him down. That was the last place on earth he wanted his imagination to go!

What would the prissy red-head think if she found out that Wes was *always* packing heat? He wasn't about to make that information widely known. There were laws about such things. Wes smiled sardonically. Laws were what law abiding people tried to follow, never understanding that they were living in a lawless world. Wes understood the lawlessness all too well. The world was a dangerous place and he had every intention of being equipped to face the danger when it reared its ugly head.

He doubted Rhonda Weaver knew anything about danger. She lived in her fairy tale world of teashops and happily-ever-after. If she understood danger then she wouldn't be dating Blake Dalton. That guy was bad news. Unless he had changed. Hadn't Rhonda told him just yesterday that things around Atlanta had changed? Maybe Blake had outgrown his impetuous, free-wheeling streak.

Closing his eyes, Wes saw a halo of copper curls and blue eyes the color of Lake Superior on a sunny August day. His heart kicked again so he forced himself to conjure up the memory of her broken sobs at Brian's funeral. How old had she been?

Help Me, Rhonda

Fifteen? Poor kid. She had been Brian's shadow from the time she could walk. Wes remembered often resenting her distracting presence when there were chores to be done. Chores that more often than not Brian left Wes to finish alone while he and Rhonda went and climbed apple trees or built forts or whatever childish pastimes they pursued while Wes worked.

Turning onto his side, Wes pushed the images of Rhonda from his mind and concentrated instead on sleep. It was a gift, the ability to fall into a deep slumber no matter his surroundings or circumstances. Wes put that gift to good use now, thinking that Rhonda had obviously gotten over her heartbreak at Brian's death, and if she did it with Blake Dalton, that was no business of his.

A mile down the road, in her upstairs bedroom, Rhonda sat at the window seat and absently ran a brush through her damp curls. She stared out at the stars in the velvety night sky, her mind as far away as the moon. Dreamily, she wondered what it was like to plan a wedding, be a bride, expect a baby. Unconsciously, her hand went to her flat abdomen as she pondered what it would be like to have new life growing inside her womb.

With a heavy sigh, Rhonda turned on the seat cushion and looked around her bedroom. The same room she had occupied for nearly all her life. Twenty-five years of memories were stored in the books on the shelves, the collection of porcelain dolls in their protective plastic boxes, the drawings on the walls. Was she destined to live out the rest of her life in this room? Caring for her aging parents? Running the farm someday?

She glanced back out at the night beyond her window as the familiar longing filled her soul. If Brian had lived, they would have been married by now, probably have started a family. But Brian was dead and it didn't look like Blake had any intention of settling down and having kids. Rhonda's hand once more covered her stomach. And if he was ready, did Rhonda want to marry him, have his babies? They had known each other all their lives and had been dating exclusively for five months now. Blake was fun, he could always make her laugh, and he had a good job, working as a mechanic at the service station. A life with him would be...

The thought trailed off into oblivion. Rhonda could not picture what a life with Blake would be like.

"O Lord, is Blake the one You've meant for me?" she whispered to the ceiling.

"Ronnie, will you braid my hair?" Becca came barging though the bedroom door without knocking, as she so often did.

"Of course, come on." Rhonda patted the cushion of the window seat and Becca quickly sat down and turned her back on her sister, handing a brush over her shoulder.

Rhonda ran the brush down the length of Becca's strawberry blond hair and thought how someday soon her baby sister would no longer need her help for braiding hair, or any of the other little things the two shared. The four older Weaver siblings were all off and married, only Rhonda's sister Val had stayed in the Atlanta area, living with her husband over in Lewiston. The oldest of the family, David, Jr., had moved down to Saginaw to work in a factory there. Brenda and her husband lived in sunny Florida and rarely came back to the cold north woods of Michigan. Todd, number three in the Weaver clan, was selling heavy equipment in Grand Rapids.

Neither of the boys had wanted to stay with farming, saying they could make a better living in the city. Rhonda would gladly have taken their place at her father's side, but she was too tiny to be much help with the heavy work farming required. Instead, her father hired a couple local men to do the work his sons had walked away from.

Rhonda missed her siblings. Although they tried to make it home for holidays, with everyone spread out so much, it was rare that all six Weaver children were together at the same time. Someday, Becca would spread her wings and fly away too, leaving Rhonda alone in this big old farmhouse with her parents for company. The thought only added to her despondency.

"You're awfully quiet tonight," Becca observed as Rhonda parted her hair and began twining the three sections into a braid.

"Sorry, I was lost in thought."

"About Blake?" Becca asked with curious amusement.

"Actually, no, smarty pants," Rhonda answered

smugly, giving a playful tug on her sister's hair. "I wasn't thinking about Blake." She didn't want to share her melancholy thoughts with her cheerful sister.

"Wes Cooper then?"

"Now why would you ask a thing like that?" Rhonda twisted a rubber band around the end of the braid and flicked it over Becca's shoulder. Becca turned on the window seat to face her sister.

"Well did you *see* him? Are you completely blind?" Becca questioned, her blue eyes wide.

"Yes, I saw him, so what?"

"So what? He's gorgeous. I thought I would just die when he walked into the kitchen," Becca stated with teenage drama. "There I was in my torn jeans and sweatshirt when Mr. GQ walks in. I wanted the floor to open up and swallow me."

"He was wearing jeans and a jean jacket, I hardly think that qualifies as GQ material. And he's nearly twice as old as you. I thought most girls your age thought anyone over twenty was ready for a nursing home."

"It depends on the guy," Becca explained. "I mean, I guess 30 *is* sort of old, way older than me, but he's still drop-dead gorgeous. He looks like one of those guys in the cologne ads, all five o'clock shadow and hooded eyes. Not that those eyes even knew I was in the room. He was too busy looking at you."

"Don't be silly." Rhonda got up from the window seat and made her way across the room to the brass twin bed. She turned down the covers. "I think your imagination was running wild. Wes barely looked in my direction."

Becca jumped down from the seat and padded barefoot to the door.

"Well, I would think *your* imagination would be running wild, that's for sure. Wes is a lot better looking than Blake, even if he doesn't drive a Mustang. Goodnight."

When her sister had left the room, Rhonda slid between the sheets and pulled the covers under her chin. She reached to turn off the bedside lamp, her traitorous imagination running wild just as Becca had said. When she drifted off to sleep, it wasn't Blake's impish smile she saw, but hard lips set in a grim line and grey eyes begging for peace.

A light tapping sound roused Wes from his sleep. In a split second he was out of bed, his hand reaching for the gun on the dresser. A quick peek from the bedroom window showed nothing but darkness beyond the glass. Soundlessly he made his way to the mud room and out into the empty back yard.

His eyes were adjusted to the blackness. He scanned the barn, the chicken coop, the tool shed. All the doors were firmly closed. He walked to each one and checked within to reassure himself that they were the way he had left them before going to bed. Everything was in place. As he walked back toward the house his gaze ran over the structure, searching for what might have woke him.

Something on the ground beneath the bedroom window shone pale in the moonlight, catching his eye. Wes squatted down. White quartz stones, the kind often used in landscaping, had been arranged to form a word. *Brian.* Wes reached out to touch one of the rocks. A few pebbles lay beneath the window, obviously used to wake him up.

In one swift motion he rose and spun, the gun pointed steadily out. But there was no one there. Whoever had formed the message was gone now, or hiding in the bushes along the road. They had better hope they stayed hidden, Wes thought grimly.

Unable and unwilling to go back to sleep, Wes sat on the cold cement step by the back door and stared at the barn, thinking. Who was trying to scare him off? Who was sending him letters, asking him to sell out? Were the two connected? And what did it have to do with his dead brother? Most likely whoever had a desire for this land was hoping to capitalize on the doubts surrounding Brian's murder, convince Wes they knew it was him who did it. They were probably whispering into the cops' ears, too. Get the rumor mill running and fan the flames of gossip, burn Wes out that way. Well, let them give it their best shot, Wes wasn't going anywhere.

He took a drag on his cigarette. Suddenly Rhonda's voice echoed on the night air.

"You would think if God spared you from getting killed by the enemy then you would have enough sense to not jeopardize your health with those stinky cancer sticks."

Wes looked down at the glowing end of the cigarette. When had she gotten so high and mighty, acting like she'd never seen a man smoking a cigarette before? But deep down he knew she was right. It *was* a dirty habit, one he had picked up in the service because it seemed like everyone around him did it. But there were a lot of other things the guys around him did that he hadn't done. Like drink, or sleep around with hundreds of different women. What had kept him from those?

God spared you. The words came again and Wes thought of the prayer list tucked inside his mother's Bible. Was it true? Had God spared him? Wes shook his head in denial. Growing up in the church probably had kept him from womanizing and drinking. Strong Christian mores had been drummed into his head since childhood. He had walked away from God, but some of the things he had learned in church had stuck. But that's as far as it went.

Wes took another drag before crushing the butt out on the step and tossing it into the darkness, and with it the memory of Rhonda's judgmental tone. It was none of Rhonda Weaver's business what he did with his own body. Maybe someday, if he felt like it, he would quit, but not tonight.

CHAPTER FIVE

When Rhonda arrived at the Spot of Tea at her usual time of 9 a.m. Monday morning, Emma had already been hard at work for hours. Fresh baked muffins filled the glass-fronted case beneath the cash register and the heady aroma of freshly ground coffee filled the air.

"How are you feeling?" Rhonda asked Emma as she tied a clean apron around her waist.

"Fine, really," Emma threw a smile over her shoulder as she took china cups and saucers from a shelf and arranged them on a large, black tray.

"Do you want me to start coming in earlier, be here at five to help you open up?"

"Not yet. But maybe soon, if I start getting bad morning sickness. And eventually it will be hard for me to be on my feet so much. We might need to adjust as things go along, if that's okay with you. Right now, I just feel a little tired around mid-morning, but I haven't felt too nauseous yet. But that could change any day. I'm only about six weeks along."

"So when is your due date?" Rhonda reached for a whistling tea kettle and filled the pot Emma had waiting on the tray.

"November twenty-first, almost right on our anniversary. Wouldn't that be a great first anniversary gift, a baby?"

"Yeah, the best. Better than diamonds." Rhonda said, squashing the bud of envy that burst forth.

"Rhonda?"

"Hmmm?" Rhonda turned from the stove to look at her boss and best friend.

"Is everything okay?"

"I thought I was supposed to be the one asking you that."

"You already did, and I told you, I feel great. But you seem, oh, I don't know. A little distant."

"I'm sorry, I don't mean to. I'm fine, really."

Rhonda put on a bright smile, not wanting Emma to know about the longing in her heart that she couldn't seem to pray away. Wes Cooper coming back to town had brought back the pain of Brian's death. Emma's pregnancy was one more reminder of all Rhonda had missed out on. It felt as if someone had laid a heavy pack on her shoulders, but Rhonda didn't want anyone else to know.

"Now, move out of the way and I'll carry this tray in for you. Which table?"

"Don't be silly, I can still carry a tray. It will be a long time before I can't serve my own customers, if ever." Emma proved her point by effortlessly lifting the cumbersome tray and heading toward the dinning room. "The Delands are at table five if you want to get their order, thanks."

Rhonda watched Emma walk away, still slender as a whip and tried to imagine her waddling through the dining room, heavy with pregnancy. She took a deep breath and held it for several seconds. Exhaling, she tried to let out all her pent up longings. This was an exciting time for Emma, Rhonda vowed she would not ruin it by being depressed.

Wes pitched another forkful of moldy straw into the wheelbarrow outside the chicken coop and turned in a rhythmic motion to scoop up another. Resting for a moment, he leaned against the pitchfork and looked around the interior of the tiny structure. The roof was still tight, the two tiny windows letting in sun were snug. Soon they would gleam with cleanliness. The roosting boxes would be filled with clean straw and in a few days the coop would resound with the clucking of a flock of Rhode Island reds. His firsts farming venture. Wes' mouth watered at the thought of fresh eggs for breakfast.

The previous evening he had sat and talked to David Weaver for well over an hour, discussing his plans for the farm. Mr. Weaver had been deeply interested in Wes' plans to start a herd of angus beef cows and his ideas for raising them organically. Wes had been doing research for the past couple of years and had carefully crafted his plans for the farm. David had seemed genuinely impressed by the wealth of knowledge Wes possessed and enthusiastic as Wes outlined his plans. It had felt good to be accepted, to talk man-to-man with someone about his dreams and visions and have that person understand.

They had come to a mutually beneficial agreement about the land use. David would continue to farm a good portion of the fields in exchange for feed and hay for Wes' livestock and a nominal fee, depending on crop yields. That would leave Wes free to concentrate most of his energy on raising cattle, which is where he felt there was the most profit to be earned. Wes retained full ownership of the land and would have enough unplowed acreage for pasture for his herd.

Wes pitched another forkful of straw and pondered his night visitor. Was David trying to scare him off his land? The thought was discarded with the forkful of dirty straw. The man Wes had spoken with the night before didn't appear to covet his land. The letters Wes had received had come through his lawyer, the same man who had handled all his parents' affairs and had looked after all the financial and legal aspects of the farm while Wes was away. They had been anonymous and requested Wes to respond to a P.O. box in Gaylord. If David Weaver wanted to buy the land, he would have openly made Wes an offer, not sent anonymous messages filled with underlying threats. And he was a little too old for sneaking around after midnight. So who?

Shaking his head, Wes leaned the pitchfork against the side of the chicken coop and pushed the wheelbarrow to the manure spreader. He hefted the full barrow with ease and emptied the contents. As he lowered the wheelbarrow back to the ground, he heard a car door slam. Walking toward the chicken coop he caught a glimpse of a uniformed figure coming across the lawn. Wes quickly removed the pistol from his belt. Reaching into the chicken coop, he shoved the gun into a roosting box full of straw. Probably not a good idea to meet the local police fully armed.

The tall man in the brown uniform spotted Wes coming up the drive and headed his way. Wes stopped in the middle of the gravel and waited. Stopping in front of him, the man put a hand to the bill of his cap and nodded.

"Wes, I heard you had moved back to town."

Wes eyed the man, his mind shifting through faded memories to place a name with the face.

"Nate. I didn't realize you had become a cop," Wes finally said, placing his hands on his hips instead of offering one to his visitor in greeting. If the police were visiting him already, it couldn't possibly be good.

"Yeah, I've been with the sheriff's department about six years now." Vibrant eyes raked Wes from head to foot. "You're looking well. Looks like army life agreed with you."

"The army made me what I am today," Wes responded, crossing his arms over his chest. "Is this an official visit?"

"No," Nate shook his head. "Rhonda just happened to mention you were back. I thought I'd come out and say hello. It's been a long time. My condolences about your parents. We all thought you would be back for the funerals."

Wes turned away from Nate and headed back toward the chicken coop. He picked up the pitchfork and went back to his task of forking straw. He could feel Nate's eyes burning into his back and knew full well this was not just some friendly visit to welcome him home. The deputy wanted Wes to know he was watching him. His night visitor probably *had* been whispering in the cop's ear.

"I wasn't exactly near a metropolitan airport at the time," Wes finally spoke. He turned and leaned against his pitchfork, appearing relaxed but coiled as tight as a spring inside. "If you want to know, I was in the remote mountains of Afghanistan. It was a week too late by time I got the news and would have been even longer before the army could get me home. I didn't see any reason to bother by then. I had a mission to do, I figured I should see it out. I could do more good there than here. I was in close contact with Ken Morris, the family attorney, who saw to all the details about the farm."

"The place looks good," Nate observed, looking around. "Considering it's been empty for two years."

"Dad always kept the place up. As you probably know, Mr. Weaver's been leasing the land and Ken kept an eye on things, too. Kept the family from raiding the place until I got back."

"So, why did you come back? Why didn't you just stay in the army?"

"That would have made your job a lot easier, wouldn't it, Nate?" At the deputy's questioning look, Wes smiled bitterly and pushed the wheelbarrow once more toward the manure spreader. "Look, we both know this isn't a casual visit." Wes hefted the wheelbarrow up and dumped the contents as Nate watched, silent. "You think you have a murderer living in your midst and you want me to be fully aware that you're watching me. Point taken. The Montmorency County Sheriff's Department knows I'm here. If I make one wrong move, you'll be on me faster than hogs on slop."

Wes rested against the handles of the wheelbarrow and looked Nate straight in the eye.

"You really want to know why I cam back, Nate? I've been killing people for ten years. I'm tired of killing. That's why I came home."

A knock at the kitchen door had Rhonda lifting her head, shifting her attention from the delicate china in the sink. Nate stood at the door. At his bright smile, Rhonda shook her head and, drying her hands on her apron, went to let him in.

"Nate, what are you doing here after hours?" she asked, pulling the door wide.

"Came to say hello," Nate answered, removing his hat as he entered the kitchen. "Is Emma around?" he asked, craning his head to look toward the dining room.

"No, actually. She wasn't feeling so great this afternoon. I think morning sickness hit her a few hours late. When we locked up she took the cash and receipts home to count. I told her I could finish up by myself. You need her for something?"

"No, not really." Nate shook his head and

relaxed back against the counter. His vivid blue gaze pinned Rhonda to the floor. He turned his hat around in his hands. "I stopped in to see your new neighbor today."

"Wes?"

"Yeah."

"Why?" Rhonda turned back toward the sink and resumed her dishwashing. Nate had a way of unnerving everyone with his stare.

"Just to check things out. I thought it would be good, you know, just to let him know we're aware he's home."

"Oh Nate, for pity's sake. Hasn't the man been through enough?" Rhonda took up a towel and began drying cups and saucers, feeling agitated for reasons she couldn't quite explain.

"He's still basically a suspect in his brother's murder, Rhonda. I've been looking at the file and I'm telling you, there's enough there to throw suspicion on Wes, even if it's not enough hard evidence to arrest him. I want you to be careful. Tell your dad to be careful, too. I don't quite trust him. He was pretty bold, admitting to all the killing he's done."

Rhonda thought of the pistol Wes had greeted her with and his cocky challenge the night before. Right there in her own house! Saying Wes Cooper was "bold" was a major understatement!

"He's been in the army, remember, fighting terrorists all over the world. I would expect that would involve killing people now and then."

She had no idea why she was defending him. Hadn't Wes admitted he was very good at killing?

She should probably warn Nate about that, and about the gun, too. But for some reason, misplaced loyalty to Wes had Rhonda biting her tongue.

"Maybe that's all he was referring to, maybe not. Just be careful, that's all I'm saying. I wouldn't want anything to happen to you or your family."

After Nate left, Rhonda finished the dishes, her mind on Nate's warning. A painful tug-of-war started in her heart. One part of her knew Nate was right. Wes Cooper spelled danger with every breath he took. The other part of Rhonda's tender heart protested, saying that Wes was a hurting man, a lost soul who just needed the soft comfort of someone's love. God's love.

Locking the door behind her, Rhonda looked up and down Atlanta's Main Street. On impulse, she left her truck in the restaurant parking lot and walked the short distance to the service station on the corner. The service bay doors were up and two cars were parked inside. She walked in and saw worn, oily work boots sticking out from beneath a black sedan. She prodded a booted foot with her toe.

Dolly wheels rolled and a blue uniform came into view, followed soon by Blake's smiling eyes and blond curls. Rhonda waited with bated breath, hoping for some romantic sensation to consume her.

"Hey sugar, what's up?" Blake asked, staring up at her from his prone position.

Absolutely nothing happened. Disappointed, Rhonda smiled down at him tremulously and tried to think of an excuse for stopping. She had never just popped in on Blake at work before, but it seemed like something couples did. After all, Blake came into the Spot of Tea most mornings.

"Nothing. I just thought I'd stop in and say hello."

"That's nice, but I'm kinda busy here." Blake pointed with a wrench to the car at his head then swiped a forearm across his brow. "I promised Kelly Clark that I'd have her car done by six. You know how ex-homecoming queens can be when they're kept waiting." He winked.

"Oh, yeah, sure. Sorry. I didn't mean to interrupt," Rhonda said, backing toward the door. "I'll see you later?"

"Sure, sugar, sure." Blake was already rolling himself back under the car, his voice growing muffled. "I'll talk to you later."

Back out on the sidewalk, Rhonda sighed heavily, chagrined. She and Blake had been dating for several months. Had he ever made her skin get tingly or goose-bumpy in anticipation? He must have.

"Lord, is he the one I'm supposed to spend my life with?" she found herself asking again, looking up at the robin's egg blue sky.

No answer boomed down from heaven. Shaking her head, Rhonda turned and continued down the sidewalk, past the hardware store and the tavern to the very last building on the main business block. A red brick colonial house with white shutters and gleaming windows stood square to the street. A sign hung from the porch roof, swaying in the breeze. A Stitch In Time. Rhonda trotted up the steps of her mother's quilt shop and walked across the deep porch to the front door.

A chime sounded when she pulled the door open and stepped inside. The walls of what had once been a stately home were now covered with bolts of brightly colored fabric of every conceivable print and pattern. Florescent lights lit the room, making it easy for a shopper to match thread and fabric. To the left was an archway into what once was a parlor. Now the walls were covered with shelves holding a variety of patterns and books. Plush chairs were arranged invitingly around a low table offering a variety of quilting magazines and catalogs.

Voices drifted from the back of the shop. Rhonda headed that way, poking her head into the former dining room where a group of ladies were seated around a quilt frame, stitching away busily while chatter filled the room.

"Hi, Ma," she said, entering. Several pairs of eyes turned her way. Mary Weaver smiled and held out one arm. Rhonda quickly went to her and accepted the hug, placing a kiss on her mother's weathered cheek.

"What brings you in this afternoon? Come to help us finish this thing?"

Rhonda smiled, looking down at the star pattern of the quilt and ran a finger over a row of squares in patriotic colors.

"You know good and well I can't stitch straight to save my life. If you want to get any money out of this thing at the Memorial Day raffle, you'd better keep me as far away as possible. Leave it to the professionals here." She motioned with her left hand to the other women sitting around the quilt.

Jeanette Hughes grabbed Rhonda's hand and looked pointedly at her ring finger.

"What? No engagement ring yet?" she asked. "What's Blake waiting for?"

Rhonda felt herself bristling. After the discussion she had just been having with the Lord out on the sidewalk, she really didn't want to defend her situation to Atlanta's quilting circle. She gently pulled her hand from Jeanette's grasp.

"We've only been dating a few months."

"Officially maybe," Gwen Talbert put in her two-cents worth, "but you've known each other all your lives."

"You're not getting any younger you know," Jeanette observed, sniping off a thread.

"I'm only twenty five," Rhonda protested.

"Twenty five," Happy Brubaker said, nearly snorting. "My Sissy had three kids by the time she was twenty five."

Happy left out the fact that Sissy's three kids all had different fathers and Sissy hadn't been married to any of them. Not exactly the example Rhonda wanted to follow.

"Rhonda and Blake are in no hurry. What's wrong with that?" her mother finally came to her defense. "And David and I are in no hurry for her to leave us. She's such a help around the farm and with Becca. I don't know what I would do without her." Blue-green eyes met Rhonda's and smiled.

"I guess it's just not the Lord's time yet," Rhonda

said, backing toward the door. "I need to run. Mom, I'll get dinner started, so stay as long as you need to."

"Okay hon, thanks," Mary called, turning her attention back to the quilt in front of her.

"So, Mary, what do you think of having that Was Cooper for a neighbor?" Rhonda heard Gwen ask as she stepped out onto the front porch. "Can you believe his nerve..."

Rhonda shut the door firmly, cutting off the sound of Gwen's voice, and took a deep breath. Poor Wes, already the topic of town gossip, she thought as she headed back down the sidewalk toward her truck. Well, better him than me.

She's such a help with Becca and the farm. Her mother's words echoed in Rhonda's head. But instead of encouraging her, they suddenly made Rhonda feel like a very old maid.

CHAPTER SIX

Spring could not decide if she wanted to stay in northern Michigan or not. Rhonda drove home through a cold rain, contemplating the weather. Squinting through the curtain of grey, she thought she could see green buds on the trees, but in this dismal downpour it was hard to tell. Yesterday had been warm enough for a t-shirt, the day before that she had driven to work with mittens on her hands and a scarf tied around her hair. Her truck hit a pot hole in the rutted dirt road and threw up a tail of brown mud.

"Soup, these roads are just soup," she muttered to herself, amazed as always at what a few hours of rain could accomplish. "Hmm, soup sounds good, maybe that's what I'll make for dinner when I get home."

Yellow light shone through the sheet of rain and Rhonda slowed, looking toward the Cooper farmhouse. Even after a couple of weeks, she still wasn't used to seeing signs of life at their neighbor's house.

Help Me, Rhonda

Rhonda took her foot off the gas and let the truck come to a stop at the end of the Cooper driveway.

Who was taking care of Wes? Who was making sure he had a hot meal at the end of a cold, miserable day like today? And who was taking care of the house, dusting the nick-knacks and mopping the floors? Her father had told the family of Wes' ambitious plans for the farm. Rhonda figured he was far too busy with chores to worry about housekeeping or cooking. She pictured him sitting alone at the dining table and her heart nearly broke. How sad, to live life totally apart from the rest of the world.

Wes had rarely ventured into town since he came home and Rhonda couldn't blame him. The rumors were already flying. It seemed everyone who came into the Spot of Tea wanted to talk about Brian's murder and Wes Cooper's audacity in showing his face in Atlanta after all these years. Her mother admitted it was the same at A Stitch In Time. It made Rhonda's blood boil. Where were the words of compassion for a man who had lost his whole family? Why did no one remind the citizens of this great town to judge not, that you be not judged? No wonder Wes walked around his own home armed with a gun.

Forgetting Nate's warning, Rhonda turned the steering wheel and pressed the gas pedal, shooting up into the drive. Parking next to Wes' truck, she slid down to the muddy driveway and dashed through the rain to the house. Under the protection of the front porch she shook water from her jacket and knocked on the screen door with a hand nearly numb with cold. In moments, the front door swung wide. Rhonda held her hands up, palms out, as if in surrender.

"It's just me Wes, don't shoot," she said, laughing nervously. Steely eyes stared at her through the screen.

"What do you want, kid?"

The use of the old nickname immediately put Rhonda's back up.

"I'm not a kid anymore, Wes. And can I come in? It's freezing out here."

Wes reached out a finger and unlocked the screen door, leaving Rhonda to let herself in. She gladly did so, pushing the door quickly closed to stand dripping on the entryway rug.

"So, what do you want?" he asked again, crossing muscular arms over his broad chest.

Rhonda couldn't help but notice the way his biceps bulged or the way his black t-shirt stretched across his shoulders. Suddenly an odd tingling sensation began at the top of her scalp. Rhonda immediately recognized it as the feeling that had been sadly lacking when she was with Blake. She pressed cold fingers to her cheeks, trying to make the sensation stop. Why was she here?

"I was just passing by, going home from work, you know, and I saw the light and wondered who was taking care of you. You know, making you dinner and cleaning the house and stuff, and I just felt bad, you being here all alone and I just stopped to check on you." Rhonda chatted aimlessly, knowing that her nervous tongue had taken over and she would have to find some way to rein it back in. "I was thinking about going home and making some soup, that sounded so good on a cold day like today and then I thought of you and wondered who was making sure you eat right and all that and so I..." She stared into his cold, hard eyes. "Stopped," she finally finished lamely.

"As you can see, I'm not starving to death."

"Yes." Rhonda blinked hard and tried to tear her eyes away from his very fit form. "Yes, I can see that." She nodded in agreement and looked around the living room, biting her lip. A pile of clothing lay on a chair.

Wes turned his head slightly to follow her gaze.

"I was just going through some of my parents' things," he explained. "I figured it was time. I gave a few things to my aunts and uncles, but there wasn't much they wanted."

"Do you need some help? I could help you if you want."

"No." Wes turned his back on her and lifted a sleeve, seeming lost in thought. "No, I don't need any help."

"Are you sure?"

"There is one thing." Wes spun and once more Rhonda was pinned to the floor by his serious stare. He took a step toward her and she found herself cringing back against the door, suddenly afraid. "Brian's things. Do you know what my mom did with them?"

Rhonda swallowed and nodded once.

"There was a family," she started to speak, finding it nearly impossible to get words out now that her runaway tongue had been bridled by fear. Why had she stopped here? Hadn't Nate warned her to be careful? Didn't she know first hand that the man in front of her carried a pistol? Her eyes roved to and fro over the room, looking for the weapon.

"What family?" Wes prompted. He rocked back on his heels, tucking his thumbs into the back pockets of his jeans, and the menacing stance evaporated.

"The Gibsons," Rhonda answered, relaxing back against the door. "They had a house fire about a year after you left. They lost everything and didn't have insurance. They had a boy Brian's age, Jacob, and your mom decided to give him Brian's clothes and some of his other things. It was hard for her, I remember helping her sort through things and how she cried." Rhonda closed her eyes, remembering her own tears. "But she felt it was best, to have Brian's things used and appreciated, rather than letting them go to waste just sitting in his room, or being packed away in the attic. She kept several things, mementos and things that had special meaning. They should be in a trunk in the attic. I could probably find them for you, if you want."

One broad shoulder lifted in a shrug. "It's not that important. I was just curious."

Rhonda noted that several pieces of furniture in the living room were still covered with white sheets and those that weren't were covered with a fine layer of dust.

"About the house. I know you're really busy with the farm now. Daddy told me about the angus cows you plan to raise. With all the other farm chores, I know you don't have time to worry about housekeeping. If you want, my sister and I could come by some afternoon and take care of it for you. It would give you one less thing to worry about."

"I thought you already had a job."

"I do. But I don't work on Sundays. We could come after church."

"Isn't that breaking some sort of Sabbath law?" he asked with a twinge of sarcasm in his voice.

"We don't live under the law, but under grace, remember? Even Jesus himself said it was okay to do good on the Sabbath."

"How much would this cost me?"

"Nothing! Doing a neighborly good deed doesn't require payment."

"Hmm. I've learned that everything costs in one way or another."

Rhonda raised an eyebrow at his bitter tone, but didn't say anything. "Okay, Sunday," Wes surprised her by agreeing. "You want to clean, knock yourself out. You're right, I've got better things to do."

Wes stood at the living room window and watched as red tail lights disappeared beyond the curtain of falling rain. You could have knocked him over with a feather when he swung the door wide to see Rhonda standing on his porch, looking for all the world like a drowned rat. But even soaked to the skin and dripping on his rug, Rhonda had given his heart a jolt.

What was he doing, agreeing to let her be his housekeeper? She belonged to another man! Nothing good could come of having her hanging around. And just wait until the gossips in town found out! They would both be in for it then. Wes wasn't stupid. He heard the whispers, knew what was being said about him around town. His heart went cold. What if Rhonda was part of a bigger plot? The way she had babbled nervously. Had she been sent here on a mission? Maybe she had volunteered her services because she was the town spy. If so, anything she heard or saw would be relayed immediately to Nate Sweeney and the sheriff's department. Wes took a deep breath. He was being set up.

Turning from the window, Wes looked around the living room and smiled slyly. Okay, so Rhonda was probably being sent to spy on him. What better way to turn the tables? Spy on the spy?

A more sinister thought gave him pause. Perhaps Rhonda wasn't the town spy. Maybe she was in alliance with the person trying to run him off his farm. His dark brows drew together at the thought. The mischief had continued over the past week. Just small things, but there was always some sort of message attached to the high-jinks. Just this morning he had awakened to find someone had broken into the tool shed and left several implements out in the rain to rust. Most prominently displayed was a very lethal looking pair of garden sheers. Was Rhonda connected with the person responsible for these occurrences? The thought left a dull ache in his chest.

Wes rubbed the spot and shrugged a wide shoulder, telling himself it didn't matter. As long as Rhonda was hanging around, he could keep an eye on her. That wouldn't be such a hardship. He thought of how her freckles had stood out on her pale face framed with damp curls. No, it wouldn't be such a bad thing at all.

With a stab of guilt, Wes remembered that Rhonda had been his dead brother's girlfriend. Well, he had no intention of getting involved with her. His only plan was to turn the tables on whatever game Miss Weaver was playing. And in the meantime, Wes would get something he needed out of the deal, a clean house.

Having loved military discipline and order, the mounting clutter in the house was bugging Wes. But he was quickly learning that running a farm alone was a difficult task. He had his chickens now and had been working steadily on putting up fence and preparing the barn for the angus calves that would be arriving next week. There were so many things that needed his attention outdoors that he hadn't even had time to get all the sheets off the furniture. He ran a finger over an end table, leaving a furrow in the dust. If a surprise inspection was sprung on him right now, he definitely would not pass muster. The thought rankled.

Rhonda would fix all that. Maybe she was being used by the local police to keep an eye on him. If so, she wasn't going to see or hear anything she could go tattling to Sweeney. And in the meantime, Wes would use her for what he needed. A perfect arrangement as far as he was concerned.

What had she just done? Rhonda gripped the steering wheel with white-knuckled fingers and berated herself. Hadn't Nate told her to be careful? And what had she gone and done but volunteered herself as Wes Cooper's housekeeper! Not only that, she'd included her baby sister in the deal as well! Wes was a possible killer. He carried a gun. If anything happened to Becca, Rhonda would never be able to forgive herself.

What had she been thinking? The truth was, she hadn't. Her tongue had become like a runaway freight train, heading Rhonda straight for disaster.

"O, Lord in heaven, help! What have I done?" Rhonda spoke into the silence. "Jesus, I know this is all my fault. I didn't think, I didn't stop to pray, I just jumped in. What should I do now?"

You shall love your neighbor as yourself.

The words of the commandment were whispered by a silent voice to Rhonda's heart. Suddenly words from 1 Corinthians 13, Rhonda's favorite Bible passage, drifted across her mind.

Love is kind, love does not behave rudely, love thinks no evil.

Rhonda began to relax and her hands loosened on the wheel. Okay, she would reach out in Christian love to her neighbor. But that's all it was, Christian love, obeying God's commandment. There was no romantic love involved, no matter the tingling she had felt! She would be kind, she wouldn't think evil, she would believe the best about Wes unless someone could prove she should think otherwise.

Once home, she took off her jacket and went straight to the kitchen to begin preparing dinner. Her wayward thoughts strayed once more to Wes. Maybe if there was enough soup left over, she would freeze it and take it to him on Sunday.

The aroma filling the house soon lured Becca to the kitchen.

"Mmm, soup," she said, leaning over the pot on the stove and taking a big sniff. "Perfect day for it."

"I thought so too," Rhonda said, stirring spices into the broth. "Hey, don't make any plans for Sunday afternoon."

"Why not?" Becca asked, picking slices of carrot from the cutting board and popping them in her mouth.

"Because I'm afraid I volunteered you for something. I know I shouldn't have, but it sort of popped out without me thinking and it's not like I can go alone, so I'm afraid you're stuck."

"With what?"

"I've volunteered us to clean Wes' house. Today, with the weather and everything, I don't know what got into me, but I started to feel bad, him living there all alone and no one to cook for him or anything. I stopped in and the place is a mess, half the furniture is still covered with dust cloths, the rest is just covered with dust. He has his hands full trying to get the farm up and running. So I said we would come over Sunday afternoon and help him. Do you hate me?"

"Well, cleaning's not exactly my favorite thing."

"I know, but it wouldn't be proper for me to be over there alone. People would talk. But I feel we should do something kind for Wes. He's been through so much already and people are being so standoffish to him. Someone around here needs to show him what the love of Jesus really is."

"Plus he's cute," Becca said, smiling at her sister from across the kitchen.

Rhonda pictured Wes and felt the tingling again. She busily stirred the soup, trying to dispel the sensation.

"Daddy says Wes has chickens now and probably will have chicks soon. Maybe he could use some barn cats. We should take a couple of the new kittens over, you think?"

Her sister's ready enthusiasm warmed Rhonda's heart.

"I think that would be a great idea," she agreed. Even Wes Cooper's stone-cold heart couldn't possibly resist a cuddly kitten.

CHAPTER SEVEN

What was it about spring that made everyone want to talk about love? Rhonda wondered as she drove home from church. They were two months past Valentine's day, so why had Pastor Bennett chose today to preach on the subject of true love that lasts? Of course, he was referring to being the bride of Christ and that kind of true love, but he had used enough romantic imagery to choke a cherub. It must be all those June weddings he had coming up.

It didn't help matters that Blake had not show up at service again today. Rhonda sighed. It was time to face facts. No tingling, no church attendance, no hint of a long-term commitment. Her relationship with Blake was a dead end. She was going to have to stop seeing him, and without Blake her prospects looked pretty bleak.

By the time Rhonda reached home, her mood had sunk to an all-time low. Becca and her parents

Help Me, Rhonda

had returned from their own church service and Becca quickly pounced on Rhonda as she entered the kitchen.

"Daddy let me pick out two kittens to take over to Wes and I've got food in this bag right here." The teen held up a zippered bag bulging with kitten chow. "If Wes says no, we can just bring them home, but Daddy agreed that with chicken feed in the barn and cows coming soon, Wes is going to need a couple good mousers."

The reminder of Wes and Rhonda's pledge to show neighborly love caused her black mood to darken. Neighborly love! Was that all her life was destined to consist of? Family love and neighborly love? And what had she been thinking, volunteering to give up her Sundays to clean house for a murder suspect?

"I don't know why I even said we would do this in the first place," Rhonda grumbled, opening the refrigerator and pulling out a can of cola. "It's not like we don't have better things we could be doing."

"Because you wanted us to show him Jesus' love, and not be like other people around here who are being mean to him because of something that happened a long time ago," Becca reminded, looking at Rhonda with clear blue eyes.

Rhonda immediately heard Pastor Bennett's voice reciting a verse from Ephesians that he had used in his sermon.

And walk in love, as Christ also has loved us and given Himself for us, an offering and a sacrifice to God, for a sweet-smelling aroma.

Convicted, Rhonda was instantly contrite.

"I'm sorry Becca, you're right. I guess Pastor's sermon got to me today and I came home in a foul mood. Let me go upstairs and change and I'll put on a sunnier attitude along with my work clothes."

Rhonda carried her can of pop up the stairs, thinking. Christ's love was sacrificial. Hadn't Pastor talked just this morning about how Jesus loved the church so much that He gave Himself up for it? He paid the price so that Rhonda could be His bride. His love would last forever. Wasn't that what it was supposed to be all about? Looking toward eternity with Jesus, and in the meantime walking in love while on this earth.

In her room, Rhonda quietly closed the door and dropped to her knees beside her bed.

"Lord, forgive me. It is all about You and Your love. If I never find true love here on earth, help me to always remember I'm Your bride, and Your love never ends, never grows old or cold. And Lord, help me show Your love to my neighbor."

The kittens cavorted around the cab of Rhonda's truck on the short drive to the Cooper farm, unsure of whether to be frightened or delighted by this change of environment. Becca finally gave up attempting to keep the two feisty felines corralled in the cardboard box she had brought.

"You two aren't going to make a very good first impression on your new owner if you don't settle down," Becca scolded.

"I hope a mile is enough distance and they don't try making their way back home," Rhonda said, removing a set of claws from her jean-covered thigh as she drove.

"With two together, they should be okay. And if Wes feeds them proper and gives them plenty of attention, they'll stay. If not, we'll just keep bringing them back until they get the idea."

Rhonda pulled into Wes' drive and parked beside the house. She could see his pickup down by the barn. The slam of doors brought Wes to the big double doors, wiping his hand on a rag. At the sight of them, he began making his way up the gravel driveway. Rhonda watched him approach, her heart beating heavier with each step Wes took. She wondered if he owned anything besides black t-shirts.

"Hi Wes, we brought you kittens!" Becca announced, holding up the box. The two cats were already trying to climb over the side and were in danger of falling to the ground. Rhonda caught one just in time and set it back inside the box.

"Kittens, huh?" Wes stopped a few feet from them, one eyebrow raised in question. "I don't have time for pets."

"Oh, these aren't really for pets," Becca explained. "They're for your barn, to catch the mice. You've got chickens now and that means corn, which means mice. These two are all weaned and their momma is a real good mouser, so they should be, too. We even brought some kitten food and some milk, so you don't have to worry about what they'll eat for awhile. They're tame enough to pet, but not house cats. I'm going to take them down to the barn and help them get settled in."

Becca hurried down the hill toward the barn. Wes looked at Rhonda, his steely eyes nearly twinkling with amusement. The sudden sparkle made him appear much more human and Rhonda felt the unwelcome sensation at the top of her head again. *Neighborly love,* she reminded herself.

"And who's the little talking tornado?" he asked.

"Don't you remember Becca, my Mom and Dad's mid-life surprise?" Rhonda asked, smiling as she watched her sister take the kittens out of the box and place them inside the barn door. "I guess you wouldn't, she was only five when you went away. She's supposed to be my helper today, but with the kittens, who knows how much work I'll get out of her. If it's okay, I'll just get started in the house. Anything in particular you want me to do, or not do?"

"No." He shook his dark head. "Have at the whole place. I've got nothing to hide." His gaze seemed to convey a deeper meaning that Rhonda didn't quite understand. "I'll be in the barn if you need me for anything."

"Okay." Rhonda headed for the front door. "Don't let Becca chat your ears off. If you've got a radio out there in the barn, I suggest you turn it up, loud."

Wes walked toward the barn, his eyes on the slender teenager kneeling in the dust outside the barn door. So much like Rhonda at that age, only with straight hair that wasn't nearly as red. He stopped and looked down at her, hands on hips. Becca looked up at him and smiled.

"You like the kittens okay?" she asked.

Help Me, Rhonda

He watched the two skitter beneath a pile of hay only to come out sneezing, bits clinging to their fur. He gave a slow nod.

"They'll do."

"This one's name is Peanut," Becca picked up the tan and orange ball of fluff. "Because she looks sort of like peanut butter, plus she was the smallest one of the litter. Her sister here I call Camo Kitty, because she sort of looks like she's covered in camouflage." Becca picked up the calico kitten and held it up for Wes to inspect. "We brought two females so you don't have to worry about inbreeding. When they grow up, a tom will probably come along and before you know it, you'll have more kittens than you can shake a stick at."

"Then what do I do?" Wes asked.

"Buy more food," Becca answered with a laugh. She got up from the ground and brushed dirt from her knees. "Daddy said you have chickens. Can I see them?"

"Sure, they're right over there." Wes pointed across the farm yard to the coop that was now surrounded by a neat fence of chicken wire. Bright red plumage sparkled in the sun.

"Cool." Becca took off like a shot toward the chicken yard. In the blink of an eye she had opened the gate and was inside, kneeling, clucking to the chickens who turned their heads and eyed her quizzically.

Shaking his head and nearly cracking a smile, Wes entered the barn and walked through to the double doors at the far end. He was putting the finishing touches on the lean-to shelter for the cows that would be delivered in just a few days.

"I see some of the hens are brooding. You'll have chicks in no time."

Wes spun at the unexpected sound of Becca's voice behind him.

"That's the idea." He picked up his hammer and resumed pounding nails into the plywood sides of the lean-to, securing it more tightly.

Like an agile monkey, Becca climbed the ladder to the hay loft and peeked over the edge at him.

"You should get some ducks, too, and geese," she informed him.

"Too messy."

"I suppose you're right. But goose eggs are all the rage now." In the space of a breath, Becca had swooped down from the loft and scooped up one of the kittens which promptly clawed its way up to her shoulder and sat looking at Wes with wide eyes. "You should see some of the things they do with goose eggs. We went to this big craft show over in Alpena at Christmastime and this lady there, she had these goose eggs and they were all decorated up so fancy, like those Russian eggs you hear about all the time. What do they call those?" Becca's brow scrunched up, thinking. "I can't remember now, but anyway, they were unbelievable and the price! Whew. She said finding a perfect goose egg is like hunting for the perfect diamond. Can you imagine, comparing goose eggs with diamonds?" Becca giggled.

Wes couldn't imagine anybody being able to talk as much or as quickly as Rhonda's sister apparently could. So much like Brian in the old days. Leaving her sister to do all the work while she played and had fun.

"I heard you were in Iraq. Is that true? I haven't met anyone who was in Iraq before. There's this girl at school, her cousin's been to Iraq, but I don't know him. Was it hot there? Did you see people get blown up?"

The flip question sent a cold sensation washing over Wes.

"Aren't you supposed to be helping your sister in the house?" he asked, the steel back in his voice.

"Oh, yeah, I suppose so." Becca seemed to deflate, like a bicycle tire that had run over a nail. Suddenly she brightened once more. "Rhonda promised she'd bring me one of Emma's chocolate chip muffins tomorrow for helping. Have you had Emma's muffins yet? They are the best. You haven't lived until you've had Emma's muffins." She turned and made her way through the barn. "Talk to you later, Wes."

"Please, no," he muttered, hammering a nail to within an inch of its life. "I don't think I could take anymore."

Once inside the house, Rhonda stood for a long time, listening to the quiet, trying to decide where to start. She had always loved this house. Unlike the Weaver home which was a traditional clapboard farmhouse that had been added onto over the years as the family grew, the Cooper home was built of native rock, rising up from the ground as if it were part of the earth. Rhonda loved the way the quartz in the rock sparkled in the sun and how the rocks changed into a rainbow of different colors when it rained.

Moving about the living room, she began pulling sheets from the different pieces of furniture, tossing them into a pile to be washed. A fireplace built from the same rock as the house was centered on one wall surrounded by barn siding faded to the softest shade of grey. In front of the fireplace was arranged sturdy furniture covered in a plaid material that wore like iron. In one corner Rhonda pulled a dust cover off a spinet piano. A memory assailed her, of sitting on the sofa munching popcorn while Mrs. Cooper pounded away on the piano and Wes played the guitar as they all sang a rousing rendition of "She'll be coming 'round the mountain."

Rhonda sank down on the arm of the sofa, clutching the sheet to her chest. Closing her eyes, she could almost feel Brian's adolescent arm around her shoulders. She fought the sting of tears and took a deep breath. There was bound to be more such moments to come. She could handle it. She made herself think of Wes, living in this house, facing the memories each and every day. If he could do it day in and day out, she could manage for an afternoon.

Joined by Becca, the two soon began to make progress as they dusted, ran the vacuum cleaner, scrubbed the bathroom from top to bottom and mopped the kitchen. A clean sparkle replaced the dull film of neglect that had hung over the house. Finally, Rhonda stood back to admire their handiwork.

"Well, I think that just about does it," she told her sister, running a damp rag once more over the kitchen counter. "I've left some soup in the refrigerator, and some of Mom's bread. Maybe I should start making an extra casserole or something to bring over."

"That's probably a good idea," Becca agreed. "I've heard army guys eat a lot. Can I go say goodbye to the kittens before we go home?"

"Sure, go ahead."

Becca shot out the back door. Rhonda opened a cupboard and stuck her head in, examining the contents.

"Find anything interesting?"

The voice had her spinning around, banging the cupboard closed guiltily. Wes stood in the kitchen doorway eyeing her with suspicion. Rhonda felt her heart rate begin to increase and unfortunately it wasn't because she was scared.

"You know, you really should throw away all those spices," she said nervously, hooking a thumb over her shoulder at the cupboard behind her. "They really shouldn't be used after six months or a year. They're probably full of bugs."

"Okay, but it's not like I was planning on making any gourmet meals or anything." Wes looked around the now gleaming kitchen. "Looks good, thanks kid."

"I'm not a kid, remember? That's my sister. And you're welcome." Rhonda began backing toward the living room, her heart beating faster with each step. "I left you some soup in the fridge. I'll, um, I'll see you later." With that she turned and fled through the living room and out the front door, but this time it wasn't painful memories that were chasing her.

CHAPTER EIGHT

A misty veil of fog hovered just above the grass, giving a surreal, dreamlike quality to everything. Wes stood on the front porch in jeans and a flannel shirt, watching as the sun slowly rose. He sipped his coffee, staring across the road at the herd of deer grazing in the hay meadow. The animals appeared to float like shadows through the early morning mist. Wes relaxed against a post and took another sip of coffee, enjoying the view. How he had missed the wildlife of northern Michigan! The sight of the deer brought a certain calmness to his spirit that Wes had not felt in a long time.

A chicken materialized around the corner of the house, pecking absently at the greening grass. Wes pulled away from his perch and stared, blinking his eyes at the sight. What was a chicken doing out? Realization hit him like a bullet and he slammed his cup down on the rail and shot off the porch. The chicken squawked and ran, feathers flapping.

Help Me, Rhonda

Speeding around the house to the farmyard, Wes slid to a halt, seeing his flock of chickens scattered about the yard, bright spots of color in the drab morning fog. He approached the coop and saw clearly that the fence had been cut down. His anger mounting, he stepped through the wire and went straight to the coop, knowing what he would find. The brooding eggs were smashed all over the inside of the chicken house. There would be no new chicks.

Standing in front of the narrow door, Wes drove a fist into the plank siding of the chicken coop. A splinter embedded itself into his hand and that's when he saw it, the word carved into the wood.

Death

The small dining room of the Spot of Tea was nearly full with the breakfast crowd. Rhonda rushed from the kitchen with a full tray just as the bell above the door gave out its silvery ring. Rhonda glanced over her shoulder and saw Blake enter.

"Hey sugar," he said, his ready smile turning up the corners of his impish mouth.

"Be there in a minute, Blake," Rhonda called as she continued toward the table where hungry customers waited.

Did Blake ever call her by her given name? she wondered. His constant habit of calling her "sugar" or "baby" all the time suddenly annoyed Rhonda. She honestly thought she would prefer being called "kid." The thought brought a picture of Wes popping into her mind and Rhonda could feel the hair on her arms stand on end. She glanced toward Blake, lounging against the glass fronted counter by the cash register. The odd sensation immediately disappeared.

"Hey," she said, coming to stand behind the counter where Blake lolled indolently. Rhonda blew a curl out of her eyes. "It's sort of busy right now Blake, is there something you wanted?"

"Yeah." He turned and leaned his forearms on the counter, gazing deeply into Rhonda's eyes. "I wanted us to go out tonight. There's a new Matthew McConaughey movie playing in Gaylord that I thought we could go see."

"I don't know, Blake..." Rhonda started to hedge. "You know I don't like all that swearing and violence."

"I know. I checked it out, it's an adventure film. No gratuitous nudity or flying body parts. Come on, baby." Blake's smile turned to a pout. "I was workin' all weekend, I need to blow off some steam. What do you say?" He waggled his eyebrows up and down.

"I..." Rhonda hesitated.

She really didn't want to go, but maybe, just maybe she would feel it this time, the tingle that had been missing between her and Blake and that seemed to appear with maddening frequency whenever she saw or thought of Wes.

"Okay," she finally capitulated.

"Great, pick you up at six. See ya." In the blink of an eye he was out the door, setting the silver bell to tinkling and leaving Rhonda with an empty feeling in the pit of her stomach.

Kneeling on the hard ground just outside the tool

shed, Wes hammered together the frame of a new gate for the chicken yard. He had managed to put up new fence and herd the traumatized chickens back into their pen. He could only hope that chickens had short memories and that the hens would soon be laying again. He heard the quiet crunching of gravel behind him. His hand reached for the gun tucked into the waistband of his jeans. Slowly, he peeked over his shoulder.

"Hi, Wes!" It was Rhonda's sister Becca, wearing a smile as bright as the spring sunshine.

Wes eased his hand away from the butt of the gun and pulled the tail of his flannel shirt lower to conceal the weapon.

"What are you doing here, kid?" he asked gruffly.

"I asked the bus driver to let me off here. I wanted to check on the kittens."

At the sound of her voice, the two kittens came bounding from the tool shed. Becca giggled and dropped her backpack at her feet, scooping one up in each hand.

"Watcha doin'?" she asked, leaning to peer over Wes' shoulder.

"Making a new gate for the chicken yard."

"What was wrong with the other one? It seemed okay to me."

Wes glanced up at the teen. What if she were part of the plot to destroy his farm? The sunshine behind her made her hair glow like a copper halo. Innocent blue eyes looked down at him in question and Wes shook off the suspicion.

"Something got into the chicken coop last night," was all he would say. No need to get the girl alarmed. "I thought a better gate might make it a little more secure."

"The brooding eggs?"

Wes just shook his head and stood, standing the gate upright and testing its strength.

"Aw," Becca buried her face in the kittens' fur. "Poor baby chicks. Poor, poor things."

She sniffed and set the kittens down. They promptly pounced on her shoestrings.

"It was probably a fox," Becca reasoned. "Or an opossum or a raccoon. You should think about getting a dog. I know you said you don't have time for pets, but a dog can be a real asset when it comes to keeping critters out of things. There's an animal shelter at the sheriff's office now. They put an ad in the Tribune every week, of dogs that need adopting. You should look into it."

Becca reached down and untangled claws from her shoestrings.

"You guys stay here with Wes. I've got to go home and do my chores." Becca headed down the drive toward the road, swinging her backpack up onto her shoulder. "See ya later, Wes."

Wes carried the new gate to the chicken yard and began setting it into place. Becca was right, a fox had gotten into the henhouse, but not the four-legged kind.

CHAPTER NINE

Rhonda sat in the darkened movie theater next to Blake and stared unseeing at the screen. She hoped there wouldn't be a pop quiz afterward or she was in big trouble. If anyone asked her the plot of the movie or the names of any of the characters, she wouldn't be able to answer. Her mind had been too preoccupied to concentrate on the action taking place on the screen.

Blake laughed and Rhonda glanced over at him. What was wrong with her? They had been dating for five months and Rhonda had always enjoyed his company. What had happened in the past few weeks to cause this sudden case of discontent? Was it Penny and Nate's fast-approaching wedding? Or Emma's pregnancy? That seemed absurd. She was dating Blake when Penny and Nate got engaged, and she had known from the beginning that Emma and Tyler were eager to start a family. So, if not those things, then what?

What else had happened recently? Rhonda questioned.

Wes Cooper had come home.

Like a bow hunter's arrow finding its mark, the answer embedded itself deep in her mind. But that was ridiculous. What could Wes Cooper's arrival in Atlanta have to do with her sudden longing for something more than the relationship she had with Blake? She didn't even know Wes. But his coming home had stirred up all the old memories of Brian. Brought to the surface all the childhood dreams and unfulfilled yearnings she thought had been buried long ago.

Blake draped an arm over her shoulder and smiled down at her. Rhonda smiled weakly in return. She forced herself to lay her head on his shoulder and willed some sort of emotional response to spring from her heart. Nothing happened. With a discouraged sigh, she turned her attention back to the movie, trying to drown out the cry of her soul with the action on the screen.

"You've been awfully quiet tonight," Blake commented as he drove her home.

"I'm sorry," Rhonda apologized. "It was a really busy day at the shop. I guess I'm just tired."

"Must have something to do with spring. We've been really busy at the service station, too." Blake glanced across the seat at her, his brown eyes glowing in the light from the dashboard. "You going to be able to handle working more hours for Emma?" His sudden concern touched Rhonda.

"Yeah, I think so." She looked out the window as Blake turned his Mustang down the rutted dirt road that led to the Weaver farm. "Cleaning Wes' house yesterday probably didn't help matters."

Blake slammed on the brakes, locking up the wheels and causing the car to skid several feet before coming to a stop in the middle of the road. Draping a wrist over the steering wheel, Blake turned dark eyes her way.

"What do you mean you cleaned house for Wes yesterday?" he asked quietly.

"How many meanings can there be for the words 'cleaning house?'" Rhonda asked, suddenly short tempered. "Becca and I went over after church and cleaned the house. Dusted, vacuumed, mopped the floors. That's what I meant."

"So he paid you?"

"No," Rhonda drew out the word. "We did it as a favor. It seemed like the neighborly thing to do. Wes has been awfully busy trying to get the farm up and running and doesn't have time for things like scrubbing the toilet. People around here have been snubbing him pretty badly, so I thought it would be the Christian thing to do, to help out. You know, like the Bible says, love your neighbor as yourself."

Love was probably the wrong word to use. Blake suddenly grabbed Rhonda by the arm and pulled her close, staring straight into her eyes.

"You stay away from Wes, Rhonda. You hear me?" He shook her slightly for emphasis. "I can't believe your daddy didn't have the good sense to tell you and Becca to stay away from that place. Don't you know the man's a murderer?"

"That has never been proven, and I suggest you let go of me right now," Rhonda commanded, her voice low.

Blake loosened his grip but didn't let her go completely. A horn sounded and Rhonda glanced over her shoulder to see headlights shining behind them.

"There's someone behind you, you'd better get moving."

Blake turned back under the wheel and stomped on the gas, causing the car to shoot forward and pressing Rhonda back against the leather seat.

"I mean it Rhonda, stay away from Wes," he warned again.

In her state of pique, Rhonda missed the fact that Blake had used her given name.

"You don't own me, Blake," she said coldly as he pulled into the Weaver driveway. "I'm not your wife, you don't have any right to tell me what to do."

"That's what this is all about then?" he asked, slamming the car into park. "Everyone else is getting married and you're not? You think a murderer like Wes Cooper is a better prospect than me?"

The question hit a little too close to home for Rhonda's piece of mind.

"Would you stop calling him that?" she cried.

"Everyone around here knows you had a thing for Brian. I would think you would hate Wes for what he did."

"There's never been any proof that he killed Brian," she said quietly, staring out the windshield at the night sky.

"Proof or not, everyone knows that he did. Even Nate Sweeney thinks so. He's been poking around, asking questions about the case. Promise me you'll stay away from Wes."

"I won't promise any such thing," Rhonda said firmly. "We're neighbors. My father is in a land use agreement with him. No matter what Nate Sweeney might think, the law says you're innocent until proven guilty and the Bible says judge not, that you be not judged. I follow God's orders, Blake, not yours. Good night."

With that she got out of the car and slammed the door. Hurrying to the front porch, she turned just in time to watch Blake go squealing down the road, his car fishtailing as he went.

Sitting at the kitchen table, Wes pushed aside the empty bowl in front of him and reached for the Montmorency County Tribune. He had eaten the last of Rhonda's soup for supper and had to admit she was a pretty good cook. It had been thoughtful of her to bring him a meal. Or had she just been trying to soften him up?

Shrugging the thought aside, he opened the paper to the classified ads, looking for a dog. He had seriously considered Becca's suggestion and the more he thought about it, the wiser it sounded. A dog would bark if anything came creeping around the farmyard in the middle of the night. A dog would sound the alarm if any visitor, wanted or unwanted, showed up at his door. But he wanted something big.

He didn't have time to raise and train a puppy to be a guard dog. At the rate things were going, he didn't have much time before it all came to a head. No, he needed a full-grown dog, something with a little bite to its bark.

An insistent knocking rattled the front door. Wes looked up from the paper in surprise. Picking up his pistol from the table, he tucked it into his jeans at the small of his back. He doubted the nighttime prowler would come announcing themselves at his door, but Wes lived by the motto of always be prepared. The knock sounded again, louder this time, as if his visitor was growing impatient.

"I'm coming," Wes muttered, releasing the chain from the front door and turning the lock. He pulled the door open to see a very belligerent Blake Dalton standing, arms akimbo, on the porch.

"Blake."

"You stay away from my girl, Cooper, you hear me?"

Brown eyes lit by the fire of anger stared at Wes through the screen door.

"I don't have any idea what you're talking about," Wes said slowly. He tucked one hand behind his back, feeling the cool steel of the gun. Blake had always been a hot head and it appeared, despite Rhonda's assertions to the contrary, that some things *hadn't* changed.

"Don't play dumb with me," Blake said, thrusting a forefinger against the screen. "You saw us together, you know good and well that Rhonda is my girl. You may have her fooled about your innocence, but the rest of us around here know the truth. You just stay away from her." Blake turned and stepped off the porch. Heading toward his car, he called over his shoulder, "I'm warning you Wes, stay away from Rhonda or you'll be sorry."

"And I'm warning you," Wes said quietly as Blake slammed his car door and roared down the driveway. "Stay off my property or you'll be sorry."

Easing the gun from the waistband of his jeans, Wes weighed it in his hand as he swung the front door closed and turned the lock. Heading back toward the kitchen he made a decision. He was definitely getting a dog.

Tiredly, Rhonda climbed the stairs to her bedroom. She needed a hot shower and bed. Maybe after a good night's sleep, the scene in Blake's car wouldn't seem so ugly. He was obviously jealous of her friendship with Wes. Shouldn't that make her happy? Blake wouldn't be jealous unless he had deep feelings for her.

Throwing herself across her bed, Rhonda thought about Blake's order that she stay away from Wes. Maybe she should. Everything would be so much easier if Wes wasn't in the mix. But the thought of not seeing Wes again left a cold, empty hole in Rhonda's heart, similar to the way she had felt after Brian died. The thought gave her pause. No, she didn't have those kinds of feelings for Wes. She just wanted to be a good neighbor. It was Christian love that motivated her to do good deeds for Wes, nothing more.

Not that it was any of Blake's business! Who did

he think he was, thinking he could tell her who to see and what to do? Remembering Blake's dictatorial tone put Rhonda's back up all over again. If Blake thought he could order her around, he had another think coming.

Pushing herself up from the bed, Rhonda gathered her nightgown and headed for the bathroom. A hot shower would help clear her muddled thinking and tomorrow she was determined that she would set Blake Dalton straight on a few things concerning their relationship!

CHAPTER TEN

Rhonda stood at the counter of the teashop's kitchen assembling a sandwich, glancing now and then at the green order ticket in front of her. She heard the bell ring out as someone entered the Spot of Tea but didn't rush out to see who it was. Emma was working the front counter and the lunch crowd had been fairly thin. Whoever had just come in, Emma could easily handle it.

"Hi sugar."

Rhonda turned her head to see Blake standing in the doorway, looking contrite.

"I asked Emma if it was okay if I came back and talked to you. She said it was."

Rhonda looked away from him, turning her attention once more to the order she was filling.

"I don't have time for this right now, Blake."

"Look, I know I owe you an apology." He walked farther into the kitchen, stopping at Rhonda's shoulder. "I'm sorry about last night," he said quietly.

Rhonda glanced up into his soft brown eyes that shone with repentance. Her heart softened somewhat.

"I was wrong to lose my temper about the thing with Wes. You're right, it was the Christian thing to do and I was wrong to get angry about it. I guess I was just jealous, that's all."

"Why in the world would you be jealous?" Rhonda demanded, slapping a piece of bread atop the sandwich. Peeling off the sanitary gloves protecting her hands, she threw them down on the counter in frustration. "It's not like we're serious about each other. We've been dating all these months and you've never hinted at wanting anything more than a fun time."

She turned and went to the stove to retrieve a steaming tea kettle.

"I'm more serious about you than you know, Rhonda. I've been crazy about you my whole life."

The confession caught Rhonda off guard and she once more turned her gaze up to look into Blake's eyes, searching them for sincerity.

"Will you at least forgive me for last night?"

"Of course I forgive you," Rhonda said, hefting the laden tray. "But I think we both need to give some thought to where our relationship is going."

Rhonda headed toward the dining room, Blake close on her heels.

"Do you want me to ask you to marry me, is that what you want?"

All heads in the dining room turned their way. Rhonda's face immediately turned crimson.

"No! And especially not in front of the customers

of the Spot of Tea," Rhonda turned and hissed. "We both need some time, Blake. Just go back to work and let me do the same, okay?"

Rhonda headed toward the table where an older couple couldn't quite hide their curiosity. She heard the bell set to tinkling with a vengeance and knew Blake had left the shop. Glancing out the front windows, Rhonda saw him stomping down the sidewalk toward the service station.

"You okay?" Nate Sweeney asked, reaching out a hand to stop Rhonda as she headed toward the kitchen with her now empty tray. Off duty, he was sitting at a table near the front door wearing jeans and a denim shirt.

"Yeah, I'm fine." Rhonda couldn't quite meet his eyes.

"That was quite a spectacle he managed to make," Emma said, putting a comforting arm around Rhonda's stiff shoulders. "I didn't know he was going to upset you or I never would have allowed him back in the kitchen."

"I'm not really upset. We just had a little set-to last night, he came to apologize," Rhonda explained.

"You aren't seriously considering marrying him, are you?" Nate's laser-beam blue eyes bored into Rhonda's. "I mean, I know you two have been going out, but marriage? You know how much trouble Blake's been in with the law in the past, Rhonda."

"That was a long time ago, Nate," Rhonda felt the need to come to Blake's defense.

"Leopards don't change their spots," Nate said.

"Oh, that's real Christian! Is that why you've

been poking around Brian's murder?" Rhonda asked, her temper rising. "You think Wes is another leopard who hasn't changed his spots?"

"I don't think this is a good time..." Emma tried to soothe.

"Well, I do!" Rhonda interrupted. "I think it's high time that someone came to Wes' defense. All these people around here claiming to be Christians, and yet they are the first ones to judge, or to hold unforgiveness. I'm tired of it! And I'm tired of people trying to tell me what to do. First one person wants to know why I haven't married Blake yet and now you're telling me not to marry him at all." She pointed a finger at Nate. "Then I've got you and Blake breathing down my neck, telling me to stay away from my own neighbor when the Bible is telling me I'm supposed to love him like I love myself." Rhonda turned and stomped back toward the kitchen. "I'm tired of it, I'm telling you, I'm just sick and tired of it!"

"Well, we're here," Wes said, putting his truck into park and turning off the ignition.

He looked across the seat to the German shepherd sitting on the passenger side, ears perked forward. Wes slowly reached a hand over, allowing the dog a good sniff before scratching him behind the ear.

"Think you'll like it here?" he asked. The dog tilted his head as if listening.

Wes had nearly changed his mind about getting a dog. He had told Becca before that he didn't have time for pets and that was true. But then this morning, as he stepped out on the front porch, something happened that changed his mind.

On the porch was the lid of a heavy cardboard box, and inside the lid someone had painstakingly reconstructed a miniature scene of a car accident. Mounds of salt were made to look like snowdrifts and a blacktop road was covered in a substance that resembled ice. Upside down in the "snow" was a tiny toy car, the same color as Wes' parents. A note had been attached to the box.

You will be next.

Sitting back on his heels, Wes contemplated the message. Was it insinuating that his parents' car accident hadn't been an *accident?* Or was it merely warning Wes that he could find himself in an unfortunate "accident" if he wasn't careful?

In a fit of sudden fury, Wes had stood and with a vicious kick sent the deadly diorama flying off the porch. He was tired of games. Why couldn't his enemy just come out and face him in the open instead of skulking in the shadows?

"There's a lot of vermin around these parts," Wes said now to the dog beside him. "You think you're up for the challenge?"

The German shepherd whined in response.

"Okay then, lets get to it."

"You okay?" Emma asked Rhonda as the two straightened the dining room after the day's business.

"Yeah, I'm fine. I'm sorry about earlier." Rhonda removed a soiled antique tablecloth from a table and tossed it into a pile to be washed.

"Apology accepted," Emma said, lifting chairs in preparation for sweeping the floor. "And you were right about us judging, both Wes and Blake. I hope you know it's because we care about you. We aren't trying to tell you what to do. Tyler and I and Nate, we want you to be happy. I guess we have a tendency to look at you as a little sister, and that makes us want to protect you, especially Nate. He's in the protection business, you know."

"I know." Rhonda dropped into a nearby chair and pulled the ponytail holder from her hair, letting the curly mass fall around her shoulders. She rubbed her scalp, suddenly feeling very tired. "Can I ask you a question?"

"Sure."

"How did you know Tyler was the right one? I mean, we all know that Nate had a thing for you for a long time, but you never gave any indication that you felt anything besides friendship for him. Why Tyler and not Nate?"

"Hmm, that's a very good question."

Emma pulled out the chair across from Rhonda and sat down, her hand automatically going to her still flat stomach, as if reminding herself of the life she and Tyler had created.

"You're right, I did know that Nate was attracted to me. And for awhile, when everything was happening, you know, with the vandalism and all the threats," Emma said, referring to the previous summer when a young man from Atlanta had nearly destroyed her home and business and kidnapped and attempted to rape her.

"During that time, I tried to force myself to feel something for Nate. I thought, if I could just feel something for him, then I would be safe, with him being a policeman. But I never had any romantic feelings for Nate. But Tyler." Emma laughed. "That's a different story. He seemed to turn my heart upside down and inside out from the minute he drove into Atlanta."

Rhonda cringed. Wasn't that what Wes had done, turned her life upside down and inside out since he came back to town?

"But what did it *feel* like?" she asked, needing to know.

"Oh, I guess I had all the classic romance novel symptoms. You know, I felt all light headed when he smiled at me, like that feeling you get going down the first hill of a roller coaster, where your stomach's up to about here." Emma held a hand under her chin. "Just the thought of seeing him could make me all weak in the knees and I thought about him *a lot*." Emma smiled. "I was just drawn to him. I wanted to do nice things for him, help him out, be with him all the time."

Rhonda nearly groaned. She was a goner.

"But don't you think a couple can make a good marriage without all those giddy feelings?" Rhonda asked, hopeful. Maybe there was still a chance for her and Blake.

Emma's brows drew together in thought.

"I suppose they could," she answered slowly, then she began to smile slyly. "But I don't think it would be nearly as much fun. I guess I've heard about success stories, you know, of arranged marriages, or marriages of convenience, where the two people weren't head over heels in love, but eventually built a sturdy and lasting relationship built on mutual respect. I know that Pastor Bennett warned us during counseling that those heady, romantic feelings can come and go, and that we shouldn't base our marriage on that. A lot of people get divorced nowadays because the spine-tingling sensations have a tendency to wax and wane and when they wane, people think that means they aren't in love anymore."

Rhonda grasped the flimsy straw Emma offered. That was the problem! Her feelings for Blake were only waning right now, that didn't necessarily mean their relationship was doomed, even if Wes did turn her knees to mush.

"Why are you asking me all this?" Emma asked.

Rhonda shrugged a shoulder. "I was just curious, that's all. I'm not sure how I'm supposed to know Mr. Right when he comes knocking at my door."

"You don't think Blake is your Mr. Right, do you?"

The straightforward question didn't catch Rhonda by surprise. Her boss had an uncanny knack for discerning the truth about people.

"I never said that," Rhonda hedged, scratching her thumbnail against the table top. "I want him to be. I mean, why wouldn't he be my Mr. Right? He's everything a girl could want. Good looking, fun, a hard worker," she said with a decided lack of enthusiasm. "We used to have a lot of fun together."

"Used to? Are you saying things have suddenly changed between the two of you? Let me think, this doesn't happen to have anything to do with Wes Cooper, does it?"

Rhonda's head snapped up and she stared at her boss. She should have known Emma would see right through her!

"I wouldn't have guessed except for you getting so angry about people assuming he's guilty," Emma explained with a nonchalant shrug. "I did the same thing when people accused Tyler of being the one threatening me."

"Being around him seems to cause a lot of those feelings you described," Rhonda admitted. "But Wes, he's a dangerous man, even if he isn't guilty of Brian's murder. Even if Blake doesn't make me feel all giddy, at least he's safe. He may be the best shot I have if I ever want to have a husband and kids."

"Oh Rhonda, don't say that!" Emma reached across and squeezed Rhonda's hands where they lay on the table top. "I'm sure the Lord has someone for you. If not Wes or Blake, then someone else who will share your love for Jesus. You know, the Bible has a lot to say about peace. It tells us to seek peace, that Jesus is the Prince of Peace, that the peace of God will keep our hearts and minds. You asked me how I knew Tyler was the one for me. I guess I would say I had that perfect peace in my heart. I just *knew*. Just like I somehow knew Nate *wasn't* my Mr. Right. And now isn't Penny glad of that?"

Emma laughed, causing Rhonda to relax and

smile too.

"My advice to you would be to follow peace. Pray, ask the Lord for His direction and He'll put that peace that passes understanding in your heart. If you don't have peace about your relationship with Blake, then don't go marrying him hoping it will materialize somewhere down the road. You'll just be miserable. As far as Wes is concerned, he *is* still a suspect in his brother's murder. All I can tell you is be careful and pray."

Emma put both hands flat on the tabletop and pushed herself to her feet.

"Now, let's get this place cleaned up so I can go home to my husband."

CHAPTER ELEVEN

Wes gave the nail a final whack, sinking it firmly into the wood, then stood back to admire his handwork. His new companion sat a few feet away, eyeing the doghouse curiously.

"What do you think, Ranger?" Wes asked.

The dog had come with the name Rocky, but Wes had decided to change it, naming Ranger after his old profession. The dog seemed to already recognize his new moniker as he cocked his head, tongue lolling out the side of his mouth.

"I hate to keep you chained up outside, but I'm afraid you won't do me much good as a guard dog sleeping in the house."

The kittens came to explore the new addition to the farmyard. Ranger rose from his haunches and trotted over, putting his nose down to sniff Peanut. The orange ball of fluff turned and began spitting and hissing at the dog.

"Easy there, now." Wes put his hand on the back of Ranger's neck and the dog immediately sat. Squatting down, Wes scooped up the two kittens and held them for Ranger to inspect. Tiny claws tried to imbed themselves in Wes' hands as Ranger gave each kitten a lick for good measure. "You guys all have a job to do, you are going to have to learn to get along," Wes admonished. He set the kittens back down and they shot inside the doghouse.

Walking to his truck with Ranger at his side, Wes retrieved a long length of heavy gauge chain.

"This is only for during the night," he assured the dog.

He began to chuckle. He must sound like Dr. Doolittle, talking to the animals. As long as they didn't start talking back, he thought. Back beside the doghouse, he began attaching the chain. Ranger lay down in a patch of sun and soon both kittens were curled up at his side. Wes couldn't help but smile.

"I see you took my advice," he said. Ranger opened one eye and looked at him balefully. "Just don't let the enemy see you like that," Wes warned. "You're supposed to be scary. I brought you here to protect stuff, don't you forget it."

He reached over a hand and patted the dog on the head before rising and gathering his tools. Ranger got to his feet, leaving the disgruntled kittens in the dust.

"Okay, I'm gonna put this stuff away and then we'll have some dinner. How does that sound?"

A short while later, Wes stood in the kitchen staring into the refrigerator. He never thought he would see the day when he missed army food. It had been so easy, just go to the mess hall and get chow. Or some evenings he and his buddies would order a pizza, or go to the NCO club. Either way, he had rarely fixed anything more than a bag of microwave popcorn. He had told Rhonda he wasn't starving, and that was true enough, but man, he was tired of trying to figure out what to eat. Warming up Rhonda's soup for two days had been a welcome respite.

A knock sounded, sending Ranger bounding for the front door, barking ferociously. Wes followed.

"Good boy, good boy," he praised, swinging the door open.

As if conjured up by his thoughts, Rhonda stood on the porch clutching a foil-wrapped packet and staring wide-eyed at the snarling dog at Wes' side.

"Good boy, Ranger, sit." Wes placed his hand on Ranger's collar and the dog sat obediently.

"When did you get a dog?" Rhonda asked, still staring at the German shepherd.

"Today."

"I thought you didn't have time for pets."

Wes watched her carefully through the screen, his pretty little spy. He hoped the intimidating canine at his side would make her think twice. But then he remembered Blake's words, that Wes had Rhonda fooled about his innocence. Did the red-headed pixie on his porch really think he was innocent of his brother's murder? Or was she just trying to lull him into a false sense of security? The thought made his stomach churn, especially when he remembered the rest of Blake's tirade, his warning that Wes was to stay away from "his girl."

"I changed my mind," he finally said, he tone purposefully cool. "You know, it's probably not a good idea for you to just show up here unannounced."

"Because he bites?" Rhonda asked, motioning toward the dog with the packet in her hands.

"Well, I'm hoping he does."

Rhonda's gaze swung to his in alarm.

"What about Sunday?"

"What about it?"

"Becca and I were going to come clean the house again on Sunday," Rhonda explained.

So, she wasn't giving up her spy games that easily.

"Oh, that." Wes nodded. "Don't worry, I'll tie him up out back while you're here."

"I'm not quite sure why you want to have a dog that bites. You know if he bites someone, you're home owners insurance is going to go through the roof."

"I want him for the same reason I pack heat, as you like to call it. Protection."

"You don't honestly think there's anyone around here that you need to protect yourself from, do you?" Rhonda asked, incredulous.

Her blue eyes seemed to shine with innocence. If only Ranger could protect him from the affects those eyes were having on his heart.

"You would be surprised," he answered.

"Well." Rhonda hesitated, as if searching for a way to respond. "I brought you a casserole. I figured the soup was probably gone by now."

She held the foil packet toward the door and Wes opened it. Spy or no spy, he gladly accepted her offering. His dinner dilemma was solved.

"And here," she reached into the deep pocket of

Help Me, Rhonda

her quilted jacket and pulled out a muffin wrapped in plastic wrap. "I even brought you dessert."

"Is this one of Emma's famous muffins?" he asked, taking the confection from her hand. Rhonda only nodded. "Becca told me I hadn't lived till I ate one. I guess this will take care of that problem."

"Yeah, well, I guess this is the last one you'll get, unless you come into the teashop. I won't risk getting bit in order to satisfy your hunger."

Wes relented some in his assessment of her when he heard the anxiousness hovering near the edges of Rhonda's words.

"I'll make sure you get good and acquainted Sunday, then you won't have to worry," Wes found himself reassuring. He looked from Rhonda to the dog, finding it much easier to keep his eyes on Ranger rather than the vulnerable woman on the other side of the screen. He cleared his throat. "I never did thank you for the soup. It was good. And I appreciate this, too." He held up the casserole. "A man gets tired of his own cooking real quick."

"You're welcome," Rhonda said. "I have to go."

She spun and hurried across the porch and down the step. Standing in the doorway holding the warm casserole in his hands, Wes watched her climb into her pickup truck, feeling a new kind of hunger building, a longing that had nothing to do with his stomach.

Rhonda drove home in a swirling vortex of emotions. What was happening to her? It had started the minute Wes had swung open the front door wearing his signature black t-shirt. Her head had started feeling light and her heart had lifted until if felt like it was blocking her throat. Then the tingling had begun, despite the ferocious looking dog sitting at his side.

Pulling into her own driveway, Rhonda drove her truck past the house, down to the pole barn situated at the very edge of the farm's yard. Several strands of hot wire surrounded three sides of the barn. Getting out of the truck, Rhonda made her way to the door of the barn and slid it back on its well-greased wheels. She found the light switch and flipped on the glaring overhead lights. A buckskin mare looked out over a stall door, tossing her head up and down in greeting. Rhonda strode quickly down the barn's center aisle and patted her horse's forelock.

"I know Daddy already fed you, so don't be thinking to fool me into giving you more oats," Rhonda scolded as the horse nudged the front of her jacket. The mare lipped the coat pocket, searching for a treat.

A whinny sounded from the next stall and Rhonda stood on tip-toe to glance down at the white Shetland pony who impatiently pawed the straw.

"You two act like you've never been fed," Rhonda complained with a laugh. "Okay, I guess it won't hurt for you to have a little treat."

She moved to the tack room and dumped several sugar cubes from a box into her hand. Returning to the horse, Rhonda held the sugar out on the palm of her hand. Sandy greedily lipped up the cubes, tickling Rhonda's palm with her fuzzy whiskers.

"Smokey's turn."

Rhonda unlatched the pony's stall door and knelt

in the straw, holding out the treat. As Smokey nuzzled her palm, Rhonda ran the fingers of her other hand through the white mane, combing out snarls.

"Smokey, you know anything about love?" she asked the pony. Smokey merely nudged the front of Rhonda's coat in reply, nearly tumbling her back into the straw. "No? I didn't figure you did."

Standing, Rhonda brushed straw from her knees before exiting the stall and latching it firmly behind her. She leaned against Sandy's door, deep in thought. The horse sniffed her hair and Rhonda absently pushed her head away before giving Sandy a scratch behind the ears.

"According to Emma, I seem to have all the fatal symptoms," she finally admitted out loud. "I want to do nice things for him, I think about him an awful lot, and he definitely makes it hard for me to breath. But he's my old boyfriend's brother! Isn't that just too weird?" She looked deep into Sandy's eyes. "Isn't it? Isn't that just weird?" Sandy tossed her head up and down as if in agreement. "And what if he did murder Brian? I mean, I'm all for giving him the benefit of the doubt, but I have to keep in mind that it's possible he's guilty. No, it doesn't matter the physical symptoms," Rhonda determined, heading toward the door. She flicked the lights off and rolled the door closed. "I absolutely refuse to fall in love with Wes Cooper."

"Dinner is served," Wes declared, dumping a scoop of dog food into Ranger's bowl. The dog fell upon the food and inhaled it in less than thirty seconds then stood looking up at Wes for more.

"Sorry, buddy, my turn now."

Wes sat at the kitchen table and pulled the foil off the casserole. Steam rose from the top, carrying with it the aroma of basil and oregano.

"Mmm, Italian," he commented, spooning a large serving of pasta covered in sauce onto his plate. "You're German," he reminded the dog who sat shamelessly begging. "You don't eat Italian food. Go lay down." Ranger immediately obeyed, going to lay by his now empty dish.

Wes dug into the food on his plate.

"Not a bad cook, for a spy," he said. Ranger lifted his head as if listening. Wes looked down with suspicion at the pasta on his fork. An alarming thought suddenly occurred to him. "What if this is poisoned?" he asked, turning the fork around and around, looking at the bite of food from every angle. "Maybe I should have let you taste it first," he said to the dog.

Ranger sat up, as if ready and willing to oblige his master.

"Well, I suppose if she was going to poison me, she would have done it with the soup," Wes reasoned. "Do you think she really is a spy? She's awfully cute for a spy. I didn't remember her being that cute."

Wes put the forkful of pasta in his mouth and chewed, remembering Rhonda as a skinny, freckle-faced kid with wild red hair. She was still pretty skinny, and she was still freckle-faced and she still had all that curly, red hair. It just wasn't as wild. And those Lake Superior blue eyes. They seemed to reflect everything she was thinking and feeling. If the town had chosen her as their spy, they had made a bad choice. Wes swallowed a bite of pasta and with it the truth, he really didn't want Rhonda to be a spy.

Looking around the empty kitchen, Wes remembered happier days when the house had been filled with love and laughter and the smell of freshly baked cookies. He fast forwarded to the future, imagining it being that way again. For so long all he had cared about was getting home, but now Wes realized he didn't want to live here alone for the rest of his life.

During his time in the army he had managed to avoid romantic entanglements. As a Ranger who was frequently deployed to dangerous places around the globe, he had seen what his job did to other guys in the unit with families. And worse, what it did to the families of those soldiers who didn't come back. But he was no longer fighting the world's battles. Rhonda Weaver suddenly had him thinking about hearth and home and children.

Then Wes remembered Blake's warning. Rhonda was Blake's girl. The code of ethics said that Wes should keep his hands off. Then there was the little matter of who was trying to drive him off his farm. He might not be fighting the world's battles, but he had his own struggles that needed to be settled before he could think about the future.

"Besides," Wes told Ranger as he forked another bite of pasta into his mouth. "She was in love with my brother, and she probably thinks I killed him."

CHAPTER TWELVE

Sitting on a tall stool at the island in the farmhouse kitchen, Rhonda sipped a cup of coffee and watched the family bustle around. Becca was rushing to get ready for school as Mary packed her lunch.

"Where's my history book? Has anyone seen my history book?" Becca called frantically as she clattered down the stairs.

"Haven't seen it, honey," Mary answered.

"I think it was in the family room," Rhonda said. Setting her cup down, she slid from the stool. "I'll go get it," she told her sister as Becca grabbed her brown lunch sack and stuffed it into her backpack.

"Thanks." Becca threw her sister a look of relief. "Bye Momma, bye Daddy. See ya this afternoon."

Becca rushed into the hallway as Rhonda stepped from the sunken family room carrying the missing book.

"Here you go."

"Thanks." Becca shoved the book into her backpack and hefted the canvas bag onto her shoulder.

Help Me, Rhonda

"Hey, Becca."

"Yeah?" Becca stopped at the front door and looked over her shoulder.

"Don't be stopping in at the Cooper's by yourself, okay?"

"Why?" Her fine brows rose at the request.

"Because Wes got a dog. A very big dog. A German shepherd and it may bite."

"Oh, he must have taken my advice."

"What advice?"

"Something got in his chicken coop the other night and ate all the brooding eggs. I told Wes he should think about getting a dog. I gotta go or I'll miss the bus. See ya later, Ronnie."

"Okay, bye. Have a good day at school."

Rhonda watched her sister dash out the door. She stood for several minutes in the hallway, wondering about Wes Cooper and his new companion. When he said the dog was for protection, was it his chickens he was talking about? Rhonda got the distinct impression it was not.

"I'm getting ready to go out and do chores," Rhonda's father said, stepping into the hallway. "I saw the back pasture is starting to get some grass, you want me to put the horses out there today?" he asked.

"Actually, it's supposed to be really nice today. I was hoping to get off early and ride when I get home," Rhonda answered.

"Okey-dokey then, I'll leave them up by the barn." David headed for the back door, settling a cap more firmly on his head.

Rhonda returned to the kitchen to see her mother leaning up against the counter, cupping a coffee mug in both hands.

"Whew, I swear mornings get more hectic around here with every passing year," Mary said. "Was that only one child going out the door for school? I don't know how I ever managed when I had five of you getting ready at the same time."

"I think Becca is equal to all five of us older kids," Rhonda said with a smile. She sat once more on her stool and took a sip of her now cold coffee.

"Did I hear you say something to Becca about Wes getting a dog?" her mother asked.

"Yeah, I got to meet the beast last night when I took a casserole over there. Becca didn't seem surprised. She said something had gotten into the chicken coop and stole the eggs. That's probably why Wes got a dog."

"I hope he makes out okay over there," Mary said, turning to put away the sandwich fixings that were strewn across the countertop.

"You sound worried," Rhonda observed.

"Well, I hear things, you know. Women coming in the quilt shop are talking. There's a lot of grumbling going on about Wes coming home and taking up life as if nothing ever happened between him and his brother."

The sentiment was familiar. Rhonda had been hearing the same thing at the Spot of Tea.

"But no one knows for sure that anything did happen between Wes and Brian," she argued.

"I know that and you know that, but some people, well, they would prefer to believe the worst.

I'm hearing a lot of people saying they are calling on the prosecutor to start an investigation."

"Do you think Wes killed Brian?" Rhonda finally asked the question that had been plaguing her for years. She stared down into her cup, unsure if she wanted to hear the answer.

Closing the refrigerator, Mary sighed and turned to face her daughter. She came over and stroked Rhonda's hair.

"We never talked about it, you know," Rhonda said, emotions welling as she looked into her mother's sea-blue eyes.

"I know, and I'm sorry about that. Your dad and I, we were never very good with words. You were so devastated by Brian's death and I didn't know how to comfort you. I worried that talking about it would just make it worse."

"So, what did you think, back then I mean?"

"About Wes?" At Rhonda's nod, Mary sat on a nearby stool, thinking. "I really didn't know what to think," she finally admitted. "Wes was always a nice boy. Very polite and hard working. Captain of the football team and president of the 4-H club. When Brian was first killed, I couldn't believe Wes would do such a thing. But then I got to thinking about how strained their relationship had gotten, remembered harsh words I had heard spoken between them. Then when Wes left in such a hurry, I was like everyone else, thinking that proved his guilt. But then I changed my mind."

"Why? What changed your mind?" Rhonda wanted to know.

"Deanne. We spent a lot of time together in those days. Here she lost two sons in a matter of months. I was trying to be the best friend I knew how to be, so I spent a lot of time with her. It was like she suddenly realized what she had done, babying Brian all those years. She saw that she had cultivated a lot of animosity between the boys. Not on purpose, of course. You'll understand someday when you are a parent. You do the best you can, but you will make mistakes. We all do."

Mary sighed as if contemplating her own shortcomings as a parent.

"Anyway, Deanne was absolutely convinced that Wes had not killed Brian. She told me over and over how a mother would just know that about her son. She said that if she thought for a minute that Wes was guilty, she would be the first to turn him in. But deep in her heart of hearts, she knew he hadn't done it.

"Carl was a different matter. He had plenty of doubt for both of them. He could barely look at Wes. Deanne tried to convince him Wes was innocent, but Carl just couldn't be sure. I think now it was his father's suspicion, not guilt, that drove Wes away. He left, thinking his parents blamed him for Brian's death. He never contacted them or spoke to them again. That was nearly as devastating to Deanne as Brian's murder was. It was her conviction that convinced me Wes was innocent."

A boulder lifted from Rhonda's shoulders. "But how do we convince the rest of the town?" she asked.

"That, my daughter, is a very good question.

One I don't have the answer to. All we can do is pray that the truth wins out."

Standing in the gravel drive, wearing his dad's old, red wool hunting jacket, Wes watched the truck driver back the stock trailer into the farm yard. Suddenly the hair on the back of his neck stood on end and he had the oddest feeling of being watched. Turning, his eyes scanned the hip-roofed barn. He glanced toward Ranger who was tied at his dog house and barking at the strange vehicle pulling down the drive. Nothing out of the ordinary.

Wes tried to shake off the feeling but it persisted. He had that odd sense of déjà vu. He was back in the jungle with eyes watching him from thick undergrowth. But here there was no place for anyone to hide. He glanced once more toward the barn and the feeling evaporated. It was just his overactive imagination toying with him.

Turning his attention back to the truck, Wes watched as with expert ease the trucker placed the back end of the trailer right up to the open gate leading into the small front pasture. The air brakes whooshed as the driver opened his door and jumped down from the cab carrying a clip board.

"You Wes Cooper?" he asked. A beefy hand came up to weigh down the paper that fluttered in the morning breeze.

"Yep, that's me," Wes answered.

"Got a load of ten angus calves for you. Let's get 'em unloaded and then I'll have you sign some paperwork."

The driver laid the clipboard on the wheel well of the trailer then proceeded to swing open the back gate and let down the ramp. Ten pairs of dark eyes stared back at the men in fear and distrust.

"That's some good eatin' right there," the trucker said. "Or will be when they get some meat on them bones. Nothing better than a black angus steak, that's what I say. Git on outta there now," he said.

Removing the cap from his balding head, the truck driver climbed into the trailer. Waving the cap back and forth, he pushed a black haunch, forcing a calf to move forward. Soon all ten were clattering down the ramp and burying their wet noses in the hay piles Wes had strewn around the small enclosure. The driver secured the back of the trailer while Wes closed the pasture gate.

"Look 'em over real good, make sure they don't have no defects," the man instructed, retrieving his clip board. "Then you can sign this paper saying I delivered 'em to ya all safe and sound."

Wes did as he was told, looking over the skittish calves as they pivoted this way and that to get away from him. None of them appeared lame. Their eyes were clear and their coats glossy with good health. Wes signed the paper and the driver climbed back into his cab. With another hiss of the air brakes, the truck ground into gear and rolled back up the drive toward the road.

Standing in the teardrop of grass created by the circular drive, Wes' eyes traveled over the barn and the pasture where the calves frolicked. The two kittens chased each other near the barn door. He glanced toward Ranger who was now snoozing in the sun. He could hear the gentle clucking of the chickens in the coop. Wes felt like a king surveying his kingdom. Satisfaction rolled over him like a warm spring rain.

He turned and looked at the house sitting square and snug and safe. The windows glittered in the morning light. His home. It came again, the odd sensation of being watched. Goosebumps formed on his arms, making Wes automatically reach for the gun at his waist. Only the gun wasn't there. He had left it on the dresser. Slowly he turned his head to glance over his shoulder. No one was there. Ranger slept on. The calves remained with noses buried in the hay.

Turning fully, Wes searched farther afield, past the barn and upper pasture to the woods surrounding the cedar swamp. A sudden light shone, as if the sun had glanced off something shiny. Binoculars perhaps? So, he was being watched after all. It was good to know his instincts were still intact. Wes had a feeling he was going to need every skill he had acquired in the army to beat the enemy that was after him.

The bell over the door of the Spot of Tea rang out just as Rhonda bustled from the kitchen with a full tray. She glanced toward the door to see Penelope Scott enter, dressed in her Department of Natural Resources uniform.

"Hey Penny, have a seat. I'll be right with ya," Rhonda called as she proceeded to place a tea pot and scones in front of two elderly women sitting near the corner windows. "Anything else I can get

Help Me, Rhonda

you ladies?" she asked. When they shook their heads, Rhonda turned and walked the few steps to where Penny was seated.

"Let me guess," she said, smiling at Penny. "Hot cocoa, extra whipped cream." Penny's sweet tooth was often the brunt of jokes at the Spot of Tea.

"Ha! Shows what you know," Penny answered smugly. "I was actually thinking vanilla cappuccino sounded good today."

"Okay, coming right up." Rhonda turned toward the kitchen.

"With extra whipped cream," Penny called, making Rhonda laugh. "And a chocolate chip muffin!"

Several minutes later, Rhonda brought out the steaming beverage piled high with whipped cream and chocolate shavings. She set it before Penny who made appreciative noises in her throat.

"And one chocolate chip muffin," Rhonda said. The antique saucer she placed on the table was nearly dwarfed by the muffin. "Are you sure you aren't the one expecting?"

"Rhonda! How could you even say such a thing?" Penny's voice resounded with offense as her golden eyes glared up at Rhonda.

"Sorry, it was just a joke," Rhonda apologized. "Is everything okay? You seem a little tense," she asked, pulling out a chair to sit across from Penny.

"Yeah, everything is fine, I'm sorry I snapped at you."

Penny put a hand to the knot of honey blonde hair twisted up on the back of her head, as if checking to make sure no strands had come loose. Satisfied that all was in order, she picked up her spoon and skimmed whipped cream off the top of her mug.

"I guess I am getting a little stressed out, trying to get all the arrangements made for moving my mom here, and the wedding is only two months away and it's calving time for the elk so I'm trying to keep an eye on them because I need to include that data in the study I'm working on for the DNR. Too much to think about."

"Did you at least get to talk to Mrs. Brisby about helping out with your mom?" Rhonda asked.

"Oh, yes." Penny nodded as she took a bite of muffin. "She agreed," she said around the mouthful of baked good. Taking a sip of cappuccino, Penny wiped cream from her top lip. "Thanks for suggesting it. I think it will work out great. Now if I can just get all this wedding stuff in order."

"If you need any help, you know I'll do what I can."

"Yeah, and I hear you might be next." At Rhonda's puzzled frown, Penny explained, "Nate said Blake was in here announcing to half the town that he was going to ask you to marry him. Sorry I missed that."

"Blake wasn't serious." Rhonda waved away the suggestion and got up from the table. "Blake is rarely serious about anything. Hey." She clutched the black tray to her chest like a shield. "Has Nate said anything about looking into the Cooper murder case?"

"Rhonda, honey, get real." Penny's eyes cut quickly up to Rhonda before she went back to devouring her breakfast. "I've got a mother to move, a wedding to plan and elk to study. You honestly think Nate is going to confide in me about his investigations? Not if he wants to keep that gorgeous head of his."

"I've heard rumors that there's pressure to revisit the case."

"Didn't you guys say that murder happened like ten years ago? Why the sudden interest in it now?"

"Because Wes Cooper came back home, and some people around here won't let anything lie."

"Well, I've got other things to worry about," Penny said, getting up. She laid several bills on the table. "Wes Cooper can live out on his farm and raise cows all he wants. As long as he doesn't put a hitch in my wedding, I'll like him just fine."

CHAPTER THIRTEEN

Rhonda rode Sandy at a leisurely pace down the rutted trail that was cut into the woods between the Cooper and Weaver farms. Thankfully it had been a slow afternoon at the Spot of Tea. She and Emma had cleaned up in record time so that Rhonda could get home in time to squeeze in a rare trail ride before dark.

Reining Sandy to a stop, Rhonda pulled a tree branch close and inspected it. Yep, there were green buds on the branches. Now if they would just open into leaves, it would truly feel like spring. She nudged the horse forward once again, listening to the flutter of birds in the trees. A black-capped chickadee called out, making Rhonda smile. Like a family movie playing, Rhonda saw in her mind the many times she had ridden down this trail with her brothers on their dirt bikes or with Becca riding next to her on little Smokey.

A doe and spindly-legged fawn jumped out of the woods and dashed across the trail, making Sandy

Help Me, Rhonda

plant her hooves, nearly unseating Rhonda. Sandy snorted and tossed her head.

"Whoa, girl." Rhonda patted the horse's neck. "Did you see that? Well, obviously you did." Rhonda laughed. "What a pretty little fawn. Couldn't have been very old."

Sandy's withers continued to tremble and twitch.

"You're okay," Rhonda assured, nudging the horse's sides with her heels. "You can tell we haven't been trail riding in ages. Deer didn't used to bother you a bit."

Pulling her ball cap farther down over her brow, Rhonda searched the ground beside the trail for signs of lady slippers and pussy willows. Soon morel mushrooms would be poking up through the dead leaves, a true sign of spring. With her attention focused on the ground, she never saw the dark, heavy object falling from the tree above her head.

The air was knocked from her lungs as she landed flat on her back on the hard ground. Sandy squealed in terror and took off down the trail at a full gallop. The monster from the tree was upon Rhonda in an instant, a vise-like grip encircling her throat, cutting off all breath. She stared up at an unfamiliar face, features obscured behind camouflage paint, and tore at the hands that held her down. Searing pain ripped through her lungs. She was dieing. The face above her began to spiral out of focus. A hand left her throat long enough to pull the ball cap from her head, spilling her hair on the ground around her.

"Rhonda! What in the world are you doing?" It was Wes' voice, sounding far away.

He pulled his other hand away from her throat and moved from astride her. Rhonda's hands immediately went to the place his had left, fingers plucking as she gasped for air. Still no breath came. Frantic eyes met his.

"I just knocked the wind out of you, that's all. Relax. Take shallow breaths. Easy now. You'll be fine in just a minute. Don't fight it so hard. Easy, easy. That's it."

Rhonda found she couldn't look away from the grey eyes looking down at her with compassion. Despite the war paint, his eyes looked nearly human. If she could move, she would scratch them out!

Slowly, painfully, her lungs began to fill. Rhonda struggled to sit up.

"Here, take it easy." A hand came behind her shoulder, easing her up.

Rhonda shrugged the help away. She rubbed the back of her head, picking sticks from her hair. She could feel a goose egg already forming. Wes handed her the ball cap and she snatched it from his hand.

"What is wrong with you?" she screeched when she was finally able to get a full breath. "Are you nuts or something? Swinging down from the trees like Tarzan trying to kill me?"

"I didn't know it was you." No apology and no remorse in the steel of his eyes now that she had regained the ability to breath. "And you are trespassing."

"Trespassing?!"

Rhonda looked at him in disbelief. He wore camouflage pants and the black t-shirt she was becoming so familiar with. But all romantic notions had fled the minute he had nearly killed her.

"Trespassing?" she asked again. "Since when? We've been using this trail as long as I can remember. Your parents never complained."

"My parents don't own this land anymore, I do. I don't take kindly to trespassers."

"Fine. As soon as I catch my horse, I'll get off your stinking land."

Rhonda got slowly to her feet and looked around for Sandy. Every fiber of her body hurt. She was going to be feeling this for days. She shot a seething look at Wes who stood watching her, hands on his hips. Her fickle heart chose that moment to give a painful squeeze and her breath suddenly felt short again, only this time she couldn't blame having the wind knocked out of her. The tingling sensation at the top of her head made her temper flare.

"You know, if you would have just let me ride on by, I would have been off your property a long time ago," she said huffily as she shoved the cap back on her head.

Spying Sandy a short distance up the trail, Rhonda gave a low whistle The horse raised her head and stared at her owner, reins hanging to the ground.

"Come on, girl, it's okay," Rhonda called to the horse in a sing-song voice. She walked forward slowly, fishing in the front pocket of her quilted jacket for a handful of sugar cubes. Sandy shook her head and backed a step away. "Don't you even dare," Rhonda said in the same sweet, crooning voice. "Come on, Sandy, want some sugar?"

Rhonda held her hand out, palm flat, letting Sandy get a good look at the treat. The horse stretched out her neck, sniffing.

"That's it."

Sandy took a slow step forward and lipped up the sugar while Rhonda grabbed the reins. Leading the still skittish horse, she walked back up the trail to where Wes stood, hands in the pockets of his camo pants. She met his cool stare and searched his face, seeking what, she was not sure. The black and green paint was a mask, hiding the real man who lay underneath.

"You said you didn't know it was me coming down the trail. Who were you waiting for up there, ready to knock them on their backside?"

Grey eyes scanned the treetops and blue sky above before answering.

"Somebody."

"Well, that narrows it down."

"You wouldn't understand." His eyes met and held hers again. Something in their cold, hard depths called out to Rhonda's heart.

"I might," she said softly.

He turned from her. Stomping a few paces up the trail, he stopped and kicked at the dirt. For a moment he stood still, hands on lean hips, head hanging down. Rhonda stared at the black t-shirt stretched across broad shoulders thick with muscle. She fought the urge to go to him and run a hand across those shoulders, easing the tension she saw there.

"I'm not your enemy, Wes Cooper," she said instead. "I know you feel you've been fighting them all your life. I know you think half the town is against you, but I'm not one of them."

His head came up, as if he were listening. Sandy stomped an impatient hoof. Finally, Wes spun to face her.

"Somebody's trying to run me off."

The accusation didn't really surprise Rhonda. "Who?"

Wes merely shrugged.

"I thought maybe you could tell me."

His gaze was cold and hard. Rhonda's temper flared for the briefest moment before common sense smothered the flame. She knew what was being said around town. Wes had good reason to be suspicious, even of her.

"I told you Wes, I'm not your enemy. If you tell me what's going on, maybe I can help."

His defensive posture evaporated one muscle at a time. "Someone was out here in the woods this morning, watching me. I wouldn't have known except I saw the sun glint off binoculars. I found footprints in the wet grass."

"It could have been anybody. Maybe a bird watcher," Rhonda reasoned. "It's migration time, a lot of people are out bird watching."

Wes just shook his head. "There's been other things," he said firmly.

"Like what?"

"How do I know I can really trust you?" Wes' head snapped up, his eyes boring into hers, his gaze once more laced with suspicion.

"Nate Sweeney is my friend, but I never told him

you held a gun on me that first day we met. I could have. I probably *should* have," Rhonda emphasized. "But I didn't."

"Okay." Wes nearly smiled. "It actually started before I even came home. After my parents were killed. Someone started sending anonymous offers to buy the farm. Offers veiled with threats about Brian's murder." Wes sighed and looked up at the treetops once again. "Since I've been home, I've had a visitor. Someone's lurking around, watching me, moving things. It's been one thing after another, always with some sort of message attached." He gave a short run-down of some of the things that had happened on the farm.

"I didn't think you got a dog to protect your chickens," Rhonda said.

"In a way, I did, just not from the kind of critter Becca thought. Whoever it is, they don't have any idea what they're up against. I've been trained to kill. Quickly, silently. I can snap a neck like that," Wes snapped his fingers.

An involuntary shudder wracked Rhonda as she stared at those fingers that had so recently been wrapped around her neck. Wes could have ended her life in a heartbeat. She pried her gaze away from his lethal hands, instead looking into his cold, calculating eyes.

"So, it's probably best if you don't ride these trails for awhile."

"Why don't you just go to the police?"

"Ha!" The humorless bark echoed through the trees. Sandy's head came up and she snorted.

"Spoken like a true innocent. Have you forgotten that the police fully believe me to be a murderer?"

Rhonda knew the truth behind his statement. Hadn't she asked Penny just that morning about Nate investigating Brian's murder? If Wes went to the police with his suspicions, would they believe him?

"But why? Why would someone try to run you off?"

"Money." The blunt word took Rhonda aback.

"But farming doesn't hardly make a body a living anymore."

"No. But Ken Morris, my attorney, has being doing some digging for me. Seems there was a geological survey done of this area just before my parents were killed. It appears my 150 acres holds some gold, in the form of a very large pocket of natural gas."

"But you could sell out and retain the mineral rights."

"This person seems to think I can be persuaded to give up the mineral rights along with the land."

"Because of Brian's murder." It was a statement, not a question, as the pieces of the puzzle began to click into place in Rhonda's mind.

"Yep. Whoever wants this land seems to think they have enough evidence to put me away for life. They want to make a little deal, my freedom for my land. Only problem is, I don't make deals."

Rhonda looked deep into those frozen eyes, then down at the hands on his hips, hands that had held her to the ground like she was a butterfly on a pin.

Hands that could kill in the blink of an eye. She agreed with Wes' earlier observation. Whoever was playing this game, they had no idea who they were up against.

Wes gave Rhonda a leg up onto the buckskin's bare back. She was light as a feather. He was thankful he hadn't broken her bones when he knocked her from her horse. He looked up into her deep blue eyes and his heart tripped. He immediately looked down and cleared his throat.

"Don't tell anyone what I told you," he warned, looking at her jean-clad thigh. It occurred to him that he could easily span her leg with his hands. He looked away, into the forest. "It probably won't be safe for you, either, if whoever is doing this finds out that you know about it."

"I'm not afraid," Rhonda stated.

Small, but tough as nails, Wes thought.

"I'm not going to stop coming to clean the house or bringing you meals. That would look even more suspicious. Besides, two pairs of eyes and ears are better than one. I'll be honest with you, I've heard rumors around town. There's pressure on the prosecutor to re-open the investigation into Brian's death. Don't be surprised if the police come around asking questions. I know I told you things around here had changed. The truth is, some things have and some things haven't. But you do have friends here, Wes. Whatever happens, don't forget that. I'll let you know if I find out anything else."

She reined the horse around and went trotting

Help Me, Rhonda

down the trail. Wes watched her ride away, her red curls bouncing on her shoulders. Maybe she was a spy, a spy on his side. It eased his troubled mind to know he had a friend. Making his way back to the house, Wes realized he wanted Rhonda as more than a friend. His whole life he had thought of her as Brian's girl. But Brian was dead and Wes was alive.

"What do ya think, Bri?" Wes asked, stopping to look up at the sky. "Could Rhonda and I make it together? You already hated my guts before, guess I wouldn't win any points ending up with your girl, huh?"

Purposely, Wes buried the idea of trying to win Rhonda's heart. It would never work. Brian would always be between them in one way or another. Better to keep it as friends.

Fingers trembling, Rhonda pulled the bridle off Sandy's head with one hand while slipping a halter onto her with the other, a trick she had mastered years ago. The well-trained horse stood motionless in the center aisle while Rhonda hooked cross-ties to each side of her halter. Her stomach felt as if a dozen jumping bunnies had taken up residence. It must be some strange, delayed reaction to what had happened out on the trail.

"It's not every day I get knocked off my horse by G.I. Joe," Rhonda said to Sandy, picking up a brush and running it over the horse's tan hide. "It's amazing he didn't break my back. First he threatens me with a gun, then he threatens to sic his vicious dog on me and then he practically gives me a concussion by attacking me from the trees. The man is danger with a capital D."

Unhooking the cross-ties, Rhonda led Sandy to her stall before going out to let Smokey in. She dumped oats in the horses' feed buckets before filling their hay racks. All the while she tried to dispel the memory of Wes sitting astride her hips with his hands around her throat. Yep, he was definitely dangerous.

Then why had she offered to help him? It was obvious he didn't need her help. He was trained in the art of killing. What could she possibly do that would help him? Helping him only meant she was putting herself in danger, and not just the physical kind. Because Rhonda had to admit, once Wes had helped her up and the threat of him choking her to death had passed, she still had all those annoying symptoms of being attracted to him, camouflage paint and all.

"Emma said let peace be my guide," Rhonda confided to Sandy who had her nose buried in hay. "That seems to be a lot easier said than done. Wes seems to think he's at war with somebody. How are we going to find peace in the midst of that?"

CHAPTER FOURTEEN

Rhonda sat in the pew and stared at the simple wooden cross that hung behind the pulpit. She glanced down at the Bible that lay open on her lap to First Corinthians, chapter 14 and re-read the verse she had been meditating on.

For God is not the author of confusion but of peace, as in all the churches of the saints.

Rhonda knew that Jesus promised in the Gospel of John, "Peace I leave with you, My peace I give to you; not as the world gives do I give to you. Let not your heart be troubled, neither let it be afraid."

Rhonda's heart was definitely troubled. Emma had advised her to follow peace. But what if she couldn't *find* it? Then what?

The other people in the pew began shifting and Rhonda looked up from her Bible to see Blake squeezing his way toward her. He was looking stylish is dark blue jeans and a black collarless jacket with a white shirt and black string tie.

Help Me, Rhonda

"Hey, baby," he whispered as he sat down on her right.

Rhonda just stared at him with wide eyes for several seconds before glancing once more at her Bible. She scanned the passage one last time before confusion descended, tangling her emotions in a sticky spider web. Blake draped his arm over the back of the pew, his hand resting lightly on Rhonda's shoulder.

When the congregation stood for a time of worship and praise, Blake stood right along with everyone else and Rhonda was shocked to hear his rich voice blend with hers. She slid a glance up at him but his eyes were focused on the overhead screen displaying the words of the song. Blake Dalton could sing!

Throughout the sermon, Blake paid rapt attention to the pastor's words. He even nodded his head in agreement from time to time, and looked over Rhonda's shoulder at the Scriptures Pastor Bennett referred to.

After the service, Emma and Tyler, Penny and Nate were all standing in the parking lot in the warm spring sunshine when Blake and Rhonda emerged from the church. Blake kept his hand lightly on the small of Rhonda's back, guiding her toward the other couples.

"Good to see you here today, Blake," Emma said.

"Thanks. Hey, I hear congratulations are in order." Blake reached down and gave Emma a brotherly hug before extending his hand to Tyler. "A baby on the way. You must be really excited."

"We are, thanks," Emma replied.

"And how about you guys?" he asked, turning to Nate and Penny. "How are the wedding plans coming along?"

"Great, just great," Nate said, crossing his arms over his chest.

"Easy for you to say!" Penny laughed, punching Nate lightly on the arm. She tossed a golden wave of hair over her shoulder and smiled easily at Blake. "Thankfully, Emma just went through this not too long ago, so she's been lots of help. You and Rhonda going to be next?"

Rhonda stood slightly behind Blake's elbow, violently shaking her head, but Penny paid no attention. Blake smiled down at her and Rhonda put a smile on her face, covering her nay-saying by suddenly fluffing her hair.

"I'd like nothing better," Blake said, causing Rhonda's jaw to drop in astonishment. "You want to go get some lunch?"

"I, um, I can't today, Blake," Rhonda stuttered. "I'm, I mean, Becca and I, we promised to clean house for Wes again today." She steeled herself for his angry reaction and let out a breath of relief when it didn't come.

"Oh, that's right." He nodded and the sun bounced off his white-blonde curls. "I should have remembered. Well hey, that's okay. That won't take you all day, will it?"

"No, probably only a couple of hours," Rhonda answered slowly.

"Well then, how about if I come by later this

afternoon? We can go out for ice cream or something. This day's too glorious to waste," he said, squinting up at the clear blue sky. "See you guys later." Dropping a kiss on the top of Rhonda's head, Blake raised a hand to the two couples then turned and headed toward his Mustang.

"Wow, I think he's finally getting serious," Penny observed, staring intently at Rhonda.

"Or putting on a really good act," Nate said suspiciously.

"What's that supposed to mean?" Rhonda wanted to know, her head still reeling with confusion.

"Didn't you feel it?" Nate gave an exaggerated shiver. "It was all weird, like he was trying too hard. Acting like he's part of our group."

"So, what if I do marry him?" Rhonda questioned. Though she had her doubts about a future with Blake, Nate's judgmental attitude made her feel angry and hurt. "I guess we won't be hanging out with all of you, since we obviously aren't good enough." Rhonda turned to go toward her truck.

"No, Rhonda, wait. That's not what Nate meant," Emma pleaded, reaching out to grab Rhonda by the shoulder.

"Oh, isn't it?" Rhonda spun and looked accusingly at each of the four people standing in front of her. "We just came out of church where Pastor Bennett talked about how only God can see a person's heart. Funny Nate, I didn't realize you were God." She looked straight into Nate's eyes. "You think you've got Blake all figured out, but you don't know him nearly as well as you think you do. He's a lot of fun and he has a good heart. But I guess you'll never find that out for yourself, since you're so much better than he is."

"Rhonda, I…" Nate started to defend himself but Rhonda cut him off.

"Oh, save it! First you complain because he doesn't come to church, and then he does and you accuse him of being a fake. If that's the way it works, then why should he even bother? Isn't church supposed to be for the ones who need it the most? Didn't Jesus come for the sick, not for the well?" Rhonda shook her head in frustration. "Forget it, I've got to go." She hurried toward her truck, feeling disappointed with the people she had come to respect and admire the most.

Leaning over the downstairs tub, Rhonda scrubbed at the tile and continued to seethe over the scene in the church parking lot. She closed her eyes for just a moment, picturing Blake as he made his way down the pew, looking for all the world like Bo from the Dukes of Hazard. The sight of him should have sent her heart reeling. So why had she remained unmoved? And if she didn't have any emotional attachment to Blake, then why had she so quickly jumped to his defense?

Sighing, Rhonda sat on the side of the tub, the damp rag hanging between her knees. Had Blake's pious demeanor only been an act? Was he only trying to impress her, suddenly serious about winning her hand? She thought back to her conversation with Emma. People could, and did, make good marriages without all the giddy, romance-novel feelings. She liked Blake, and she did feel a very strong sense of loyalty toward him. For the most part he was easygoing and attentive, even if he wasn't the flowers-and-chocolates kind of guy. If Blake did propose, Rhonda would be assured of having a husband who would take care of her, provide for her, even cherish her, in his own way. How could Emma deny her the same love and security she herself had found?

Slapping the rag against her palm in frustration, Rhonda got up and walked to the sink. She wiped the faucet then moved a few items on the vanity. Picking up a bottle of aftershave, she casually unscrewed the top and took a sniff. She immediately recognized Wes' scent and her heart lifted as if it had suddenly sprouted wings. Screwing the cap back on, she slammed the bottle down and spun from the bathroom, uselessly trying to evade the emotions the mere scent of aftershave had caused to erupt.

Where, oh where, was the peace she was supposed to have?

Still annoyed, Rhonda went to the kitchen and began wiping down the countertops. Why was she so angry all of a sudden? She was mad at Blake for sending mixed signals about their relationship. She was upset at Nate for his quick judgment of Blake. She was even angry at Wes! After all, it was him coming home that had stirred up this whole hornets nest! Everything had been going along just fine until he showed up. Why hadn't he just stayed in the army and left all of them alone?

Moving the coffee maker, Rhonda spied the pack of cigarettes. Stupid, filthy habit! she thought angrily. She looked around the kitchen, listening. Ranger barked outside and Becca's lilting giggle was carried through the kitchen window on the spring breeze. In her fit of temper, Rhonda snatched up the pack of cigarettes and hurried to the sink. She turned on the tap and dumped the offensive things down the garbage disposal. With a flip of the switch, the motor ground them into dust.

Satisfied, Rhonda turned off the disposal and rinsed out the sink. Picking up the now empty cellophane packet, she shoved it all the way to the bottom of the trash can. Brushing her hands off, she reached for the broom in its narrow closet and began sweeping the kitchen floor.

Within minutes she heard the back door squeak and the sound of someone wiping their feet on the mat in the mud room. Rhonda peeked over her shoulder to see Wes enter the kitchen.

"Getting warm out there," he commented as he went to the refrigerator and pulled out a can of cola.

"Maybe spring is going to come, after all," Rhonda said, forcing her eyes away from the sight of his neck as Wes tipped his head back, drinking deeply from the can. His Adam's apple bobbed with each swallow. Slowly he wiped his mouth with the back of his hand. Rhonda could smell the musky scent of him drifting across the kitchen and busied herself with sweeping. "Sounds like Ranger and Becca have hit it off."

"Yeah, they're running each other ragged with

that tennis ball. Doesn't seem like Becca's helping you much."

"That's okay, I mostly asked her to come, you know, as a chaperone. It wouldn't seem proper, me being here by myself."

"I didn't think anyone worried about being proper anymore."

Rhonda looked up from her sweeping and their eyes clashed across the room.

"Well, I do," she stated simply.

Leaning back against the counter, Wes turned and began searching the space Rhonda had just cleaned. He moved the coffee maker a fraction and Rhonda felt the dread of confrontation spiral up her spine.

"You seen my cigarettes?" he asked.

Rhonda ignored the question and bent to sweep the dirt into the dustpan.

"Rhonda, what did you do with my cigarettes?" Wes demanded.

Rhonda stood and bravely met his eyes. No use trying to deny it.

"I dumped them down the garbage disposal," she declared self-righteously, turning to tip the dustpan into the trash can. The wrapper seemed to glare accusingly up at her from the bottom of the trash bag.

"You what?!"

Seeing the storm clouds gathering in his grey eyes, Rhonda hurried to put the broom away and high-tailed it into the living room.

"Now wait just a doggone minute!" Wes yelled, following after her.

The vacuum cleaner sat in the middle of the

carpet. Rhonda grabbed it and turned it on. The roar of the motor drowned out his angry words. Wes reached down and yanked the plug from the outlet. The sweeper whined into silence.

"You had no right messing with my cigarettes, Rhonda. This is my house!"

"Yes, it is your house," Rhonda said, turning to confront Wes head on. Her own temper, which had been simmering all afternoon, flared to life. "But I won't be coming over here cleaning it anymore if you're going to have it stinking like smoke!"

"I only smoke outside," Wes defended.

"Well, you shouldn't be doing that, either. That barn is full of hay and straw. You could start a fire in the blink of an eye!"

"I spent ten years handling dangerous ordinance and high explosives, you think I'm going to be careless with a cigarette?"

The vein on Wes' forehead throbbed with fury as he stood over her, so close Rhonda could smell the mingled scents of sweat and aftershave on his skin. Her stomach lifted with that same funny feeling you get when you go over the top of a Ferris wheel. Rhonda's anger fizzled as quickly as it had flared and she felt an odd calm envelope her.

"Then there's your body to consider," she said in a now rational voice. Considering Wes' body made her stomach do that weird thing again, but she went on anyway. "You are the temple of the Holy Spirit. I hardly think God wants to be breathing in that awful smoke."

"Rhonda..." Wes warned.

"Well, it's true. I was there the day you got baptized, Wes Cooper. The Spirit of God dwells within you, whether you want to accept that fact right now or not. Besides." She looked up into his eyes and forgot that just a moment ago she had wished he hadn't ever come home. "I know you think no one around here cares whether you live or die, but that's not true. There's a lot of people who care what happens to you, me included."

Wes still stood over her, but his intimidating stance melted away as his eyes looked deeply into hers.

"Rhonda..." he warned again, softer this time. He touched a finger to her cheek.

Insistent knocking on the front screen door broke the spell that had fallen over the two of them. Wes and Rhonda turned in unison to stare down the hall toward the entryway.

"Hello! Anybody home?" Blake called.

Wes followed Rhonda to the front door. Ranger came flying around the corner of the house, barking furiously.

"Whoa!" Blake held up his hands in surrender as Ranger slid to a stop only a few feet from him.

"Ranger! Sit!" Wes commanded, pushing around Rhonda and out the screen door. Ranger immediately obeyed the command but continued to growl, his lips pulled up to expose menacing teeth. Becca stood wide-eyed at the end of the porch.

"That's quite a dog you have there," Blake said, lowering his hands.

"What do you want, Blake?" Wes asked, staring coldly at the unwanted visitor. He hadn't forgotten Blake's threat to stay away from "his girl." Had the man seen how close Wes had just come to kissing that same maddening girl?

"I just stopped by to see if Rhonda was finished. After church we made plans to go out for ice cream. I don't remember seeing you there, at church I mean," Blake observed, tongue in cheek. When Wes just continued to stare at him, Blake smiled casually and went on, "I just thought with all your years in the army, you know, that now you would want to be in the army of the Lord."

"I've had enough of being in anyone's army," Wes answered.

"Oh really, that's too bad," Blake replied. His smile grew wider. "But I guess I don't have to worry so much about Rhonda being over here then. You know, I was feeling just a mite jealous, but I know Rhonda won't look twice at someone who's not on fire for the Lord, isn't that right, baby?"

He put a possessive arm around Rhonda's shoulders and looked down at her for confirmation. She stared blankly up at him.

"Now me, I never served the United States government, but I proudly serve my Savior, Jesus Christ."

Wes had to bite the inside of his cheek to keep from laughing out loud. He didn't believe Blake Dalton had ever served anyone but himself his entire life. And if Blake's behavior on his front porch a week ago was any indication of how those in the

Lord's army behaved, then Wes wanted no part of it.

"Anyway, about that ice cream. What do you say, squirt?" He looked beyond Wes, to where Becca still stood at the end of the porch. "You want to go for some ice cream?"

"Sure!" Becca was quick to accept.

"Why don't you go hop in the 'stang?" He motioned with his head toward the car. "We'll follow Rhonda home so she can leave her truck."

"Cool!" Becca tossed the tennis ball down on the grass and ran toward the sports car sitting in the drive.

"I still have to put the vacuum and stuff away," Rhonda said, turning to go back in the house.

"Don't worry about it," Wes told her cooly. She turned surprised eyes his way. "I'll take care of it. You go on. Your boyfriend seems anxious for your company."

"Wes," Rhonda began to protest.

"Thanks, Wes, you're a gem!" Blake declared. He took Rhonda's elbow and led her off the porch. "Come on, baby, let's go enjoy this sunshine. I've been looking forward to ice cream all day."

Wes watched the two as they walked toward their vehicles. Rhonda craned her head to look at him over her shoulder. Was that desperation he saw in her eyes? Wes shrugged the thought away and pulled open the screen door. Blake's arrival had been fortuitous, stopping Wes before he could make a fool of himself.

"You're a good dog, Ranger," he said, scratching the top of the animal's head as they walked into the house. "That's just the kind of varmint I want you chasing off this property."

CHAPTER FIFTEEN

Sitting across the table from Blake in the pizza place which also doubled as Atlanta's ice cream parlor, Rhonda took a bite of her turtle sundae then glanced over to where Becca played video games. Blake had continued to surprise her when he reached into his jeans pocket, pulled out a handful of quarters and handed them to Becca, encouraging her to have fun. His odd behavior definitely had Rhonda puzzled.

"Blake, can I ask you a question?" she asked.

"Sure, shoot." Blake spooned a bite of banana split into his mouth.

Rhonda's eyes ran over his curly blond locks, his twinkling brown eyes and his elfin chin. Blake was nice looking and he had an easy charm about him that had attracted Rhonda from the start. He raised an eyebrow at her, waiting.

"Since when are you on fire for the Lord?" she blurted.

Blake's smile grew wider and he sat back on the hard plastic seat of the booth.

"Baby, I know you've questioned my commitment to the Lord, but honestly, I've always loved Him just as much as you do. I'm just not as good at expressing it as you are. It's true, I've let things get in the way of coming to church on Sunday, but I know how important it is to you and I vow I'm going to do better from now on." He leaned forward and took Rhonda's hands in his own.

"I've been doing a lot of thinking about what you said, about where our relationship is headed," Blake said earnestly, running his thumbs lightly over the back of her hands. "I guess I've always thought of us as being so young, you know. I'm only twenty-six and it seemed like we had all the time in the world to be grown up. I figured we could just keep having fun. I never looked at it from your perspective and I see now I was being pretty selfish. I understand you're at that point where you want to start thinking about settling down and starting a family."

"Blake, I..."

"Whew! That was fun!" Becca came to a sliding stop at the end of the booth and picked up her milkshake, taking a long draw from the straw. "Thanks, Blake."

Rhonda sent up a silent prayer of thanks for the timely interruption. She was far too confused to deal with a proposal at this point in time.

"You're welcome, squirt. Now, if you ladies are done here, how about a stroll in the park while the sun is still shining?"

Help Me, Rhonda

Briley Township park was located in the middle of downtown Atlanta, on the banks of the Thunder Bay River. A paved walkway followed the curves of the river and a large gazebo sat in the middle of the park. Becca decided fifteen wasn't too old for swings and set off to see how high she could make herself go. Rhonda and Blake walked sedately down the path, watching the fishermen who cast their lines from the low dam at the end of the park. Blake took her hand and Rhonda didn't pull away. It was such a nice day and Blake was being so sweet. She didn't want to spoil it.

Blake stopped in the middle of the path and looked around. He brought their joined hands up between them.

"Rhonda, I'm not going to pop the question in the middle of the park with your sister and half the town looking on. But I want you to know, I'm thinking about it, and I want you to be thinking about it, too. When the time is right, I plan on asking you to marry me. I pray you'll give me the answer I'm wanting to hear."

Leaning into the open refrigerator, Wes spied an unfamiliar plastic bowl sitting on the glass shelf. He pulled it out and pushed the door closed with his foot. Setting the bowl on the counter, he pried up the airtight lid to find slices of roast beef smothered in gravy, along with roasted potatoes and carrots.

"Rhonda, you are an angel," he said to the empty kitchen as he carried the bowl to the microwave. The appliance beeped as he pushed the buttons, bringing

Help Me, Rhonda

Ranger trotting into the room. "Our next door neighbor has left me a veritable feast," he informed the dog. "If you're lucky, I just may leave a bite or two for you."

When his dinner was warm, Wes carried the steaming bowl to the table and sat down. He cut through the fork tender beef, putting the bite in his mouth and chewing slowly.

"Mmm, she sure cooks like an angel. What do you think she sees in that devil, Blake Dalton?" he asked. For some reason Wes had not been able to get that question out of his head all afternoon. Ranger tilted his head, listening. "You sure didn't seem to think much of him. Can't say that I blame you. I don't think much of him, either. But if that's Rhonda's choice, who are we to criticize?"

It wasn't like he had a chance with her. Wes chewed in silence for several minutes, digesting that truth. He could still see Rhonda standing in the middle of his living room, red curls blazing, blue eyes snapping with temper.

"Guess it was kind of silly to think she might fall for us, hey Ranger?" He set the nearly empty bowl on the floor and Ranger quickly trotted over and finished the left-overs. Wes looked down at his hands. "A man can't kill as many people as I have and expect to come home and win the heart of the prettiest girl in town. Especially a pretty *Christian* girl."

Wes patted the pocket of his t-shirt then stood and went to the counter, searching for his cigarettes. Then he remembered, his *angel* had dumped them down the garbage disposal. Looking at the clock on the stove, he saw he had plenty of time to run to town and buy another pack.

I was there the day you got baptized, Wes Cooper. The Spirit of God dwells inside you.

Wes heard Rhonda's voice as if she were standing in the room and suddenly he was transported back, to that hot August day when he was fourteen, standing on the bank of the Thunder Bay River, his bare toes curling into the damp sand. His parents had been there, too, of course, and Brian and spindly-armed, frizzy-haired Rhonda, along with a good many others from their church. Wes closed his eyes and re-lived the moment when he had come up from the water, having just been baptized in the name of the Father, the Son and the Holy Spirit. He had never felt as close to Jesus as he had at that very moment.

Wes opened his eyes, coming slowly back to the present. He hadn't felt close to Jesus in a very, very long time. He doubted the Spirit of God was dwelling in him any longer, not after everything he had done.

"Guess it doesn't matter." Ranger was still licking the bowl clean and Wes snagged it from the floor and set it in the sink. "God or not, I've been saying for awhile I should quit. Guess now's as good a time as any."

After making sure the animals were safely bedded down for the night, Wes clipped Ranger to his chain and headed for a hot shower and bed. Several hours later he was awakened from a deep sleep by the distant ringing of the telephone. In a heartbeat his feet hit the floor and he made his way quickly to the kitchen where he snapped up the receiver.

"Yeah." Wes squinted through the kitchen window, seeing nothing but blackness beyond the glass.

"Wes, it's David Weaver. You'd better get dressed and come over. Your cows are loose."

Rhonda walked up the aisle on her father's arm, the train of her wedding gown rustling softly on the white runner that covered the carpet. Blake stood at the altar, smiling, holding his hand out to her. As Rhonda reached for his hand, she looked beyond Blake's shoulder. Wes stood there in his BDU pants and black t-shirt, staring coldly at Rhonda. Her puzzled gaze ran between the two men. Blake continued to hold his hand out to her invitingly.

"Wes?" Rhonda said, still not reaching for Blake's proffered hand.

Wes merely turned and walked silently down the aisle and out of the church. Blake still waited, hand outstretched. Rhonda reached to put her hand in his...

Pounding on her bedroom door brought Rhonda slowly out of the dream. She sat up in bed, listening again for the noise that had woken her up. The knocking sounded again.

"Rhonda? Rhonda, wake up!" It was her father's voice on the other side of the door.

Rhonda's bare feet hit the floor and her nightgown billowed as she hurried to let her father in, her heart nearly bursting with fear. With one hand held

Help Me, Rhonda

to her pounding heart, she threw the door wide. Her father stood in the hall in work jeans and heavy flannel shirt.

"What is it? What's wrong?" she asked breathlessly.

"You need to get dressed and get Sandy. Wes Cooper's cows are loose and running all over. We'll need your help rounding them up."

"Good grief, Dad, you scared me half to death!" Rhonda wailed.

"I'm sorry, honey, I tried calling quietly and you weren't waking up. Besides, there's no time to waste. If we don't hurry, those calves could get tangled in wire, or hit by a car or taken down by a coyote." David turned and headed toward the stairs. "I'll get Sandy bridled for you."

Rhonda closed the door and reached for the jeans she had left laying over a ladder-backed chair. Her heart slowly returned to its normal rhythm as she stared bleary-eyed at the clock. Two a.m.! How in the world were they supposed to round up ten black calves in the middle of the night? She sat on the bed to pull on a pair of heavy socks. Suddenly it hit her. Was this another in the long line of "incidents" Wes had told her about?

"O Lord, help us," she muttered the prayer as she pulled on a sweatshirt and went clattering down the stairs. "Help us round up these cows, and watch over Wes."

Half-way down the steps, Rhonda stopped abruptly, remembering the dream. She had been about to marry Blake. If Wes had said one word to stop her, she wouldn't have gone through with it, but he had walked away. Did the dream mean anything? Was she supposed to marry Blake?

Shaking her head, Rhonda jumped from the last step and hurried to retrieve her jacket from the mud room. Now was not the time to be contemplating Blake's forthcoming proposal.

Rounding up the calves was more than just a challenge. Rhonda began to think it was an impossible task. Sandy was skittish and uncooperative, unhappy with being pulled from her stall in the middle of the night. Though Rhonda had at one time competed in western riding events, it had been years since horse and rider had done any herding. Riding without a saddle, Rhonda almost became unseated more than once when a terrified calf came plunging from the undergrowth. It seemed to take hours before Rhonda had several of the cows heading in the general direction of the Cooper farm.

Her father, who was fairly adept with a rope, was able to lasso two of the calves which he tied to the back of his pickup truck and drove slowly toward Wes' place. Between the three of them they had managed to round up seven of the ten calves.

Rhonda sat tiredly upon Sandy's back and watched as Wes led the last calf into the barn and shut him into one of the stalls along with his six companions. A floodlight on the barn's exterior lit the farmyard up nearly as bright as day. Every light inside the barn was ablaze as well, adding to the surreal feeling of the moment. Rhonda glanced to the east and could barely make out the slightest hint of pink on the horizon. Ranger sat alert in front of his dog house, watching the proceedings.

"I'm sorry about all the trouble, Mr. Weaver," Wes said, approaching Rhonda's father. "The fence," he glanced quickly at Rhonda and then away. "I don't understand what could have happened."

David shrugged. "Could have been lots of things. Something probably got them running and they went right on through the hot wire." David placed a reassuring hand on Wes' shoulder. "You might as well wait until daybreak to try and find the others. Hopefully you'll find them before something else does." David walked to his truck and opened the door. "Want me to lead the way home?" he asked, looking at Rhonda.

"Yeah, I'll follow you."

David got in the truck and slammed the door. In a moment the engine roared to life. Rhonda looked down at Wes. He was wearing a red wool work jacket that had seen better days. His shoulders slumped wearily.

"The fence was cut?"

Wes nodded his head once, still staring into the depths of the barn.

"What about Ranger? He didn't bark?"

"No. The calves' lean-to is at the back of the barn. Whoever cut the fence, they did it at the back. It looks like they coaxed the cows out that way with hay. Ranger must have slept through the whole thing. After your dad called, when I came out, he was curled up in his dog house, snoring. Some guard dog he turned out to be."

"I'm sorry, Wes. When it gets light, I can ride the woods and see if I can find anymore of the calves for you."

Wes shook his head. "You've done enough already. I'll go out and see if I can find them. And I guess I'll have to call the sheriff's office, just in case they wander onto someone else's property or get hit by a car." He ran a hand over his hair in frustration. "I don't know how I'm supposed to fight this guy!"

Rhonda's heart wept as Wes turned worried eyes up to her. She wished she had some profound words of wisdom to offer.

"Don't worry Wes, it will all work out," was all she managed to say. Glancing toward the truck, she saw her father motion for her to get a move on. "I've got to go." She nudged Sandy who moved forward. "It will all work out," she called over her shoulder to Wes as he stood in the middle of the gravel drive. "I'm praying for you."

But would it all work out? Rhonda questioned as she rode home behind her father's truck. She honestly didn't see how Wes would be able to protect his farm. And then there was the investigation into Brian's murder. And what about Blake? She recalled with vivid detail the wedding that had been taking place in her dream. Was she destined to marry Blake? Her tired mind couldn't answer any of her own questions.

"Dear Jesus, help us," Rhonda prayed. "Help us all."

CHAPTER SIXTEEN

Prayer, ha! Wes nearly laughed out loud as he beat the brush in the lowland around the cedar swamp. Obviously is was going to take more than prayer for him to find the three missing calves. He had called the sheriff's department and reported that there were three black angus calves on the loose. So far none had been reported trespassing on anyone's property and no accidents had been called in. That was something anyway.

It wasn't so much the financial loss Wes was worried about. During his years in the service, he had been very frugal with his money. While other guys in his unit bought fancy cars or other luxury items, Wes had been socking every cent he could spare in the bank. Overseas deployments meant extra income and hazardous duty pay which was invested wisely and tended to carefully. After his parents' death, Wes had known he would return to work the farm and he also knew it would take a couple of years before he saw a profit. He had an initial investment in the calves that would be lost should they not be recovered, and then the potential profit down the line when they were sold for slaughter. But that was not what occupied Wes' mind.

What consumed his every thought was the person who was out to destroy him. Every new incident had Wes feeling more violated. The fact that someone was walking freely around his property causing damage made Wes see red. What was even more frustrating was that he didn't have a clue who it might be.

Sharp thorns sank into the flesh on Wes' arm as he pushed blackberry bushes out of his way. More snagged the fabric of his shirt and held. Muttering an oath under his breath, Wes stopped to untangle himself. He should have accepted Rhonda's offer to help him with this search.

I'm praying for you. Rhonda's voice seemed to drift on the breeze and Wes looked around. She was probably praying for him right now. For once Wes didn't respond to the thought with a sarcastic laugh. He remembered his mother's prayer list, tucked away inside the worn cover of her Bible. Had her prayers been answered? Were they the reason Wes had come home alive?

Finally freeing his clothing from the brambles, Wes pushed deeper into the underbrush, pushing aside thoughts of prayer. He had seen too many people die. Seen good men get their limbs blown off. Men he was sure had someone, somewhere praying for their safe return. Obviously there were a lot of prayers that didn't get answered. Even his parents' own faith hadn't prevented them from being killed in that car wreck.

A sound that didn't quite fit with the woodland surroundings whispered through the brush. Wes stopped, listening. He heard it again, a lowing off to his left. Forging ahead through the grasping, tangled growth, Wes finally broke out into the tiniest of forest glens. Three black heads turned toward him in surprise and snorted.

Wes felt the unfamiliar urge to fall to his knees right then and there and thank God. Instead, he reached slowly for the length of rope he had slung over his head and shoulder.

"Easy now fellas, easy," he spoke soothingly as he slowly approached the calves.

The three were obviously worn out from their long trek through the woods and didn't shy or run away. They stood docilely as Wes fashioned the rope into a series of loops that he slipped over each calf's head. Feeling like an old-fashioned cowboy without the horse, Wes began pushing his way out through the brush, his three charges following quietly behind.

"Do we have any pickles in here?" Emma asked, coming into the teashop's kitchen.

Rhonda stood at the counter assembling a customer's sandwich to go. Emma opened the refrigerator door and pulled out a jar of dill spears.

"Ooh, sour cream, that sounds good, too." Emma plopped the carton down on the counter next to the pickles.

Help Me, Rhonda

"I thought pregnant women were supposed to crave pickles and *ice* cream," Rhonda said. She watched in amusement as Emma ladled a heaping spoon of sour cream onto a plate before dipping a pickle into it and taking a huge bite.

"Mmm," Emma murmured, dipping again.

"Anything else I can get you?" Rhonda asked with a smile.

"I think I could eat an entire jar of peanut butter."

Rhonda reached into a cupboard above her head and set the jar down in front of her boss. Emma quickly unscrewed the cap. Rhonda held out a spoon which Emma snatched from her hand and plunged into the jar.

"If you dip your pickle in that, I'm going to throw up," Rhonda warned.

Emma looked at her wide-eyed, holding the spoonful of peanut butter aloft.

"I thought throwing up was my job," she said with a smile.

"Tiredness, throwing up, craving weird food, you've got me having second thoughts about wanting kids," Rhonda said, envy beating in her breast even as she spoke the words.

She quickly wrapped the sandwich in paper and put it in a white sack. She left Emma munching her pickles and went to the front counter where she handed the bag to a waiting customer. When the woman had left, the dining room was empty. Rhonda headed back to the kitchen. Emma had climbed up on a tall stool at the counter and was licking peanut butter from the spoon. She watched as Rhonda began putting away the sandwich fixing she had used.

"Nate felt awful about upsetting you after church yesterday," Emma finally spoke.

Rhonda paused at the refrigerator door. Slowly, she opened it and set the sandwich fillings inside.

"Yeah, well, I owe him an apology," she admitted. "I shouldn't have lost my temper. I just get so frustrated. I feel like nothing I do is right anymore."

"Nate realized he shouldn't have criticized Blake for coming to church. It's something you and I have been praying for. And you were right, if people come to church and then are rejected, then why should they even come? Perhaps Blake really is turning over a new leaf. It's not for any of us to judge his motives."

Rhonda leaned back against the counter and crossed her arms over her chest, replaying the proceeding day's events. She was exhausted and it all seemed like a giant blur to her.

"He took me and Becca out for ice cream. He said he's going to try harder to come to church and stuff. He said he loves the Lord just as much as I do, he just has a harder time showing it."

"And did you believe him?" Emma asked.

Rhonda shrugged a shoulder. "I don't have any reason not to. He has seemed different lately. More serious about things. More caring and attentive. He..." she hesitated and looked at Emma, trying to decide how much she should confide. "He said he's going to ask me to marry him, when the time is right, and he prays I'll say yes."

"And will you?"

"I don't know!" Rhonda cried, pushing away from the counter. She went to the sink and began running water into it.

"You told me just the other day you had doubts about Blake being your Mr. Right. Have you changed your mind? Are you in love with him?" Emma spun around on her stool to look at Rhonda.

"I told you, it seems like nothing I do or say is right anymore. I'm very mixed up. Blake is a great guy. He works hard, he's good looking, he says he's crazy about me. It seems like I would be a fool *not* to marry him."

"It seems to me you would be more of a fool to marry someone you don't really love."

"I never said I don't love him," Rhonda protested.

"Okay then, turn around, look me straight in the eye and tell me you are head over heels in love with Blake Dalton," Emma challenged.

"Emma," Rhonda sighed heavily, her shoulders sagging. "I am very, very tired. I really don't want to have this argument. Can we please just leave it be for now?"

"Are you tired because you were awake all night trying to decide if you should marry Blake? I told you God would give you peace. If you couldn't sleep because of it, then you don't have God's peace about it."

"I was up half the night because of Wes Cooper's cows," Rhonda answered.

"What do Wes Cooper's cows have to do with anything?" Emma asked, obviously confused.

Rhonda glanced over her shoulder at Emma, trying to decide how much she should divulge. In her delicate condition, it probably was best not to get Emma any more upset or worried than she already was.

"They got out in the middle of the night," Rhonda answered briefly. "I had to get up and play cowgirl. Something I haven't done in a very long time. I've been up since two this morning."

"Why didn't you say something? I would have sent you home. Why don't you go now, go home and take a nap. I know what it's like to be on your feet when all you want to do is lay down and sleep."

"No way." Rhonda shook her head. "I'm not going home and leaving you here by yourself. I'm supposed to be taking care of you, not the other way around. I'll drink some coffee and be wide awake in no time. I just..." she turned and looked straight at Emma. "I just don't want to argue about Blake anymore, okay? The emotional stuff, that makes me even more tired than being up all night."

"I understand," Emma agreed. "I'll keep praying that the Lord will give you direction concerning Blake. Remember, He is not the author of confusion but of peace."

Rhonda looked at her boss in wonder. "That's the verse I was reading yesterday morning when Blake showed up at church," she said in awe.

"Well then." Emma smiled. "Maybe the Lord's trying to tell you something, huh?"

The bell at the front of the shop gave a ring, alerting the two they had customers.

"I'll go see who that is," Emma said, turning toward the dining room.

"No, I'll go." Rhonda stopped her. "You clean up your disgusting snack." She pointed to the pickles and peanut butter still sitting on the counter before hurrying out front.

Wes stood just inside the door of the Spot of Tea and surveyed the empty dining room. So, this was where Rhonda spent her days. His eyes took in the delicate looking tables and chairs grouped cozily in front of the wide, front windows. The scent of strong coffee mingled with cinnamon, creating an aroma that immediately sent his mouth to watering. But his mouth quickly went dry when Rhonda appeared through the doorway behind the counter. Upon seeing Wes, she stopped dead in her tracks, staring at him with those depthless blue eyes.

"Wes, uh, this is a surprise." Her hand went to her neck to fidget with the simple, gold cross necklace hanging there.

"Hi." Wes nodded and stepped forward. Why was his heart racing?

"What brings you in here?" Rhonda asked. She dropped her hand from her neck and walked behind the glass-fronted counter. "Did you decide you couldn't live without some more of Emma's muffins?"

Wes eyed the variety of baked goods in the case below the cash register then raised his eyes to look

Help Me, Rhonda

at Rhonda. Her hair was pulled back in a ponytail high on the back of her head. Purple smudges darkened the skin beneath her eyes. Wes felt a twinge of guilt at how tired she looked.

"Actually, I came by to thank you for your help this morning. I really appreciate what you and your dad did. It, it meant a lot to me. I know you lost a lot of sleep because of it."

"That's what neighbors do, help each other out. Any luck finding the others?"

"Yes, actually." Wes nodded, stuffing his hands into the front pockets of his jeans. "I found the other three out beyond the cedar swamp."

"Well, praise the Lord!" Rhonda said, slapping a hand down on the counter in excitement. "I told you I was praying you would find them."

"Yeah, well, whatever." Wes shrugged a shoulder in discomfort. "I'd be happier if they had never gotten out in the first place."

"Any idea yet who it might be?" Rhonda asked, leaning her elbows on the counter.

"No, but this came in today's mail."

Wes reached into his back pocket and pulled out the envelope. He held it out to Rhonda who straightened slowly away from the counter, looking at it as if it were a rotten piece of meat.

"What is it?" she asked suspiciously.

"Another letter. Go ahead, read it," he prompted.

Rhonda reached out and took the envelope between her thumb and forefinger, as if afraid it was contaminated. She pulled out the piece of plain white paper and her eyes scanned the page.

"One thousand dollars an acre?" she asked, incredulous. "Is this guy trying to rob you blind?"

"I don't believe my financial well-being is his primary concern," Wes replied with a wry smile.

"If we do not hear from you by May first," Rhonda proceeded to read aloud, "we will assume you remain hostile to our overtures and will respond accordingly." She met his eyes across the counter. "That sounds like a threat. And May first is day after tomorrow. I think you should take this to the police."

Wes watched as she refolded the paper and replaced it in the envelope. She handed the letter back to him.

"There's something else," he said, slipping the envelope into the back pocket of his jeans.

"What?"

Rhonda's blue eyes, so clear and open, held his. Wes felt an odd tripping of his heart. He swallowed hard, trying to dislodge the feeling. He glanced around the empty restaurant, assuring himself that they were still alone before dropping his voice to a whisper.

"I asked my attorney to get me a copy of the accident report from the crash that killed my parents. I told you about the diorama I found on the porch. I couldn't figure out if it was implying I could have an unfortunate accident or if my parents' accident wasn't really an accident after all."

Wes took a deep breath, reliving the pain he had felt upon uncovering the awful truth.

"I've read the report over and over again and I'm convinced what happened to my parents was no accident. I think they were murdered, just like Brian."

CHAPTER SEVENTEEN

Murdered! Rhonda stood rooted to the spot as the word sank into her tired brain. From the corner of her eye she saw a group of customers approaching the entrance to the Spot of Tea and quickly reached out and grabbed Wes by the sleeve.

"Come into the back," she ordered, motioning with her head toward the kitchen.

"No, I..." Wes balked.

The bell above the door rang out as the two couples entered the restaurant.

"Be right with you," Rhonda called with forced cheerfulness, smiling over Wes' shoulder at the customers. "I really think you should come back into the kitchen," she hissed under her breath.

She turned and moved toward the kitchen, not giving Wes any choice in the matter. Emma's eyes went wide when she saw who was following Rhonda.

"The Crammers and the Simmons just came in,"

Rhonda explained to Emma. "According to my mom, Shirley Simmons has been in the quilt shop a lot lately, kicking up a fuss about Wes. I really didn't want there to be a confrontation out in the dining room."

"I'll take care of it." Emma headed that way.

"Thanks. This will only take a minute," Rhonda assured. When Emma had left the kitchen, Rhonda turned to Wes. "You can't be serious about your parents!" she insisted. "The police would have noticed if it wasn't an accident. I think your imagination is running away with you."

"No."

Wes shook his head stubbornly and folded his arms across his chest. Rhonda couldn't help but notice that he looked just as good in green and black checked flannel as he did in his usual black t-shirt.

"I'm not making it up, Rhonda. I went out to the crash site. It would have been very easy for someone to cause an accident at that curve, on an icy, snow-covered road."

"Even so, even if someone did cause the accident, how could they have been sure your parents would be killed? No matter how well they planned it out, there was no way to know they would go down that ravine and roll a bunch of times."

Wes just shrugged. "Maybe they took their chances and hoped for the best. Or the worst, as the case may be," he amended. "The report stated there was a set of tire tracks coming off the side road. What if someone waited and purposely pulled out in front of them, causing my dad to hit the brakes, skid on the ice and lose control, going down into the ravine?"

"But even if that did happen, there's no way to prove it was on purpose. It was dark. That curve is treacherous even during the day. If someone pulled out in front of them, it was probably a mistake," Rhonda insisted.

Wes refused to be convinced.

"I don't think it was a mistake. I can't explain it, it's just a gut feeling I have. In the army I learned to trust my instincts. Sometimes that's all I had to go on. Now those instincts are screaming loud and clear that my parents' death was no accident."

Rhonda heard the bell out front ring again. Emma hurried to the kitchen door.

"I need two chocolate mint cappuccinos and two decaf coffees," she called.

"I'm on it," Rhonda answered. "I've got to get back to work."

She looked into Wes' eyes, eyes that had been so icy and cold that first day he had returned home. Now they held a strange warmth that made Rhonda's heart tumble over in her chest.

"Yeah, I need to get back and keep an eye on things."

Wes stepped toward the dining room. Rhonda caught the back of his sleeve, stopping him. He gave her a quizzical look over his shoulder.

"Not that way. Go out the kitchen door." She motioned to the back door of the shop.

"Don't want the upstanding citizens of Atlanta to see me here, huh?" he asked, the frostiness back in his voice.

"No." Rhonda shook her head and gave a gentle tug on his shirt sleeve. "I don't want to see you getting treated badly by those upstanding citizens. Plus, Emma's pregnant, I don't want anything causing her to get upset."

Wes threw one last look at the entrance to the dining room.

"I can take them all on, you know."

"I know you can, but now isn't the time or the place. You know, the Bible tells us that the Lord is our vindicator. If you give it all to Him, eventually He will make sure you're cleared. And in the meantime, I still think you should go to Nate. If you have questions about your parents' accident, you should tell him. He was with the department when it happened. Even if he didn't investigate the accident, he could probably find things out for you."

Wes moved toward the kitchen door and turned the knob. He stopped with his back to Rhonda.

"I doubt the good Nate Sweeney would believe my suspicions anymore than you do." And with that he was out the door, closing it firmly behind him.

Rhonda stood for several seconds, watching Wes disappear around the corner of the building. Her heart ached with sudden emptiness. Was Wes right? Had his parents been murdered, just like Brian? And if so, what did that mean for Wes? Could he be next? Despite the warmth of the sun shining through the window of the kitchen door, Rhonda shivered. Dread crawled down her spine. Wes could be the target of a killer. The thought left her cold.

Help Me, Rhonda

Wes contemplated Rhonda's advice as he drove back to the farm. She seemed to hold a lot of store by Nate Sweeney. Maybe he should go to the police, or at least discuss his suspicions with Ken Morris. The attorney only knew there had been several letters expressing interest in buying the farm. He didn't know the contents of those offers, or about the series of incidents that had occurred since Wes had returned home. Wes was sure if he discussed these issues with the lawyer, he would insist Wes go to the police. So, why didn't he?

Pulling his truck into the driveway, Wes immediately saw the white county sheriff's cruiser parked next to the house. He hadn't gone to the police, so the police had come to him. He almost smiled, but then remembered Rhonda's warning. There was pressure to re-investigate Brian's murder. People in town were making noise. Was that what this visit was all about?

Wes slammed his truck door closed. Ranger barked and strained at the end of his chain. A tall, uniformed figure walked around the corner of the house. Nate approached Wes with a smile that didn't quite reach his eyes.

"Sweeney, what can I do for you?" Wes asked, leaning back against the grill of his truck and crossing his arms.

Nate stopped a few feet away. Cocking a hip, he pushed back the bill of his cap with a thumb and sighed.

"I've got to be honest with you, Wes. Some

people aren't happy about you being home. The prosecutor has been getting calls, we've been getting calls." Nate placed his hands on his hips and shook his head. "You know how it is around here. People don't forget anything. It pains me, but I've been sent out here to ask you some questions about your brother's death."

"I figured as much," Wes admitted. "I didn't have anything to hide back then and I don't have anything to hide now. What do you want to know?"

"Can you take me to the scene of the crime?"

"Sure." Wes pushed himself away from the hood of his truck. "I don't see what good it will do you though. It's grown over in the last ten years. It's not like you're going to find any evidence there now."

Nate shrugged. "Maybe not. But I'd like to get a feel for it anyway."

Wes led the way past the small upper pasture. The black angus calves stood and watched them pass. Silently, the two men made their way across the greening lower pasture. Wes slid a glance toward the man in uniform walking next to him. What would Nate do if Wes just stopped and spilled out all that had happened since he returned home? What if he told the deputy his beliefs about the accident that had taken his parents' lives? What would Nate say?

His mind clicked through all the myriad possibilities and as they reached the cedar swamp, Wes made the decision. He would keep his own counsel, for now.

The trail leading to the pond seemed a little more

overgrown now that the bushes were budding out. Wes pushed his way down the trail, hearing the branches slapping against Nate's arms and legs. They finally stepped out into the clearing.

"Here we are," Wes stated.

He looked toward the oak tree and felt the familiar guilt and pain rise up, trying to smother him. He hid his emotions beneath a veneer of cool control.

"Brian was killed there."

He pointed toward the oak. Sweeney walked over to the tree, removing a small notebook and pen from his pocket.

"Where was he found?"

"Pretty much right there, laying on the ground."

"And you found him?"

Nate turned his head and pierced Wes with his laser-beam eyes. Wes felt the oddest sensation wash over him and was suddenly transported back, to a training exercise several years before. The objective of the exercise was to evade capture by the "enemy" and if you were captured, to successfully avoid giving away any information to the captors. Wes had eluded the enemy for three days. Finally, out of food and water, he had made a stupid error and was immediately seized. He was forced to endure some of the most brutal interrogation tactics he had ever encountered. One of the interrogators, a special forces captain in real-life, had had eyes as penetrating as Nate Sweeney's.

"You were the one who found him, weren't you?" Nate asked again.

"Oh, yeah." Wes shook himself and nodded. "I

found him." He opened his mouth to say more then closed it abruptly, remembering his training. Never volunteer information.

"He had been stabbed in the chest?"

"Yes."

"What did you do?"

"I ran back to the house and got my dad."

"Had you touched the body?"

"Yes." Wes rubbed his fingers together, once more feeling the sticky blood there. "I put my hand on his chest."

He closed his eyes, remembering in detail kneeling next to his brother's body, placing his hand over the wound as if he could stop the bleeding. Opening his eyes once more, he saw Nate making notations on his pad.

"What about the weapon?" Nate continued his line of questions.

"It was never found. Not that they didn't look. I think they turned over every inch of this farm looking for it."

Nate took one last, long look around the clearing. He took a few steps forward, standing at the edge of the murky pond. Once more he turned his piercing gaze on Wes.

"Did they dredge the pond?"

The question took Wes by surprise. He hesitated for several seconds. Nate's gaze never faltered.

"No." Wes finally shook his head. "No, now that I think about it, they didn't dredge the pond."

"Hmm, I wonder why." Nate tucked his notebook back in his pocket and turned toward the trail.

"Okay, I guess that's all I need to know for now."

Wes would have preferred to follow the deputy back up the trail, but Nate Sweeney wasn't stupid. He stopped and motioned Wes ahead of him. Wes cocked an eyebrow at the officer and smiled sardonically, reminding himself that he was a murder suspect. Nate Sweeney wasn't taking any chances.

"So," Nate broke the silence when they were once more walking across the pasture. "You told me why you came back to Atlanta, but why did you leave in the first place."

Wes thought of all his reasons for leaving and the agonizing memories of betrayal rose up, nearly choking him. He looked down at his feet as the memories of his father's accusing looks hammered his weary brain. Perhaps Nate would understand. More likely he would find a way of using it against Wes, who wasn't about to incriminate himself.

"I just couldn't stay," Wes answered, and that was all he would say.

Tired. She was so tired. Rhonda sagged against the stainless steel sink and tried to concentrate on the delicate china she was washing. She really just wanted to lay down on the floor and take a nap. Emma's pickles and peanut butter had not set well with the mother-to-be and she had ended up getting sick, guiltily leaving Rhonda to finish up from the day's business. Rhonda heaved a sigh, wishing her boss would just have regular morning sickness like every other pregnant woman.

A tapping sounded at the kitchen door and Rhonda

turned to see Blake's smiling face on the other side of the glass. Her heart plummeted to her toes. She really wasn't up to dealing with Blake's affection today. With dripping hands she went to let him in.

"Hey sugar, how ya doing?" he asked, stepping across the threshold.

"Not that great." Rhonda leaned against the edge of the open door. Blake peered closer at her face.

"Whoa, what happened? You look terrible!" He took her by the shoulders and pushed the door shut with a booted foot.

"Thanks a lot." Rhonda frowned up at him then relented. "The truth is, I'm about to fall over from exhaustion. I was up half the night chasing cows and then Emma got sick and had to go home. I'm here all by myself trying to clean up and, to be honest, I just want to lay down and die."

"My poor baby, come here." Blake pulled her into his arms and Rhonda didn't have the strength to resist. She laid her head on his shoulder. "Guess I showed up just in time, huh? I actually came by to ask you to dinner, but I guess that's out of the question. I tell you what, you tell me what to do and I'll help you with the clean up, okay?"

"You mean it?" Rhonda pulled back, looking up into eyes that overflowed with concern.

"Of course I mean it. I love you, remember." He framed her face with his hands and dropped a quick kiss on her nose. Rhonda froze. "What?" he asked, looking down at her quizzically.

"You just said you love me," she said slowly.

"Well, of course. Why should that come as such

a surprise?"

"You've never said it before."

"I haven't?" Blake looked thoughtful.

"No, you haven't." And Rhonda wasn't completely sure she wanted him to be saying it now.

"I guess I thought it was a given. I wouldn't be talking marriage if I didn't love you."

"But you never mentioned marriage until yesterday." She pressed fingertips to her forehead. She was in no shape to be having this discussion.

"Rhonda, honey." Blake put an arm gently around her shoulders and steered her toward the dining room. "I've wanted to marry you since I was about ten years old. I guess it just took me sixteen years to get brave enough to mention it. But hey, lets leave talk of matrimony for another day, huh? For now, let's concentrate on getting this place cleaned up and you home to bed. Hey." He stopped abruptly at the end of the front counter. "Why were you up half the night chasing cows?"

Rhonda's stomach clenched. She knew she could not deal rationally with a confrontation about Wes right now.

"Well, Wes' cows got out last night. Actually, it was very early this morning. I was up at two a.m. playing cowgirl."

Blake just shook his head and Rhonda breathed a sigh of relief.

"Another good reason to not want to be a farmer," he said, smiling down at her. "Aren't you glad when you marry me you'll never have to worry about that kind of thing?"

Rhonda's back stiffened. She had been raised to be the wife of a farmer. To her, there would be no greater honor.

Blake began turning chairs up on top of the tables and Rhonda found herself comparing him with Wes. If she really had to choose, who would she rather marry? Her heart beat out the answer and she turned on her heel, hurrying back to the kitchen to drown the thought in her cooling dishwater.

An hour later, Rhonda had to admit that Blake's arrival had been a godsend. He had run the sweeper in the dining room, carried the trash out to the dumpster, even mopped the restrooms. Rhonda knew she would never have been able to complete all these tasks by herself. Now he stood beside her as she locked the kitchen door.

"You going to be okay driving yourself home?" he asked.

"Yeah, I'll be fine." Rhonda nodded. "I'll just drop this money off at Emma's." She held up the vinyl bank bag. "And then head home for bed. Thank you so much for helping me, Blake. I just can't tell you how much I appreciate it."

She stared up at the soft brown eyes that had regained their teasing sparkle. He ran his fingers over the side of her face and down her neck to rest his hand lightly on her shoulder.

"It was my pleasure. You sure you're going to be able to handle all this? I mean, with Emma being pregnant and needing you to work more, and cleaning house for Wes, it seems like an awful lot for you to take on. I don't want you overdoing it."

"I won't, I promise. Emma's mid-afternoon sickness won't last forever. At least, I hope it doesn't." She laughed.

"Well, I'm just glad the Lord sent me over here just when you needed me. But next time, if you're in a bind like that, just call me, okay? You know I'll come to your rescue." He placed a gentle kiss on Rhonda's lips. "Now, go on home and get some rest. We'll go out to dinner another day."

CHAPTER EIGHTEEN

Wes walked the perimeter of his property, Ranger padding silently beside him. The night sky was dark, clouds obscuring the moon and stars. He thought back on his army days and the countless hours he had spent on guard duty. After last night's incident with the calves, and the latest letter he had received, Wes wasn't taking any chances. Even if it meant exhausting himself, he was determined to patrol the area every two hours, sleeping in short shifts in-between.

Striding silently across the plowed field, his eyes adjusted to the darkness, Wes found one portion of his brain registering everything around him while another part of his mind wandered. He thought of Rhonda's tired eyes and pale skin. For a moment he stopped and turned his head to stare in the direction of the Weaver farm. He pictured Rhonda sleeping soundly, tucked safely into bed. What would it be like to crawl in along side her, take her in his arms?

Shaking his head to dispel such crazy thoughts, Wes walked on.

Instead, he mentally revisited Nate Sweeney's appearance that afternoon. The questions about Brian's death had not lost their sting. A rock settled in the pit of Wes' stomach. He was going to be arrested for his brother's murder. He had run away once, he couldn't run away again. Rhonda seemed certain he would be vindicated. Wes wasn't nearly as sure. Nate's question about the pond had startled him. Would the pond reveal the answer to who had killed his brother?

Wes felt more than saw Ranger's ears prick forward. A low growl rumbled from the dog's throat. Wes squinted ahead to the brush-covered banks of the creek that separated two fields. A rustling erupted from the bushes as branches snapped. Ranger continued to growl.

"Easy boy, easy," Wes murmured, placing a hand on Ranger's head to keep him from bolting forward.

Like a phantom, Wes crept through the dark toward the creek, his footfalls barely a whisper across the fertile soil of the field. The quiet rustling sounded again from the brush. It was most likely a raccoon or opossum coming out for a nocturnal drink from the creek, Wes thought. Ranger's sharp bark suddenly broke the stillness of the night. The rustling immediately stopped.

"Ranger, hush," Wes whispered the command.

Ranger began to growl once more then, without warning, the dog shot forward, barking furiously as he rushed toward the creek. Wes broke into a run, following. He could hear splashing in the shallow water and could make out Ranger's silvery coat as the dog ran parallel to the creek for a short distance before pushing through the brambles and disappearing down the bank. More splashing as Ranger hit the water.

Wes shouldered his way through the thick growth around the stream and plunged down the steep embankment, not even flinching when his feet hit the water. He could still hear Ranger, somewhere ahead. The dog was running up and down the creek bed, sometimes in the water, sometimes plowing through the reeds and rushes on the sides of the stream. He came trotting toward Wes, his nose to the ground.

Not finding anything, Wes finally climbed up the opposite bank and stood staring across the field toward the north. Had it been a person walking along the creek or had it just been a nocturnal animal? Wes wondered. Ranger climbed up from the stream and stood dripping and panting beside his master. Wes squinted off into the distance, straining to see anything that might be moving across the dark field. Once more, Ranger's ears pricked forward and the dog went trotting off, more sedately this time. Wes followed, trying to make out what the dog might have seen.

His eyes caught a flash of light. Was that a person at the far edge of the field near the woods or merely a deer running into the trees? Ranger must have seen it, too. He shot forward, running full tilt toward the tree line. There was no way Wes could keep up, but his physical stamina served him well. He was barely

Help Me, Rhonda

blowing hard when he reached the edge of the woods. Ranger circled around the trees, his nose to the ground, but there was nothing to be seen. Then Wes heard it, coming from deep within the bowels of the woods, the quiet purring of a car engine.

Wes' mind quickly ran through his knowledge of the area. Where would the car exit the woods? He shook his head. He had very little memory of these woods and had no idea where the access road may be. The sound of the engine quickly faded away, telling Wes the vehicle had moved away from him and was probably out on the main road by now.

Turning, Wes whistled for Ranger and started back across the field toward home. At the creek he pulled a flashlight from his pocket and carefully went over every inch of the banks on both sides of the stream, methodically running the light back and forth across the ground.

A quick flash of color caught his eye. He paused and scanned the ground once more before stooping down. Reaching out, he carefully lifted the pack of matches. The blue matchbook cover was printed with the name of a local supermarket. Wes flipped it open and saw that none of the matches had been used. Sitting back on his heels, he glanced down and saw an unlit cigarette lying near the toe of his boot. He picked it up.

Not his brand, Wes noted. He stared off toward the farm yard, thinking. Whoever had trekked through the woods and across the field had not come all this way for a smoke, of that Wes was certain. He contemplated the matches and cigarette in the palm of his hand, convinced of one thing. Whoever had been out here had come for one purpose. To start a fire.

A mile up the road, in her upstairs bedroom, Rhonda was not fast asleep. Overly exhausted, she tossed and turned, tangling the quilts until she finally flopped over on her back to stare up at the ceiling. What was wrong with her? She sighed heavily and punched the pillow beneath her head. For the first time in ten years a man had told her he loved her. Wasn't a declaration of love supposed to make a woman feel something besides annoyance?

Closing her eyes, Rhonda concentrated on breathing evenly, forcing herself to relax and clear her mind. Then slowly she called to remembrance Blake's words, the look on his face when he said them. She mentally went over each nuance of those short moments when he had vowed his love for her. Nothing happened. Instead, Rhonda's heart remained lukewarm.

What was she going to do? Turning on her side, she buried her face in her pillow. It hadn't been all that long ago when Rhonda had wanted Blake to take their relationship to the next level. Now he was doing so and she was balking worse than a stubborn pony. Didn't she want to be married? Didn't she want children and security? It seemed that Blake was finally ready to offer her the world. So why did she suddenly have cold feet and a cold heart?

Throwing the quilt back in frustration, Rhonda got up from the bed and padded to the window seat. She stared out at the dark night, thoughts of Blake discarded as she envisioned the Cooper farmhouse to the north. Closing her eyes, Rhonda could see Wes' face as he dropped the bombshell about his parents' accident. She could hear his deep, raspy voice as he said her name. She could almost smell his aftershave. At the mere thought of him, her heart did its pirouette and her eyes flew open.

What was she going to do? Somehow she had to find a way to end her relationship with Blake, but the man her heart was yearning for was under investigation for murder!

"Jesus," Rhonda prayed quietly, "I could really use some of that peace You promised right about now."

Wes paced through the house, repeatedly driving his fist into his palm. Man, he wanted to throttle something! Never before had he felt so helpless, totally at the mercy of his enemy. He had to find some way to gain the upper hand. But how? Whoever was after him always seemed to be one step ahead. Wes had to find some way to turn the tables.

Throwing himself down on the sofa, Wes tried to think of a plan. What he wouldn't give for a couple of hand grenades and a claymore mine right about now. Booby traps. He needed to set some booby traps. But booby trap what? He had no idea where his enemy would strike next, and booby trap the wrong thing and Rhonda or Becca could get hurt. So, what was he supposed to do? Sit idly by while his farm was destroyed little by little? Wait quietly until the cops finally showed up with a warrant for his arrest?

You could pray.

A voice, sounding oddly like Rhonda's, whispered to his heart. Wes squeezed his eyes tightly shut, trying to dispel the thought. He didn't even know how to pray anymore. Didn't even know if he believed there was anyone to hear his prayers, even if he did know how.

Sitting up on the sofa, Wes straightened his shoulders. No. He had made it through this many battles on his own. He wasn't going to be defeated, even if he didn't have God's help. Not when he was finally finding something worth living for. Somehow he was going to find a way to beat his invisible foe.

CHAPTER NINETEEN

May first came and went with no occurrences of sabotage at the Cooper farm, at least as far as Rhonda knew. She hadn't had the chance to take any more meals to Wes. It seemed like she hadn't had a moment to herself all week. Emma's pregnancy was wreaking havoc with the work schedule as she continued to get sick every afternoon.

Then there was Blake. He was being overly solicitous, which should have touched Rhonda's heart. Instead, it was getting on her last nerve.

Rhonda spent a lot of time in prayer, seeking the peace God promised but which seemed to be eluding her. Her rational, reasonable mind told her she should try to make it work with Blake. After all, dreams of Wes were just that, *dreams*. Blake was flesh and blood, offering to make her dreams reality. What more could a woman possibly want?

The knot of confusion in Rhonda's heart grew more tangled the night a detective from the

Montmorency County Sheriff's Department visited the Weavers. Randy Epworth made it clear; they were formally investigating Brian Cooper's murder. Old wounds, wounds Rhonda had thought healed long ago, were slashed open as she was forced to recount the days leading up to Brian's death.

What sorts of activities was Brian involved in? Who were his friends? Did he have any enemies? What was his relationship like with his brother? The questions seemed endless. Rhonda tried to answer truthfully without implicating Wes, but it was hard. Detective Epworth was good at his job and Rhonda found herself revealing details she would rather have kept to herself.

By the time the detective left, Rhonda's emotions were raw, plowed up like the newly turned fields. Her grief felt as fresh as the day Brian had died. So much hope, so much promise, gone forever.

And Wes. Rhonda felt the now familiar surge of protection rise up within her. Things certainly did not look good for Wes.

Rhonda couldn't wait to pounce on Nate when he and Penny stopped in the Spot of Tea Saturday morning. But the deputy just shook his head and pierced her with his direct, electric-blue stare.

"It's an unsolved murder, Rhonda," was all he would say. "We have a sworn duty to protect the citizens of this county. It's our job to try and do everything in our power to bring the person responsible to justice."

It was obvious the person Nate thought responsible was Wes Cooper.

Help Me, Rhonda

Rhonda contemplated all this as she sat in her robe at the kitchen table Sunday morning. The old house was quiet. Her parents and Becca had gone off to church. Rhonda had called Blake and told him she wasn't up to attending service. She was tired, she just wanted some time alone. Blake had seemed to understand.

"Sure, baby, sure," he had said. "You just take it easy. You've had a hard week."

Rhonda picked up her mug and took a sip of coffee. She ran a hand lovingly over the tissue-paper-thin pages of her Bible then leaned forward to read the words of Psalm 9. Oh, how she loved the Psalms. They could soothe her better than anything else when her spirit was in distress. And her spirit had certainly been in distress the past week!

"The Lord also will be a refuge for the oppressed. A refuge in times of trouble," Rhonda read out loud, thinking more of Wes than herself. "Oh Lord, Wes really needs Your refuge right now," she interjected before continuing on with the Psalm. "And those who know Your name will put their trust in You; For You, Lord, have not forsaken those who seek You."

Rhonda closed her eyes and bowed her head, feeling as if her heart were shattering into a million tiny fragments. She tried to picture Brian. What would he look like now if he had lived? But her mind could not conjure up the image. All she could see was Wes. What if they dragged him off to jail? Or worse, what if the person responsible for Brian's death, and maybe his parents', caught up with him first? The thought left Rhonda feeling sick to her stomach.

"Jesus, I know Wes knows Your name. I know he isn't putting his trust in You right now, he isn't seeking You, but please, don't forsake him."

Lifting her head, Rhonda's eyes fell on verse 13 and she automatically began to read aloud.

"Have mercy on me, O Lord! Consider my trouble from those who hate me, You who lift me up from the gates of death."

Wes certainly had trouble from people who hated him! Rhonda went back to the beginning of the verse, inserting Wes' name and reading it as a prayer.

"Have mercy on Wes, O Lord!" she prayed. "Consider his trouble from those who hate him, You who lift him up from the gates of death." She began to smile as she continued with verse 14. "That I may tell of all Your praise in the gates of the daughter of Zion. I will rejoice in Your salvation."

Sitting back in the chair, Rhonda tilted her head back and closed her eyes. The burden that had been weighing down her soul began to lift as she focused her mind on the Lord. She would trust in Him. He would avenge. He would not forget the cry of the humble. And in the end, they would rejoice in His salvation. God's Word said it, Rhonda had to believe it was true.

The columns of apple trees, their boughs heavy with blossoms, stood in orderly rank and file at the bottom of the hill to the north of the Cooper farmhouse. Bees buzzed lazily among the flowers doing their job of pollination. Wes eyed the jagged stump between the last two trees of the second column. It marred the otherwise perfect formation of the orchard and he was determined to get it out. His military mind liked to have things squared away. The blackened stump stood out like a grape juice stain on a starched white tablecloth.

Walking to the back of his truck, he lowered the tailgate. Ranger jumped down from the bed of the truck as Wes reached for the long-handled shovel and an axe which he tossed beside the tree stump. The day was sunny and unseasonably mild for early May. As Ranger trotted around the trees, sniffing, Wes set the point of the shovel into the ground near the stump and began to dig. Soon rivulets of sweat trickled down his temples. He buried the shovel in the dirt and yanked his black t-shirt over his head, tossing it aside.

Wes contemplated the morass of tangled roots he was uncovering and unconsciously swatted at a bee buzzing near his ear. His life had become like those roots, all tangled up in a giant knot, until he couldn't make heads or tails out of any of it. Pulling his work gloves on more snuggly, Wes picked up the axe and took a whack at the knot. One swing, with the blade directed at the right point, and things would break loose.

He felt it was the same for him. Brian's death, his parents' accident, the offers to buy the farm, the incidents that had taken place since he returned home. Somehow it was all tangled together. If he could just cut through the mess, eventually it would all make sense. But he was running out of time.

Exchanging the axe for the shovel, Wes went back to digging. The droning of the bees was welcome background music to his work. For a moment he was transported back, to the years when the orchard rang with laughter in the fall; families coming to pick apples, ride in the hay wagon or just sip hot cider in the barn. Wes closed his eyes, his senses recalling the sounds and smells of those happier times.

Opening his eyes, Wes looked off toward the house and saw the sun glinting off copper curls as Rhonda walked toward him. His stomach tightened and he turned his full attention back to the knot of roots. His life was a big enough mess, he didn't need to add Rhonda to the mix. Ranger, who had laid down in the shade, perked his head up, watching Rhonda approach.

"Hi," she said softly, coming to stop a few feet away from Wes. Ranger got up and trotted over for attention. Wes spared her a quick glance, noticing how she barely had to bend over to pet the huge dog.

"Hi." He tossed a shovel-full of dirt aside.

"What are you doing?"

"What's it look like I'm doing? I'm digging out this stump."

"But why?" Rhonda asked.

Wes put down the shovel and hefted the axe, preparing to attempt to cut through another knot of roots.

"Because it's in the way."

"In the way of what?"

Wes ignored the question and kept chopping.

"I think it adds character," she declared.

"You would," he muttered under his breath, suddenly craving the cigarettes she had dumped down the drain.

"I remember when that tree got hit by lightening. It was split nearly straight down the middle. Fascinated Brian and I to no end, the power of nature. I think my mom used that tree to keep me in line for months afterward. If I didn't behave, I could be struck by lightening, just like that tree. Funny, but I could never figure out what the tree had done to deserve getting struck. Every time I asked my mom, she just changed the subject. Anyway, Brian and I sat right up there." She pointed to a branch above her head. "And watched while your dad cut the tree up and hauled it away. I think you should leave the stump there, as a sort of memorial."

"Well, I'm not going to."

Rhonda pulled down a branch heavily laden with blossoms and buried her nose in the white flowers.

"You know, there's a lot in the Bible about trees, especially fruit trees."

"Yeah, as I recall, they were responsible for the fall of man."

Wes dropped to his knees and stuck his hand into the hole he had dug, seeking the roots that were still intact. He glanced up to see Rhonda staring down at him with wide eyes. He looked down to see what had rendered her silent.

"Shrapnel wound," he explained, pointing at the scarred and puckered skin on his side.

Rhonda's mouth formed a perfect 'O' before she

shook herself, as if suddenly aware she had been staring. She looked away from him, off into the trees.

"I think God has a special place in His heart for farmers," she continued her dialogue. "After all, Adam and Eve were basically the first farmers. And that whole thing between Cain and Able, it was all because Cain tried to offer fruits as his sacrifice."

Wes froze at the mention of the Bible story, the one that haunted his thoughts night and day. The cold from the ground seeped into his skin as he lay in the dirt, hearing the words once again.

Your brother's blood cries out to me from the ground.

Wes shook his head to dispel the voice before standing. He brushed at the dirt clinging to his sweaty chest. Daring a peek at Rhonda, he caught her staring once more and nearly smiled. Slowly he bent down and snagged his t-shirt from the ground, lazily pulling it on over his head. When his head emerged from the top, Rhonda had turned her back on him.

"I heard somewhere that as tall as a tree is, that's how long its roots are," she said, staring up into the top branches of a nearby tree. Finally she turned and ventured a step closer to the stump Wes was removing. She peered down at the tangle of roots he had uncovered. "You think that's true?"

Wes just shrugged and resumed his digging.

"I heard it's especially true of fruit trees. They need all those roots to keep them upright when they're heavy with fruit." Rhonda held her arms out, demonstrating. "Otherwise they would topple right over in a wind. In the Bible it says we're supposed to be like trees planted by rivers of water and bear much fruit. If we have really deep roots, planted in God, then we won't get blown over by hard times when they come our way. You need to be well rooted in God, Wes."

Wes pointedly ignored the comment and continued digging. He didn't need to be preached a sermon.

" Well, I need to get up to the house and get to work," Rhonda finally said. She turned to head that way then abruptly stopped in her tracks. "You know, you should think about opening the orchard this fall. It would be a good income for you and it would be fun to have the hay rides and stuff again. I could bring the horses down and we could do pony rides, too. Wouldn't that be fun?" She turned to look over her shoulder at him.

"I'll give it some thought. If I'm here," he added deliberately.

"You'll be here," Rhonda said with confidence as she once more moved through the orchard toward the farm house. "I'm believing God you will. Oh." She spun around once more, a playful smile dancing around her mouth. "And if you have any trouble pulling that stump out with that fancy truck of yours, just give a holler. I'll come and show you what some real horse power can do!"

Twirling around, Rhonda continued toward the house, her musical laughter held suspended in the apple blossoms. Wes just shook his head as he watched her retreating back. He glanced up at the boughs above his head and thought of what she had said about being rooted in God and bearing much fruit. Rhonda must be well rooted because Wes was beginning to think she was as fruity as they come.

In the front yard of the farm house, Rhonda stopped. Hands on her hips, she drummed her fingers as she stared at the front porch, perfect for watching the sunrise, and called herself ten kinds of fool. Glancing back toward the orchard, Rhonda envisioned Wes, bare-chested, muscles rippling as he wielded the axe. She felt an odd trembling that left her stomach feeling like a bowl of underdone gelatin. Closing her eyes, she recalled her nervous rambling and grimaced. Wes was sure to be impressed by her dissertation on trees.

With a mental shrug, Rhonda climbed the porch step and entered the house. She recalled a verse from the Bible, something about how Paul planted, Apollos watered, but God gave the increase. Maybe, just maybe, her unbridled tongue had planted a seed. It would be up to the Lord to make it grow.

Now that she had gotten into a routine with cleaning, Rhonda had the house set in order in no time at all. With only one person living there, only the most basic maintenance was required. She shooed Becca off to explore, telling her she could find Wes and Ranger down in the orchard, before heading up to the attic. Rhonda had not forgotten Wes' inquiry about his brother's things, and since the investigation into Brian's death had been re-opened, Rhonda felt driven to find the physical evidence of his existence. She wanted something to hold onto.

The pull-down ladder in the upstairs hall groaned in loud protest as Rhonda pulled the chain and unfolded the steps. Cautiously she ascended into the dark upper reaches of the house. Standing at the top, she reached above her head for the string that was hanging there. With a quick tug, a bare, overhead light bulb illuminated the attic.

Three generations of memories hunkered in the shadows, pieces of an era long gone, and many from the not-so-distant past. Bending slightly at the waist, Rhonda made her way carefully down the length of the attic, between the steep trusses of the roof. A few paintings leaned against the walls. A tattered dress form stood in one corner, wearing a yellowed organdy dress. Smiling, Rhonda touched the dress with a finger, feeling as she were being sucked back through time. The Coopers had only been gone two years, but the attic held nearly a hundred years worth of heirlooms and junk.

The trunk containing Brian's things was easy for Rhonda to find. Though barely in her fifties when Brian was killed, Deanne Cooper was old-school. No modern, plastic totes for her. No, family treasures were stored in sturdy, cedar-lined chests. Kneeling in front of the trunk, Rhonda brushed her hand over the top, dislodging years worth of dust. Her heart beat heavily as she stared at the latch, suddenly afraid to confront the ghosts of the past.

Trembling fingers reached out and unhooked the simple closure. Rhonda hefted the lid and stared down at the items carefully wrapped in yellowing tissue. She pulled out Brian's green wool school jacket and held it at arm's length, gently shaking out the folds before pulling it to her chest and burying her nose in the collar. She recalled October nights, sitting in the football stands, wrapped in this coat, while Brian huddled next to her in a t-shirt, insisting he wasn't cold.

Inhaling deeply, Rhonda sought to detect a familiar scent, some essence of Brian still lingering in the cloth, but there was nothing. Only the smell of cedar and time long past. Tears squeezed from her tightly closed eyes.

Brushing them away with the heel of her hand, Rhonda quickly rummaged through the remaining items in the trunk, choosing a few she thought Wes would be interested in. There was no way she could man-handle the trunk down the attic steps. Anything else Wes wanted, he was more than capable of coming up and getting himself. Standing, she gathered the letterman jacket and other things before turning off the light and descending the stairs into the bright afternoon below.

In the upstairs hallway, Rhonda contemplated the closed bedroom doors on either side of the central bathroom. Since Wes was only using the downstairs, Rhonda and Becca rarely ventured to the upper floor except to do a cursory dusting and vacuuming. Cradling Brian's things, Rhonda turned the knob and pushed open the door to his old room. The white iron daybed was covered in a frilly comforter and dust ruffle, as far removed from Brian's brown and orange plaid bedspread as possible.

Pushing aside old memories that fought their way to the surface, Rhonda deposited her load on the bed and went to the closet for a hanger for Brian's coat. She pulled open the closet door and stared. A green military uniform hung, left sleeve out, on the closet bar. On the floor beneath stood a pair of highly shined boots; a tan beret lay on the shelf above. Slowly, Rhonda reached for the hanger and lifted the uniform down. A host of colorful ribbons adorned the left breast along with several badges. A black nametag reading simply "Cooper" was pinned on the right breast. Everything went very still and silent as she stared at the uniform. Wes' uniform.

Footsteps sounded on the stairs. The bedroom door creaked as someone pushed it wide. Rhonda turned her face toward the door.

"Rhonda, what are you doing?" Wes asked.

CHAPTER TWENTY

Standing in the doorway, Wes looked at Rhonda as she held his uniform. The eyes that met his were filled with awe and respect.

"This is your army uniform," she stated.

"Yes," Wes said simply, lounging against the door frame.

"What are all these for?" She turned the jacket slightly and pointed to the ribbons on the breast.

"Lots of different things," he replied, shrugging a shoulder.

"Will you tell me?" Rhonda moved to sit on the side of the bed, draping the jacket across her lap. "Like this one, what is this one for?" She pointed to a rainbow colored bar.

"That's an Army service ribbon. It's no big deal, everyone gets one of those."

"You're too modest. *I* don't have one!" Rhonda smiled and Wes felt the familiar band tighten around his heart. "What about this one?"

She put a fingertip against a blue, green and white striped bar. Wes pushed away from the doorway, her eyes drawing him into the room. Suddenly she didn't seem as fruity as she had out in the orchard. Bending on one knee next to the bed he answered,

"That's an Army achievement medal. This one is the global war on terrorism service ribbon. Good conduct medal," he said, pointing to each ribbon.

"You got a good conduct medal?" Rhonda teased with a laugh.

"Yeah, can you believe it?"

"What about this one?" she asked, pointing.

"That's a bronze star," Wes said quietly, not quite able to keep the pride from his voice.

"A bronze star?" Rhonda's voice squeaked with amazement. "You got a bronze star?" She laid a hand on his shoulder and Wes felt warmth seep all the way into his chest. She shook his shoulder slightly. "That's really cool. What exactly do you get a bronze star for?"

Wes swallowed hard as flashes of memories went off in his brain like firecrackers. Bombs exploding. The staccato sound of gunfire. One of his men screaming from the middle of a dusty street, blood gushing from his thigh. Rushing forward among the gunfire. Pulling the pin on a grenade. Throwing, running, explosions deafening him as he ran into the street. Grabbing the fallen soldier and throwing him over his shoulder. Running, firing his weapon with one hand, stumbling around the corner of a building while blood ran down his chest.

"Heroism in combat," he finally answered in a choked voice.

"Wow," Rhonda said softly. The hand on his shoulder became incredibly gentle. "Will you tell me about it someday?" she asked quietly.

Wes cleared his throat.

"Probably not." He risked looking into her eyes. "We'll see," he amended.

"What about this one?" Rhonda pointed to a purple ribbon with thin white stripes on each end.

"That's a purple heart," Wes answered, rising to his feet.

"A purple heart?" Wide blue eyes looked up at him in wonder. "Oh, the shrapnel wound?"

"Yeah, the shrapnel wound." Wes took the uniform from her hands and went to place it carefully back in the closet. "What's all this?" he asked, motioning to the things strewn on the bed, ready for a change of subject.

"Oh, some of Brian's things. I brought them down from the attic. Remember, you had asked about them?" She turned slightly on the bed to face him. "It's only a few things. There's still more in the chest up there, but it's too heavy for me to lift. I thought…" Her voice caught as her fingers reached out to softly caress the white leather sleeve of the coat. "I thought it would be nice to have a few of his things around. I was going to hang the coat up in the closet when I found your uniform."

Rhonda stood and carried the jacket to the closet and quickly hung it on a hanger. She reached out to touch the yellow chevrons on the sleeve of Wes' uniform.

"Is this your rank?" she asked.

"Yeah, I was an E-7 when I got out."

"E-7?"

"Sergeant First Class," Wes explained. "I was a platoon sergeant."

He didn't know why he tacked on that information until he saw the admiration in Rhonda's eyes, then he understood. He was seeking her approval.

"Sergeant First Class Wes Cooper," Rhonda said, sounding impressed. "You know, Memorial Day is only a few weeks away. There's always a parade in town for the veterans. You should wear your uniform." She stared deeply into his eyes and Wes found he couldn't look away. "You're a hero, Wes. People should know."

A bitter smile turned up one corner of his mouth. Wes couldn't stop himself from reaching out and framing Rhonda's face with his hands.

"I'm not a hero to people around here," he said coldly. "They only think of me as a murderer and if they have anything to say about it, I won't be walking around free come Memorial Day."

She had been sure he was going to kiss her. She had desperately, desperately wanted him to kiss her, Rhonda admitted to herself as she drove the short distance home. If he had, she probably would have melted into a puddle right there in the middle of the bedroom floor.

But what about Blake? He was bound to propose

Help Me, Rhonda

any day now and Rhonda still had no idea what she was supposed to do about their relationship. She didn't want to break Blake's heart, but his kisses had never made her feel like melting. Just the thought of Wes doing so had turned her insides into pudding.

Becca chatted excitedly all the way home, about the chickens, Ranger, the calves and the fact that she was still trying to convince Wes to get some ducks. Rhonda threw a glance at her baby sister, covered in orange dirt from helping Wes pull out the stump in the orchard. Becca had probably come close to talking his ears clean off while she helped him work. Rhonda recalled how she herself had rattled on about trees and inwardly cringed. She had Becca had a lot in common.

"Remember when the Coopers had the hay rides and stuff in the fall?" Becca asked as Rhonda parked the truck in the Weaver driveway. She jumped from the cab and followed Rhonda to the house. "Don't you think it would be awesome if we could get Wes to do that this year? My friends and I could have so much fun! We haven't had anything like that around here in ages."

Rhonda felt her heart sink like a stone at the thought of what the fall would bring. Wes seemed sure he would be arrested before Memorial Day. Was there even any hope he would be here to see the orchard heavy with fruit this fall? Of course there was! Rhonda straightened her shoulders. God was the God of hope.

"Don't you think it would be fun?" Becca asked again.

"Yes, I do," Rhonda agreed, putting her arm around Becca's shoulders as they walked down the hall toward the kitchen. "I think it would be a lot of fun. I actually had the same idea and mentioned it to Wes. We need to be praying he'll do it."

And that he'll still be here when the time comes, she added silently.

The phone was ringing when the two entered the kitchen. Rhonda snatched up the receiver.

"Hello."

"Hey sugar, how are you feeling?" It was Blake.

"Good, I'm feeling a lot better," Rhonda answered.

"Did you get to have a nice, quiet day at home?"

Was that a suspicious undertone in Blake's voice? Rhonda wondered.

"For the most part."

"You didn't go and clean house for Wes again today, did you Rhonda?"

It was so tempting to lie. Rhonda stared out the kitchen window. One little white lie to avoid an argument. Then her eyes fell to the table where her Bible still lay next to her empty coffee cup. She drew herself up to her full five-foot height. She had no reason to be afraid of Blake.

"Actually, I did. But it wasn't a big deal. Now that Becca and I have done it a few times, we zip right through in no time. And Wes was out working in the orchard all afternoon."

Except for that tiny space of time when Rhonda had been sure he was going to kiss her, her traitorous heart reminded. She shoved the memory aside and tried to concentrate on what Blake was saying.

"Well, I hope you'll have some time for me tomorrow then," Blake sounded petulant. "Between Emma and Wes, I'm starting to feel slighted."

"Blake, I'm not slighting you..."

"How about tomorrow afternoon then? I'll come by when you're closing up. If Emma's sick again, I'll help you with the clean up and then we can go out for a nice dinner, just the two of us. What do you say?"

Rhonda felt the time of his proposal creeping closer. And when he did pop the question, what was she going to say? Closing her eyes, she touched her cheek where Wes had laid his hand.

"Rhonda?"

Her eyes popped open and she stared unseeing out the window.

"Sure, okay, dinner tomorrow," she reluctantly agreed.

"Great, baby, see you then."

Rhonda hung the phone back in its cradle and stood chewing her bottom lip. Tomorrow would be her day of reckoning. If Blake didn't spark some sort of romantic feelings, she was going to have to break it off with him for good.

Steam followed Wes out of the bathroom as he walked through the house rubbing a towel over his wet head. His stomach rumbled with hunger. Rhonda had left a note on the kitchen counter saying his dinner was warming in the oven. Tossing the damp towel over his bare shoulder, he made his way to the kitchen. He cracked the oven door and

Help Me, Rhonda

looked in at the homemade pot pie, bubbly gravy seeping through cracks in the flaky crust. His mouth immediately began to water. What would he do without Rhonda?

Wes pictured her standing in the upstairs bedroom, holding his uniform. Thought about how she had stood still between his hands. How easy it would have been to kiss her. What *would* he do without her? He finally admitted that Rhonda, with all of her "help," had broken through his bitter shell and crept right into his heart.

After feeding Ranger, Wes sat down with his own dinner, his thoughts drifting lazily over the day. Becca had followed him around, chattering like a magpie and getting in the way more than helping, but Wes had to admit he enjoyed the teen's company. He probably should discourage her from coming around. It could be dangerous for her, too.

Wes cocked his head, as if he could hear Rhonda's laughter as she walked through the orchard. His eyes scanned the clean kitchen. Evidence of her presence was everywhere, from the potted plants thriving on the windowsill, to the food sitting in front of him. He should tell her to stay away, and keep her sister away as well. It wasn't safe for either of them to be associating with him. But Wes knew he wouldn't, couldn't do it. Rhonda was the one bright spot in the darkness of his life.

Finished with his meal, Wes went out to the front porch and sat on the top step. Dusk was settling quietly over the land. He stared away to the north, toward the Rattlesnake Hills. Though not nearly as tall or majestic as some of the mountains he had seen during his military career, the familiar sight of the hills brought a sense of comfort and serenity. Shadowy forms emerged in the hayfield across the road as the deer came out to graze. Ranger sat up and whined, his ears perked forward.

"Shhh," Wes commanded, laying a hand on the dog's collar. "Down." Ranger obediently lay down.

Out of habit, Wes patted the pocket of his t-shirt looking for his cigarettes and extracted a pack of gum instead. Unwrapping a stick, he popped it in his mouth and chewed. Not really as satisfying as a cigarette, but he figured he would get used to it. He pictured the awe in Rhonda's eyes as she held his uniform. Would she be just as impressed if she knew he had quit smoking? Wes chuckled to himself. Since when had he been so eager to impress Rhonda Weaver?

Leaning back on his elbows, Wes went over the scene in Brian's bedroom. He could have easily taken Rhonda in his arms and kissed her. The urge to do so had been strong. The only thing that had stopped him had been the sight of her caressing his brother's varsity jacket. Rhonda may be impressed by his medals and awards, but it was obvious her heart still belonged to Brian.

And then there was Blake to consider.

It was all a mess. Just like that tangled knot of tree roots he had finally managed to pull from the ground. Brian's murder, the threats to him and the farm, his possible arrest, his growing feelings for Rhonda, her involvement with Blake Dalton. How was he supposed to make sense of any of it?

Rhonda seemed to have all the answers. What was it she had said, in that sermon she had preached him down in the orchard? Something about being like trees and bearing fruit. Wes closed his eyes and heard Rhonda's voice,

"You need to be rooted in God, Wes."

Winds of adversity were beginning to blow. If he was rooted in God, would it keep him from being picked up and carried away by the storm? Would it keep him from being sent to jail for Brian's murder? Wes glanced once more toward Rattlesnake Hills, now barely visible in the deepening gloom, as words both familiar and foreign rang in his heart.

I will lift up my eyes to the hills – from whence comes my help? My help comes from the Lord who made heaven and earth.

"But I don't know how to be rooted in You," Wes said aloud. "I drifted away a long time ago. I have no roots left. Do you still love me, God? Will You still help me, even after all I've done?" he cried to the hills.

CHAPTER TWENTY ONE

Wes woke with a start and sat up on the sofa. Soft grey light filtered in through the living room drapes. Another quiet night had passed. He swung his legs down from the couch and heard a soft thump. Looking down, he saw his mother's Bible laying on the floor where it had slid from his lap. Wes reached for the Bible and held it gently in his hands. There had been plenty of time to search the passages in between his shifts of patrolling the farm. Now the words swirled around in his tired mind.

As you have therefore received Christ Jesus the Lord, so walk in Him, rooted and built up in Him and established in the faith...

That Christ may dwell in you hearts through faith; that you, being rooted and grounded in love...

But when the sun was up they were scorched, and because they had no root they withered away.

Would he be scorched? Would he wither away when the heat of the murder investigation was turned on him full force? He heard Rhonda's voice reminding him of the day he was baptized, the day he openly proclaimed Jesus as his Lord and Savior.

"The Spirit of God dwells within you," Rhonda had said.

Back then, Wes had believed it was true. But he had traveled such a long way since then.

Scratching his head, Wes walked to the kitchen and laid the Bible on the table. After turning on the coffee maker, he stretched and yawned, his eyes focused on the barn and the farmland beyond. His farm, his land, his home. He wouldn't allow it to be taken from him. He would fight to the death for what was his.

My farm, My land, My home.

The quiet voice echoed in Wes' heart and he spun around, searching the kitchen for the source. Of course, no one was there. He was alone in the kitchen and it hadn't been an audible sound. No, it was merely a whisper spoken to his spirit.

"But this *is* my home," Wes argued aloud to the empty room.

But it's My home, too, the silent voice seemed to reply. *Release it back to Me.*

Opening the refrigerator, Wes reached for the fresh eggs Becca had gathered the day before and remembered why it had been so easy to drift away from God ten years ago. Sometimes it seemed He required far too much.

A short while later, as Wes was rinsing his breakfast dishes, he could hear Ranger barking up a storm. Knocking at the front door followed a few moments later. Drying his hands on a dish towel, Wes made his way toward the front door, looking down at his worn grey sweatpants and rumpled t-shirt. Whoever was at the door, he hoped it wasn't anyone he needed to impress.

He swung the front door wide. A man in tan slacks and a baby blue, button-down shirt stood on the front porch holding a clip board. Hearing the door squeak, he turned to face Wes.

"Can I help you?" Wes asked, staring at the stranger through the screen.

"Yes, hello. I'm Bill Standish from Northland Gas. I've been sent out to do a preliminary survey in preparation for us possibly building a gas processing center here."

"I don't know what you're talking about. I don't want any gas plant here."

"And you are?" the man asked, eyebrow raised.

"The owner of this farm." Wes' fingers itched to wrap around the butt of a gun.

"And do you have a name?" Bill Standish asked, looking skeptical.

"Wes Cooper, not that it's any business of yours. My family has owned this farm for more than a hundred years. I can assure you, I never contacted you about building any gas facility on my property."

"Well, according to this," Standish said, riffling through the papers on his clip board. "The survey was requested by Energy Options, LLC, out of Gaylord. They claim to be in negotiations for buying this property."

"I've never heard of Energy Options, and this land is not for sale. Good day." And with that Wes swung the door closed, leaving a bewildered Bill Standish standing on his front porch.

Quick strides carried him to the kitchen where he snatched up the phone and punched in his lawyer's phone number.

"Ken? Yeah, it's Wes. Sorry to call so early. I need you to do some digging for me. Find out who Energy Options, LLC out of Gaylord is owned by. Yeah, that's right, Energy Options, LLC. Seems they think they're buying my farm."

Blake drove Rhonda to Lewiston's steak house for a quiet dinner, away from the hometown crowd where they knew everyone in sight. Thankfully, Emma had felt better today and Tyler had the day off from the tri-county EMT service, so he stopped by to help close up shop. Rhonda was grateful for the break.

"You're looking a little perkier today," Blake observed. His brown eyes were warm as they assessed her from across the table. "A day off did you good, huh?"

"Yes." Rhonda nodded in agreement. "I think it did me a world of good. But I have to admit, I felt sort of guilty about missing church. Did you go?" Rhonda looked at him, hopeful.

"No." Blake shook his head, looking sheepish. "I know I should have, but it just isn't the same without you there. Emma and Tyler and Nate, they don't seem to like me especially. I would have felt uncomfortable by myself."

"It's not that they don't like you," Rhonda broke off, searching for the right words. "They're just... protective."

"I just wonder when Nate will forgive me for something I did when I was 18. I mean, I know it was stupid, joy riding in that squad car. I was young and I didn't have the same kind of growing up that you and Nate and Emma had. Not that I'm making excuses for myself, I know it was wrong, what I did. That and a few other things. But that was eight years ago. I'm different now. I've grown up. If God forgives and forgets, why can't Nate and Emma?"

"They will." Rhonda placed her hands over his on the tabletop, trying to behave the same way she would have a month ago. Her feelings remained lukewarm. How could she continue with this charade?

The waitress came and took their orders. When they were alone again, Rhonda sat back in the booth and looked at Blake, studying him, trying to picture herself marrying him. What if he asked her tonight? Could she put off answering him? What if she said no? Blake had professed his love for her. How could she break his heart?

"What are you thinking?" Blake's question startled Rhonda from her woolgathering.

"What?" She turned wide, blue eyes his way.

"You seemed like you were a million miles away there for a minute. Where did you go?"

"Oh, no place." Rhonda waved a hand in dismissal

as guilt pricked her conscience. She took a sip from her water glass, trying to think of something to say. "Becca and I are trying to talk Wes into opening the orchard this fall."

Blake snorted and sat back in his seat. "I wouldn't get your hopes up."

"Why not?"

"Because last I heard, they are close to wrapping up the investigation into Brian's murder. I think they'll arrest Wes any day."

"I don't believe it." Rhonda carefully set her water glass down and crossed her arms, clutching her biceps to still her trembling hands. "I don't believe Wes is guilty. My mom doesn't believe it and neither did Deanne Cooper herself."

"Well, you three are in the minority then," Blake said matter-of-factly. "I mean, come on Rhonda, who else could it have been?"

"Anybody!" Heads turned their way. "Anybody," she hissed again, leaning across the table.

"Like who?"

Both of them fell silent as the waitress set their plates in front of them. Rhonda looked down at her fried chicken and mashed potatoes, her appetite gone.

"There aren't that many possibilities, Ronnie," Blake insisted, cutting into his steak. "You can't even name one."

"Maybe it was a drifter. That's not impossible," Rhonda argued. "Maybe someone was passing through and Brian stumbled upon him out by the pond."

"What reason would a drifter have for murdering

him?"

"I don't know!" Rhonda covered her eyes. "Please, can we not talk about this anymore."

"Okay, I'm sorry." Blake reached out and drew Rhonda's hand away from her face. He squeezed her fingers for a moment. "I didn't mean to upset you. I just can't figure out why you're so all-fired sure Wes is innocent."

"He's a hero, did you know that?" she said quietly. "He won a bronze star in Iraq. I asked my dad about it and he says they don't just give those things out like candy. He got a purple heart, too." Rhonda decided it was best to leave out the fact that she had seen the wound that had won Wes that honorable award. "I saw his uniform, it's covered with all these medals."

Blake carefully set his knife and fork down on his plate.

"You're falling for him."

"What?" Rhonda blinked in confusion.

"I said, you're falling for Wes."

"No, I'm not!" Rhonda spluttered.

"It's written all over your face. I should have seen this coming." Blake threw his napkin on the table. "Didn't I tell you to stay away from him? I was worried about your physical safety, but I should have known he'd try to steal you away from me."

"Don't be ridiculous. Wes hasn't tried to steal me away from you. He's been a perfect gentleman whenever we've been together, which is hardly ever." Unfortunately, her rebellious heart silently added.

"Well, the sooner he goes to jail, the happier I'll

be," Blake said crossly.

"Don't say a thing like that, Blake," Rhonda begged, realizing with a sinking heart that Blake was wrong. She wasn't falling for Wes. She had already fallen. Hard. O, Lord, how could this have happened? "God is very clear that judgment is His job. Instead of wanting Wes arrested so bad, you should be praying the real killer gets caught. Here." She handed him his napkin, determined she would not reveal her true feelings in the middle of this very public place. "Eat your dinner. You upset me, I upset you. We're even. Now, lets forgive each other and have a nice evening, okay?"

Picking up her knife and fork, Rhonda dug into her chicken. It felt like sawdust in her mouth. Later, after a tense ride home, she allowed Blake to kiss her goodnight but she never once felt like melting.

Ranger's ferocious barking woke Wes from where he was dozing in the living room. In a split second he was out of the chair and rushing out the back door. The halogen barn light lit up the farmyard. Ranger strained at the end of his chain, barking toward the orchard. Wes peered through the dark. Light flickered through the trees. He hesitated just a moment, deciding there wasn't time to let Ranger loose. Instead, he vaulted off the back steps and ran toward the apple trees, holding his pistol tightly in his right hand.

Someone was definitely in the orchard. Wes slowed his pace and took cover behind the gnarled trunk of a tree. The tiniest of flashlights gave off a narrow beam of light down at the far end of the orchard. Wes strained to make out the figure moving like a shadow. Obviously the intruder was covered from head to foot in black. What were they doing down there? The sound of quiet sawing drifted toward Wes. They were cutting his trees!

Silent as the night, Wes bent over at the waist and crept from tree to tree. The sound of metal biting into wood grew louder. A small branch snapped under Wes' boot and the sound stopped. The light disappeared, leaving Wes searching vainly for the phantom that melted into the blackness. He took a cautious step forward. Something cold and hard smashed into his face just above his right eye. Stars erupted in his head as he fell backward, squeezing off two rounds before the world went dark.

Pain pulsated in his temple as Wes slowly came to. How long had he been unconscious? Gingerly he opened his eyes, but only his left eye obeyed the command from his brain. Night still reigned. Wes raised his right hand to prod the injured eye, only to find he still clutched his pistol. Slowly he sat up. The earth spun, making Wes groan and clutch his head. He stilled, listening. All was quiet. Even Ranger's barking had ceased.

Easing himself to his feet, Wes searched the orchard as his head pounded with each step. It was empty. Whoever had been here was gone now and Wes couldn't even asses what damage they had done in the dark. He glanced toward the house. It seemed very far away.

Long minutes later he stood before the bathroom

mirror staring at the angry red mark that was quickly becoming lavish shades of purple and black. His right eye was swollen closed. Making his way to the kitchen, Wes dumped ice into a plastic bag and held it to his face, grimacing as the cold touched his tender flesh. His one good eye fell to the table where his mother's Bible lay open to Psalm 121.

I will lift up my eyes to the hills – from whence comes my help? My help comes from the Lord who made heaven and earth.

Wes sighed. If his help was coming from the Lord, he couldn't help but think God was running a little behind.

CHAPTER TWENTY TWO

"*Peace I leave with you, My peace I give to you; not as the world gives do I give to you. Let not your heart be troubled, neither let it be afraid.*"

Rhonda contemplated the words from the Gospel of John as she drove to the Spot of Tea. If Jesus was so adamant about giving her peace, then why didn't she have any? He was very specific about not letting her heart be troubled or afraid, but Rhonda's heart had been in a non-stop uproar for weeks.

"I gave you My peace, I did My part. Now it's your turn. Not letting your heart be troubled or afraid is your job."

Rhonda heard the silent voice speaking to her heart and conviction pierced her soul. She stomped on the brakes, her truck coming to a sudden stop as the truth hit home. She hadn't been doing her part. Emma had urged her to let peace be her guide, but Rhonda hadn't listened. Instead, she had tried to pretend her relationship with Blake was what she wanted, even though her heart longed for Wes. Rhonda knew with sudden clarity why peace had eluded her; she had been operating out of fear. Fear that she would never have the happiness that Emma and Tyler and Nate and Penny had found.

"How was your date last night?" Emma asked when Rhonda arrived at work.

"Tense," Rhonda answered as she tied an apron around her waist.

Emma turned from the counter where she was arranging tea cups on a tray.

"Why was that?"

"How busy is it out front?" Rhonda asked.

"Just two tables right now, why?"

"We'll talk when it's quieter, if that's okay with you."

"Sure." Emma hefted the tray and headed toward the dining room. "But don't think I'll forget."

A lull fell after the breakfast crowd and Emma immediately cornered Rhonda, dragging her into the now empty dining room.

"Okay, now spill," she commanded, perching on the edge of a chair. "Why was your date with Blake tense?"

"Has Nate said anything to you about Brian's murder investigation?" Rhonda asked a question of her own. Emma merely shook her head. "Well, Blake seems convinced they'll be arresting Wes any day now."

"I don't know anything about it, Rhonda, I swear I don't. Nate's being pretty closed mouthed about it."

"Well, it doesn't really matter." Rhonda shrugged. "But when Blake brought it up, I got a little defensive."

"That's happened before," Emma said with a smile.

"Yeah, I guess it has." Rhonda nodded in agreement. "It was like a light bulb went off in Blake's head and he accused me of falling for Wes."

"And how did you respond?"

"I denied it, but..."

"But?"

"He was right," Rhonda finally admitted. She sat up straighter, amazed at the relief the admission brought. "I told you before that Blake plans to ask me to marry him, and I, well, I've been trying to convince myself to say yes, even though I didn't have peace about it. Even though I knew deep down I wasn't in love with him."

"Oh, Rhonda, why? After all we've talked about, why would you do that?"

"Because I was jealous."

"Jealous? Of who?"

"Of you." Another admission. Another weight lifted off Rhonda's heart. "I was jealous of you and Tyler and the baby coming, even of your morning sickness. Jealous of Penny and Nate and their wedding coming up. I didn't want to be! I knew it was wrong to be envious of all of you. I kept trying to bury my feelings but they kept bubbling to the surface. I felt so left out. I wanted what you guys have and I was afraid I would never find it. I thought marrying Blake was my only chance."

"I'm sorry." Emma's hazel eyes looked sadly at Rhonda.

"Why? You don't have anything to be sorry for. It was me. I'm the one who's sorry. You've been the best friend a person could ever have. You've done nothing but give me godly advice and I've done nothing but wallow in self-pity and jealousy. And I've misled Blake, which is the worst sin of all."

"So, what are you going to do?"

Rhonda sat back and sighed, her fingers drumming the tabletop.

"I'm going to have to break up with him. He deserves better than what I've been giving him, half-hearted affection. It's time I tell him the truth."

"And what about Wes?" Emma wanted to know.

"What about him?"

"What if he really did kill his brother? What if Blake's right and they arrest him?"

"I guess I have to leave all of that in God's hands, and cross that bridge when we come to it."

Wes stood at the bottom of the orchard assessing the damage with his one good eye. Sawed off limbs littered the ground. He bent down and examined the base of a tree where a deep hole had been drilled. An unmarked bottle of what Wes was sure was poison lay where it had been abandoned when the perpetrator fled. Wes had no way of knowing how much poison had gotten down into the tree trunk, or if it would do any harm. Only time would tell. He would just have to wait and see. Thankfully, Ranger had sent up the alarm so only a few trees had been damaged.

Standing, Wes looked down at the container, wondering if there was any chance it might be covered with fingerprints. Probably not. His intruder appeared to be very bold and daring but not necessarily foolish. And what would he say to the police, anyway? If he told them someone was trying to run him off his farm, they would most likely assume he was trying to divert their attention away from Brian's murder and his own guilt in the crime.

He vaguely remembered shooting off a couple of rounds from his pistol, but there was no trail of blood on the orchard floor, so obviously he had not hit his target.

Snagging the bottle from the ground, Wes whistled for Ranger and headed toward the barn. Tiredness swathed him in a thick blanket. How much longer could he go on like this? He was hardly getting any sleep as it was, and still the attacks continued. He couldn't stay awake twenty four hours a day. He went over the incidents that had occurred so far and calculated their possible cost. His calves set loose and nearly lost, his chickens terrorized and their brooding eggs destroyed, a brush fire barely averted, his orchard vandalized. What would be next? Wes shied away from the question, unwilling to contemplate what the answer might be.

Was it just yesterday morning when God had demanded he release the farm back to Him? Wes wondered. Well, at the rate he was going, soon there wouldn't be much left to hold onto. Setting the bottle of poison on a shelf in the tool shed, Wes locked the door behind him then stood surveying the farmyard. He might be tired, but he wasn't defeated yet. Straightening his shoulders, Wes headed for the barn, determined he would not be intimidated, he would not be uprooted from his home, he would not turn tail and run.

But what if they arrested him for Brian's murder? The question stopped Wes in his tracks. He stared at the open barn doors. If he was taken off to jail, there would be no one here to protect the farm. All his family had built for the past one hundred years could be destroyed in the blink of an eye. The thought drove Wes to his knees.

"O, God, please!" he cried out, his hands digging into the dirt in the doorway of the barn. "This is all I have left." He clutched a handful of dirt in his fist. "Please don't take this away, too. I know my brother's blood cries out for vindication, but please, don't require it of me. This is all I have."

You have Me.

The words struck Wes' heart like a bolt of lightening and he collapsed on his haunches in the dirt.

"I haven't had You in a long time, Lord," Wes argued aloud.

I will never leave you nor forsake you.

The promise Wes had learned in his childhood rose up in his spirit.

"I've done an awful lot of terrible things, Lord. I've killed people," Wes said, looking up at the baby-blue sky. A Bible verse, memorized in his youth, surfaced in his mind.

If we confess our sins, He is faithful and just to forgive us our sins and cleanse us from all unrighteousness.

It was a start. It may not stop the madness that

was going on around him. It may not put a brake on the wheels of justice that were already turning, but it was a start. Wes had roots in this soil, it was time to get grounded in God.

Rhonda stood on the porch of A Stitch In Time and admired the quilt in the window. It had taken Atlanta's quilting circle weeks of hard work, but the saw-toothed star quilt in patriotic red, white and blue was finally finished. A hand-lettered sign taped to the glass explained that the quilt could be won in the Memorial Day raffle, tickets available inside, profits to go to the local VFW post. Rhonda immediately thought of Wes. He should be marching proudly with the other veterans this Memorial Day. He had earned the right.

Pulling open the door, Rhonda stepped into the empty shop. The door chime faded away into silence.

"Be right with you," Mary Weaver called from the back.

"It's just me, Mom," Rhonda answered, heading toward her mother's voice.

Rhonda found her mother in the kitchen, rinsing out the coffee pot.

"I was just getting ready to close up shop and head home," Mary explained. "What brings you in?"

"Oh, I just wanted to talk to you." Rhonda leaned back against the counter and watched Mary reach for a mug and run it under hot water. "I figured there wouldn't be much chance for privacy once we were at home."

"This sounds serious." Mary wiped her hands on a dishtowel and walked the few steps to the small breakfast table squeezed into a corner of the tiny kitchen. "Have a seat and tell me what this is all about."

Rhonda did as she was told. Taking a deep breath, she looked across the table at her mother and plunged in.

"A week ago, Blake told me he was preparing to ask for my hand in marriage."

"Oh, honey, what great news!" Mary's smile was radiant as she reached out and took Rhonda's hands. "You must be so excited."

"Actually, Mom." Rhonda pulled her hands from her mother's grasp and shook her head. "I've decided to break it off with Blake. I've decided I can't marry him."

"Why ever not?" Mary couldn't quite disguise her surprise.

"Because I don't love him," Rhonda answered simply. "I realized I was just using Blake. I was so afraid no one else would want me that I strung him along. Dating him was fun at first. We had a good time together. But when I realized I wanted more than fun, I also realized I didn't want it with Blake. He's good and kind and caring and he's treated me well, but Mom, I don't love him. I wanted to love him, I tried to love him, but I don't."

"Is it because of Brian?"

"No." Rhonda shook her head adamantly. "I was only fifteen when Brian died. I had always loved him, and if he had lived we would probably be married and raising babies right now. I will always cherish my memories of him, but my love for Brian was an immature love, a wonderful, childhood experience that I will treasure forever, but that's all."

"Then why break up with Blake? If he asks you to marry him, just tell him you need more time. You could still date. You never know, your feelings for him might change. You may grow to love him."

"No, I won't." Rhonda shook her head again. "I'm sure of it only because I have feelings for someone else. What I'm about to tell you could cause you a lot of problems with the women in the quilting circle if they find out." Rhonda looked solemnly at her mother. "I think I'm in love with Wes."

Mary's eyes went wide with shock. "Oh, my."

"Yes, oh my," Rhonda agreed. "I never meant for it to happen, I didn't want it to happen. I don't know if there's a chance for us or not. A lot of things stand in the way, not least of all the suspicions about Wes killing Brian. But I think there might be the tiniest hope. Now." Rhonda got up from the table. "I'm going to go home and bake a batch of cookies and take them to Wes and see if the way to a man's heart really is through his stomach. Pray for me."

Kissing her mother on the cheek, Rhonda hurried out the door, feeling happier than she had in months.

CHAPTER TWENTY THREE

Standing on the front porch clutching a plateful of cookies, Rhonda felt more scared than she had the day Wes had returned home and greeted her with a gun. She put a hand to her fluttering stomach before raising it to knock.

The butterflies disappeared when Wes swung the front door wide and she saw his bruised and battered face.

"Wes! What in the world happened?"

"I ran into a door," he said, a sarcastic smile turning up the corner of his hard mouth.

"Very funny." Rhonda reached out and snatched open the screen, walking into the house without waiting to be invited. The damage looked even worse in the bright light of the entryway. "What really happened?"

Help Me, Rhonda

Wes sighed. "I don't think I should tell you." He went to the door and stuck his head out, looking up and down the road. "And it isn't safe for you to be here. I'm pretty sure someone is keeping a very close eye on the place. If they see you coming and going, they'll probably come after you, too. And tell Becca not to stop in here anymore. I don't want her getting hurt."

"Don't be silly…"

"Does this look like I'm being silly to you?!" Wes yelled, pointing to his face. "Do you want your sister getting hit upside the head with a lead pipe?" He turned on his heel and stomped toward the kitchen, Ranger trotting behind. "I can't even protect myself, I can't very well protect you and your sister," he said, plopping into a chair at the kitchen table.

Rhonda's heart broke at the sight of his broad shoulders sagging in defeat. Her gaze ran over his black eye, swollen shut, and the angry bruises that marred his handsome face. Her stomach got that light feeling she was becoming familiar with. Sliding the plate of cookies onto the table, she took the chair across from him.

"Tell me everything that's happened," she demanded quietly. "I thought everything had been calm since you got that last letter."

"No." Wes shook his head. "It hasn't been calm. Someone tried to start a brush fire right after that last letter arrived. I was patrolling the property every couple of hours. Ranger ran them off. I found the cigarette and matches out by the creek."

"Are you sure it wasn't *your* cigarette and matches?" Rhonda asked, skeptical.

"I'm sure. You dumped my cigarettes down the garbage disposal, remember?" His one good eye bored into hers. "I haven't smoked since. I'm sure whoever was out there was figuring to make it look like I started the fire with a carelessly tossed cigarette butt. Thankfully, we stopped them before that could happen."

"You quit smoking because of me?"

"Don't flatter yourself, kid." Wes got up and went to the cupboard. Taking down two cups he filled them with coffee. "It was as good a time as any to quit."

He returned to the table carrying the full mugs and placed one in front of Rhonda. After resuming his seat, he reached for the platter of cookies.

"Wes."

His hand stopped in mid-air. Slowly he met her eyes.

"I'm not a kid anymore, remember?"

"Yeah, sorry." Wes looked away.

"And I'm glad you quit smoking, whatever the reason," she added with a soft smile. Reaching for the cookies, she removed the plastic wrap and pushed the plate his way. "So, you didn't see the person trying to start the fire?"

"No. They were parked somewhere back in that woods to the northwest. I heard the car engine but had no idea how they got back there," Wes answered.

He picked up a cookie and dunked it in his coffee. "Then yesterday morning I had a visitor. Some guy claiming to be from Northland Gas. Said he had an order to survey my property for putting a gas main in. I told him I didn't order any survey," Wes explained around a mouthful of cookie. "He said a company named Energy Options out of Gaylord ordered the survey and that they were in negotiations to buy this land."

"Really? That has to be a great lead." Rhonda leaned forward, feeling hopeful. "If you can find out who owns that company then you'll know who's threatening you and you can go to the police."

"I wish it were that simple." Wes took a sip of coffee and sat back in his chair. "Ken Morris is looking into it, but the company was registered by an investment group, not an individual. Ken is trying to get to the bottom of who's behind it, but so far he hasn't had much success. I'm beginning to think I'm running out of time."

"Why?" Rhonda asked, troubled by his ominous tone.

"Because last night someone was in the orchard, trying to destroy the trees. That's how I got this." He pointed to his face. "The blow to my head could very well have killed me and not just knocked me out. As it is, I'm pretty sure I have a concussion."

Rhonda's blood ran cold despite the hot coffee she had just swallowed.

"Did you go to the doctor?"

Wes shot her a look that said "don't be ridiculous."

"No, I didn't go to a doctor. I could just see myself trying to explain how I managed to get whacked in the face with a pipe."

"You probably should see a doctor," Rhonda

argued. "What if you broke your orbital bone, or whatever that thing is called?"

She touched her own eyebrow, pointing to the bone in question, trying to dispel the mental picture of Wes laying dead in the orchard.

"I've had a lot of first aid training," Wes reassured. "Nothing's broken. My point is that whoever was out there, they could have done a lot more damage than a black eye. I have a feeling I'm living on borrowed time. But to be honest, I'd rather be fighting that enemy than be locked away in jail, unable to protect my property. But I don't think I'll be walking around a free man much longer."

Blake's dire prediction rang in Rhonda's ears. She began to protest.

"Wes, they aren't going to arrest you. It's been ten years since Brian's murder. What evidence could they possibly have now that they didn't have back then?"

"I told you before, I've been trained to trust my instincts," Wes said, wrapping his hands around his mug. "Whoever's trying to buy me out, they seem to think they have some leverage, something connected to Brian's murder. Since I'm not cooperating with their plan, I have a feeling they'll go to the police with whatever evidence they have."

Rhonda's eyes fell on the Bible laying at the end of the table. She reached out and pulled it towards her.

"This is your mother's Bible," she stated, running a hand over the worn leather cover.

"Yes."

Rhonda looked up to meet Wes' stare across the table.

"You've been reading it." It wasn't a question.

Wes shrugged. "For all the good it's done me."

Rhonda opened the Bible and began thumbing through its pages.

"Let me show you what I was reading just this past Sunday." She found Psalm 9 and turned the book so Wes could see the page. She tapped it with her finger. "Read this. I think it will bring you a lot of comfort."

Wes lifted the Bible and began reading, his lips moving silently with the words.

"When my enemies turn back, they shall fall and perish at Your presence. For You have maintained my right and my cause," he read the verse aloud before returning to silence.

"The Lord also will be a refuge for the oppressed, a refuge in times of trouble," Rhonda quoted from memory. "And those who know Your name will put their trust in You; for You, Lord, have not forsaken those who seek You."

Wes continued to scan the words of the Psalm.

"Have mercy on me, O Lord! Consider my trouble from those who hate me, You who lift me up from the gates of death," he read. Wes lowered the Bible to the table and stared solemnly at Rhonda. "Do you think He will? Have mercy on me, I mean. Even after all I've done? I..." He hung his head. "I tried to confess it all earlier today. I felt better, cleaner than I have in years. But I still don't know how God's going to extricate me from the noose that's wrapping around my neck."

Rhonda couldn't resist reaching a hand across the table and touching his. "God's mercies are new every morning, and His love is the same yesterday, today and forever. I have faith that He's going to lift you up from these gates of death."

Wes looked down at the delicate hand resting on his and resisted the urge to curl his fingers around hers. She belongs to another man, he reminded himself. As if suddenly aware of what she had done, Rhonda withdrew her hand to her lap.

Pushing the Bible away, Wes sat back in his chair, feeling empty at the loss of contact between them.

"But there's no guarantee that I won't get arrested," he said, crossing his arms.

"No, but there is a guarantee that whatever happens, God is in control. More bad things could still happen. And whoever's responsible might get away with it. All I know is that whatever God allows into our lives, He uses it for good somehow."

Wes stood and walked slowly to the kitchen window. He stared out at the night.

"God told me yesterday to give it all back to Him. The farm, the land, everything. To release it into His keeping. But it's hard." He turned around and met Rhonda's eyes.

"Yes, it's very hard," Rhonda agreed with a nod. "But that's what it's all about. Surrender. Total surrender of everything. Our hearts, our lives, our possessions. Then trust Him for our every need."

"That's what you've done?" Wes asked. He

watched as a sad smile touched Rhonda's mouth.

"Not always," she admitted. "Matter-of-fact, just recently, there's been a pretty big need in my life that I wasn't trusting Him with. I almost made a huge mistake because of it. Thankfully, the Lord brought me to my senses just in time."

"What mistake did you almost make? Can I ask?"

Rhonda pursed her lips, thinking. Her eyes traveled around the room before coming back to settle on his once more.

"Blake. I almost made a huge mistake with Blake. I was ready to marry him, even though I didn't have peace about it. I almost sacrificed my future for a man I don't love."

Wes felt his spirit lift at her confession. So, she didn't belong to another man, after all!

"Can I ask you another question?"

"Sure, ask away. But I can't promise I'll answer."

"Are you still in love with Brian?" Wes felt his heart thudding heavily as he held his breath, needing an answer but dreading what Rhonda would say. She fiddled with the handle of her coffee cup.

"Funny, but you're the second person to ask me that today. Seems like ever since you came home, the past has been resurrected, so to speak. I've thought about Brian a lot. Where would we be now if he were still alive? The other day..."

Wes watched as pain washed across Rhonda's face and she closed her eyes.

"The other day I tried to picture his face, but I couldn't. He's been gone too long." Reopening her eyes, she took a sip of coffee. "We were just kids, you know. What did we know about love? The truth is, if Brian had lived, we probably would have gotten married, had children, grown old together. But Brian didn't live. So, obviously that wasn't God's plan for my life. I love the memories I have of Brian, but no, I'm not still in love with your brother."

A weight Wes didn't even know he was carrying lifted from his shoulders and he breathed a sigh of relief.

"I'm sorry, I had no right to ask."

"That's okay. I'm glad to get the air cleared between us. I'm not in love with Blake and I'm not in love with a memory. My heart is free."

Her blue eyes conveyed her message clear across the kitchen. Wes found himself drawn across the room. He bent down to bring his face even with hers.

"The problem is, Rhonda, very soon, I might not be."

"Well, I guess that's where we both have to trust God then, huh?"

Lying in bed, Rhonda stared through the dark at the ceiling, replaying the scene in Wes' kitchen. He had almost kissed her again. She had been sure he was going to kiss her. But the man had more willpower than a superhero. Must be all that military discipline, she reasoned. There was hope, though. It was clear that Wes felt something for her, too. He just felt it his duty to wait until things were settled with the murder investigation before pursuing it.

"Then please, dear Lord, let him pursue," Rhonda begged. "And let this thing get settled quickly. Protect Wes until the truth comes out. Lord, you said in Your Word that there is nothing covered that will not be revealed, and nothing hidden that will not be known. I pray that will be true in this situation. Whoever killed Brian, let it finally be revealed, Lord. And whoever is hiding, waiting to harm Wes, let them be known to everyone."

Rolling onto her side, Rhonda curled around her pillow and thought of Blake. She was going to have to find a way to break up with him. He was another person who deserved to know the truth.

"Lord, help me do the right thing," she mumbled before falling into a peaceful sleep.

CHAPTER TWENTY FOUR

What a relief it was to finally have taken hold of the peace Jesus promised, Rhonda thought as she got out of her truck and headed for the door to the Spot of Tea. She felt almost giddy as she thought of Wes and the possibilities of the future. Sure, there were obstacles to be overcome, but Rhonda had faith God would be with them as they faced each one.

Pulling open the door, she saw Blake's white-blond curls and heard his teasing voice as Emma refilled his coffee cup.

"Why Emma, I'd say your cheeks are positively rosy this morning," Blake said with an impish smile. "It looks like pregnancy is finally starting to agree with you."

"Pregnancy always agreed with me," Emma returned. "It just didn't agree with my stomach. Hopefully the worst is over."

Emma moved behind the counter to place the coffee pot on its warmer. Blake glanced toward the door as Rhonda stepped through.

"Good morning, sugar," he called.

"Hi, Blake," Rhonda answered, her heart suddenly beating heavily. Was this the hour of truth?

She headed for the kitchen to hang up her jacket and tie an apron around her waist. How was she going to deal with Blake? She couldn't very well break up with him in the middle of the Spot of Tea. He deserved better than public humiliation. Somehow, she was going to have to put him off a little longer until she could find a way to let him down easy. Putting on a smile along with her apron, Rhonda headed back out to the dining room.

"Something wrong, baby?" Blake asked when she approached his table.

"Nope. Everything's fine," Rhonda said.

"Can you sit down a minute?" Blake's eyes traveled around the nearly empty dining room. "There's something I need to tell you."

At his suddenly serious tone, Rhonda's heart took up its heavy drumbeat again. She pulled out the chair across from his and sat down gingerly.

"What it is?"

"Rhonda." Blake reached for her hands. She kept them limp in his, even though he began rubbing her fingers in a way that should have made her skin dance. His eyes bored into hers. "I'm sorry about the way our date ended the other night. I shouldn't have gotten so upset about Wes. It's just that…" He cleared his throat and started over. "It's just that, I don't think

I've made my feelings very clear to you over the years. Everyone thinks I'm such a practical joker that when I'm being serious, they don't necessarily believe what I'm saying. When I told you the other day that I've loved you forever, I wasn't kidding."

Rhonda wanted to pull her hands from his grasp and run from the table. She didn't want to hear this! Not now!

"When we were growing up, you were always Brian's girl," Blake continued. "And then after he died, you were so broken up, I couldn't bring myself to approach you. Then I went off to mechanic's training and when I got back, we started hanging out with friends and that was fun. I know…I know I'm a little slow at this romantic stuff. I should have made my intentions clear to you years ago."

Rhonda held her breath. He couldn't mean to propose to her right here in the middle of the Spot of Tea! How was she going to say no in front of all these customers? Her eyes darted nervously around the dining room to see if anyone was eavesdropping on their conversation. Thankfully, they all appeared to be engrossed in their coffee and muffins.

"Blake, I…" She tried to withdraw her hands but he tightened his grip.

"Let me finish," he interrupted. "I need to get this out. No jokes anymore. I love you, Rhonda. You're the only girl I've ever wanted. I know I have a jealous streak. I promise I'll work on that. I've got to stop getting so upset whenever you mention Wes' name. I realize you are neighbors, and also that you probably have a special bond with Wes because of

Brian. I'm learning to cope with that. But because of it, I think it's only fair that I tell you. I hear they're getting close to arresting Wes for Brian's murder."

"How in the world would you have heard a thing like that?" Rhonda asked quietly, her mind scrambling to process everything at once. How was she going to let Blake down easy after everything he'd just revealed to her? How could she tell him that the special bond she had with Wes had nothing to do with Brian?

"There might not be any love lost between me and Nate Sweeney, but I do have other friends in this town. They keep me informed. I tried to tell you the other night they're getting close to wrapping up the case."

"I still don't see how that could be possible," Rhonda fought to keep the edge of panic from her voice. "There's no way new evidence could have surfaced after all these years."

"We'll see." Blake shrugged. "I'm just trying to warn you, so you'll be prepared when the time comes."

"Thank you," Rhonda managed to choke out in a relatively normal voice. "I appreciate that. And everything else you've told me. I...I..." She what? What was she supposed to say? She couldn't very well shout out 'I don't love you back!' The bell over the door gave out a warning ring. "I've got to get back to work." She rose from the table.

"Okay, baby." Blake still held her hand and tugged her down for a kiss. Rhonda turned her head so the kiss landed on her cheek. When she stood upright, she saw a hurt gleam in Blake's eyes. "I'll see you later?"

"Yeah, sure, later." Rhonda hastily went to seat the arriving customers feeling like a rock had settled in the pit of her stomach. She really didn't want to see Blake later, because somehow she was going to have to find a way to break the man's heart.

Peas, tomatoes, carrots, cucumbers. Wes checked each item off his list then looked again at the piece of tilled ground that had always been the family garden. He hoped he had enough room for everything. He glanced at the piece of graph paper in his hands, trying to picture the garden in full bloom. How much of each thing had his mother planted? Was he planting too much for one person? No doubt! Maybe he could get Rhonda to can some of it for him.

His heart lifted like a balloon being carried on the breeze. Rhonda was free. She wasn't still in love with Brain. Maybe, God willing, if he could get these other matters squared away, maybe they had a chance. Wes allowed himself a moment to daydream. He pictured Rhonda in the kitchen, steam from the double boiler wreaking havoc with her already unruly hair. He imagined walking up behind her, placing his lips on her sweaty neck...

Gravel crunched, bringing Wes back down to earth. He turned his head to see a caravan of four vehicles pulling into his driveway. Two Montmorency County Sheriff cruisers were followed by a dark blue SUV and a black pickup truck. The two civilian vehicles pulled boat trailers carrying flat-bottomed skiffs.

Doors slammed as Nate Sweeney and his partner exited their car followed by a plain clothes detective and another deputy in the other cruiser. The men in the other two vehicles stayed put.

Wes watched through narrowed eyes as Nate Sweeney approached, a sheaf of white papers clenched in his hand. The bottom dropped out of Wes' stomach. So, the day of reckoning had come.

"Wes," Nate greeted with a nod. He peered closer at Wes' face. "What happened to you?"

"The cows." Wes quickly thought up the excuse. He pointed to his now open but still blackened right eye. "I had some trouble with my cows. Got trampled a little bit."

"Sorry to hear that," Nate replied, failing to sound sincere. "And I'm also sorry to tell you why we're here. We've got a search warrant to dredge your pond."

Standing silent, Wes watched as the deputies directed the SUV and pickup through the lower pasture to park at the edge of the woods. Wes glanced down and crumpled the paper in his hand. No need to bother planning a garden. No point in dreaming about the future. If Nate Sweeney had anything to say about it, Wes would be spending the rest of his life behind bars.

She had to find a way to tell Blake the truth. Rhonda contemplated the various ways she could break up with him, discarding each one in turn. A Dear John letter was out of the question. It wasn't something she could do over the phone, that was just too cold and heartless. She was too old to get away with having a friend tell him. The man had sat there and bared his soul to her, finally admitting his deepest feelings. How did a woman turn around and throw that back in his face? Especially after she had led him to believe she was looking for marriage?

"Oh Lord, I've never done this kind of thing before," Rhonda said, looking through the windshield of her truck as she drove home. "How do I break a man's heart and do it with loving kindness?"

Turning off the main highway onto the dirt road leading home, Rhonda's stomach began to tremble. The predicament with Blake was suddenly forgotten in anticipation of seeing Wes. She would stop in and see if everything was okay. Maybe she could fix him dinner, something fresh he wouldn't have to heat up in the microwave. Even if he felt they couldn't pursue a relationship until more pressing matters were taken care of, that didn't mean they couldn't spend time together. Even if Wes did think it was too dangerous for her. If she showed up on his doorstep, he wouldn't turn her away.

Plans for what she could make for dinner came to a screeching halt when Rhonda saw two sheriff's cruisers parked in Wes' driveway. She immediately pulled in and parked behind them. Her eyes stared off in the distance, seeing Tyler's truck and another vehicle with empty boat trailers parked in the lower pasture. What was going on? Without thinking, she jumped from the cab and ran toward the woods. Ranger barked, lunging and straining at the end of his chain, but Rhonda ignored the dog's pleas. Her only thought was for Wes.

The trail to the pond had been hastily widened and Rhonda careened down the path, coming to a sliding halt when she burst into the clearing. Nate and his partner, Lydia Ebersol, spun in surprise.

"What's going on?" Rhonda asked, taking in Tyler and Caleb and two other volunteer firemen in small aluminum boats. The men slowly pulled up muddy nets and began examining their contents.

"Rhonda, you shouldn't be here," Nate said, approaching her with a stern look. "We're executing a search warrant."

"You've got to be crazy." Rhonda searched frantically for Wes, finally spotting him standing under the tall oak. He turned his gaze her way and Rhonda felt the ice in his stare from across the clearing. Detective Epworth and another deputy stood on the far side of Wes, looking at Rhonda with displeasure. "You can't possibly think there's anything to be found in that pond."

A pile of mud-and-rust-covered debris lay on the shore.

"Rhonda, you can't stay here," Nate stated emphatically.

"Well, I'm not leaving." Rhonda crossed her arms stubbornly. "Arrest me if you want, but you can't make me..."

"Nate!" Tyler's shout had Nate turning to hurry toward the pond. "Found something."

Tyler and Caleb used tall poles to maneuver the skiff toward the shore. When the skiff hit bottom, Tyler jumped out and dragged the boat up onto dry land. Caleb reached into the net and handed a mud-covered knife to Nate. Rhonda's feet automatically carried her forward. Wes, too, stepped toward the deputy.

Nate rubbed silt from the handle then held up the weapon for Wes to see. The stainless steel blade still looked wickedly sharp despite its years in the water.

"This look familiar to you?" Nate asked.

He turned the knife, holding it by the blade . Rhonda immediately recognized the intricately carved handle. Her sharp intake of breath echoed in the silent clearing and her wide eyes rested on Wes. The knife had been an eighteenth birthday gift to him from his father.

"No, Wes," she plead desperately, shaking her head in denial.

"Well, I guess that answers my question," Nate said, placing the knife into an evidence bag that Lydia held open. "Wes, I'm afraid we're going to have to take you in for questioning."

Nate moved toward Wes and reached for his arm. Rhonda stood frozen, watching as Nate was suddenly flipped over Wes' shoulder to land on his back on the ground. The gun appeared out of nowhere. How stupid! She should have remembered that Wes went everywhere armed! Before she could blink, a vise-like arm was wrapped around her throat, dragging her backward, the cold barrel of the gun pressed into her temple. Rhonda stared disbelieving at Tyler and Caleb, who watched in shocked surprise. Lydia, Detective Epworth and the other deputy had drawn their guns.

Rhonda closed her eyes and prayed.

"Put the guns down or I'll blow her head off," Wes growled.

He took another step backward and Rhonda stumbled trying to keep her footing. This couldn't be happening, she thought crazily. This is just a dream. A terrible nightmare. I'll wake up and everything will be how it's supposed to be. She opened her eyes to see that the nightmare was all too real. Wes had killed Brian and now he was going to kill her!

O, God, I don't want to die! she cried silently.

The trees were at Wes' back. In one swift motion he dropped his arm from around her neck and Rhonda landed unceremoniously on her backside. She heard crashing through the brush and looked up, stunned to find Wes had disappeared. As if of one accord, the others sprang forward. Tyler and Caleb rushed to Rhonda's side as Nate and the other officers took off in pursuit of Wes.

"You okay, Rhonda?" Tyler asked, kneeling next to her. His kind, green eyes looked deep into hers.

"Yeah, yeah, I think I'm okay." She held a trembling hand to her throat as tears began to gather in her eyes. But she wasn't okay. She had just found out the man she loved was a murderer.

"There, it's all going to be alright," Tyler comforted, pulling Rhonda against his chest. She sobbed into his shoulder. "Nate will find him. It's all going to be okay."

CHAPTER TWENTY FIVE

Adrenalin pumped through his veins and instincts took over as Wes pushed deeper into the thick forest. It had never been his intention to escape. But as soon as Nate reached for him, Wes' training took over. Elude capture, evade the enemy. Wes knew if he was taken into custody, he would never see the light of day again. It was his knife. If Rhonda hadn't given it away, he could have bluffed his way out of it. There was no way to prove it was his. His prints wouldn't be on it, not after sitting at the bottom of the pond for ten years. No, if it weren't for Rhonda, he would have gone in for questioning. He would never have given anything away and they would have let him go.

Why hadn't she stayed away? There would be no hope for them now. He never should have grabbed her. Wes closed his eyes for just a moment, remembering the look of abject terror on Rhonda's face when he pressed the gun to her temple. Now it wouldn't matter what happened. Even if his name were cleared, she would never trust him again.

Wes slowed and looked around. The sound of pursuit had grown distant. Looking up, Wes grabbed the low branch of an oak tree and easily pulled himself up. Like an agile monkey, he climbed through the branches, up until he was unsure if the branches would hold his weight. There was nothing to be seen below. They would have to call in more deputies and volunteers for a search party. Wes took some small comfort in knowing that he had more training in eluding capture than the others did in searching for an enemy. But he had never dreamed he would need those skills in his own back yard.

Wes sat, straddling the branch. He leaned back against the tree's trunk allowing himself a moment to rest. He had to think and plan. He had no food or water. No friendlies in the area to give him a hand. His pistol and his wits, that's all he had to rely on. Leaning his head back against the trunk, Wes closed his eyes. He started humming then smiled sadly when he recognized the tune his mind had unconsciously conjured up. It was the Beach Boys' song, "Help me, Rhonda." He quietly sang the chorus as the truth hit home. It was too late. Rhonda couldn't help him now.

So, who did that leave? Wes searched his mind, trying desperately to remember part of the Scripture Rhonda had pointed out to him last night. What had it said? Something about the Lord being a refuge for the oppressed. He certainly needed a refuge now!

"Jesus, I know I've gone my way for a long time," Wes found himself praying. He closed his

Help Me, Rhonda

eyes, feeling weak sunshine beating down on his face. "I know I shouldn't have run away, I should have stayed and faced the music. I should have ten years ago, and I should have today. You said You'll be my refuge, that You'll lift me up from the gates of death. I know I don't have any right to ask You for anything, but I am anyway. Help me, Jesus. Please God, help me."

Night settled softly over the Weaver farm. Rhonda sat at the kitchen table staring out at the darkness, still numb. She and Becca had returned to the Cooper's to feed the cows and chickens and had brought Ranger and the kittens home with them. As Rhonda had locked up the house, she took one last, sad look around at the home she had dreamed of living in. That dream was gone now, shattered like glass. How could she have been so wrong?

Dropping her head into her hands, Rhonda fought back another wave of tears. She had cried enough to last a lifetime. She didn't even know what she was crying for anymore. The death of her feelings for Wes? The death of her innocence? Brian? Or was she crying because she had been foolish enough to fall for Wes Cooper? To believe in him even when everyone around her had tried to warn her of the truth?

Rhonda sat back in the chair with a tremulous sigh. Realization slowly dawned. Wes had never denied killing his brother. He had never once professed his innocence. Replaying their conversation from the night before, Rhonda remembered Wes asking if God would be merciful even after everything he had done. Rhonda had assumed he meant everything he had done while in the army. But now she realized he must have meant what he had done to Brian, too.

"Lord, how could I have been so wrong?" Rhonda cried, covering her face with her hands. "I thought I was finally finding peace. I thought I was going to avert disaster where Blake was concerned, but I headed right into another one with Wes."

She dropped her hands to her lap and looked out at the night.

"I've been looking for love in all the wrong places, haven't I?" she confessed. "I've been so busy wanting a man in my life, when I should have been looking to You. Being Your bride is supposed to be more important. Your love lasts forever. Father, forgive me."

Pushing up from the table, Rhonda walked out the back door and headed toward the barn. She shoved her hands deep into the pockets of her zip-up sweatshirt and stared unseeing at the night sky, trying to block out the memory of Wes pressing a gun to her head. After all she had done for him! Terror battled with temper in her soul with anger finally gaining the upper hand.

It had all been a ruse! What an actor Wes Cooper had turned out to be! How long had it taken him to concoct the story of someone trying to run him off? Rhonda thought back to the incidents Wes had told her about. She had no proof that any of them had even happened, except for the cows escaping, and he could very well have done that himself. He must have even sent himself the threatening letters! And his bruised face? Had he done that to himself, just to add authenticity to his act? Rhonda realized he must have. He had even tried to convince her his parents had been murdered, too.

And she had fallen for it all; hook, line and sinker. She was so desperate for him to be innocent that she had believed his every word. Had even believed his sudden interest in the Lord. It had all been a lie.

Swallowing hard, Rhonda closed her eyes to the sight of the stars and fought off the wave of hurt and tears that assailed her once more. Slowly, as if the stars were winking out one by one, the truth hit home. Blake had been right all along.

Hunger drove Wes toward town. Spring wasn't exactly the best time to be on the run. It was a little hard to live off the land when the land had little to offer. He knew it was crazy to head straight into the lion's mouth. There were cop cars everywhere. But what better place to hide than right under the noses of those who were looking for him? They would never expect him to be in town. They probably figured he was headed for the state line or Canada.

Wes had learned how to walk silently and to blend into the night. He had never expected to need his training once he came home. He had figured it would all be discarded, packed away like so many dusty memories. But he was glad for all those training missions he had lived through as he lay flat on his belly in a ditch as a car drove slowly by. He needed every skill just as badly now as he had in the rough terrain of Afghanistan.

The car rolled past and Wes belly crawled several more yards before getting up and sprinting to the cemetery. He moved like a ghost among the tombstones. Not much farther now and he would be smack-dab in the middle of downtown Atlanta. And then what? His stomach cramped with hunger but Wes ignored the discomfort. Sitting down behind a tombstone he gave himself a moment for his heartbeat to slow and his thinking to clear. Since escaping, he had been running on instinct. Now he had to take a minute and get his thoughts together. He felt the urgent need to pray.

"Lord," he whispered, his breath a puff of steam on the night air. "I asked You to help me, and I believe You are. I don't know what I'm doing here. Should I give myself up? If You…"

He swallowed hard. An image of Rhonda flashed into his mind and Wes knew if he turned himself in, their chance of ever making a life together would be gone for good. Despite the pain that caused, Wes continued, "If you want me to Lord, I will. For the last ten years, the only ones I've trusted were myself and my men. But tonight Lord, I'm trusting You."

Rising up, he glanced across the road where the sheriff's department was visible. An unseen force seemed to push him back down just as a white car with lights on top pulled into the cemetery. Was this God's answer to his prayer? Wes took a deep breath, preparing to surrender himself, but before he could move, the car drove around the circular drive and headed back out on the main road. Wes let out the breath he had been holding.

"Okay," he spoke into the darkness. "I'm not supposed to surrender. Then show me what I *am* supposed to do."

Back on his feet, Wes continued toward town, planning to head for Emma's shop. He knew from his visit there that it would be easy enough to break in. The memory of the counter filled with baked goods made his stomach cramp once more with hunger. Breaking and entering was wrong, but he was a desperate man. God, and Emma, would have to understand.

Traversing the town was easier than Wes had expected. The sidewalks were pretty much rolled up. Music still drifted from the tavern and a few cars and trucks were parked at the curb, but everything else was closed. Wes slunk across the road to the corner grocery store. Trees and brush grew right up against the back of the building and he crouched down among the thick cover, thinking. His eyes rested on the dumpster. Food! Maybe he wouldn't have to add breaking and entering to his list of sins after all.

With no qualms as to what may be waiting for him inside, Wes hurried to the dumpster and hefted himself over the side. He landed with a hollow thud, barely registering the stale smell of garbage. He had smelled a lot worse. Reaching out blindly in the dark, he felt a pile of flat cardboard boxes. He moved slightly in the cramped confines, his boots crunching broken glass. Come on! There had to be something in here he could eat. His hands continued their desperate search, finally landing upon a lumpy plastic bag. Wes pulled the bag from the pile and held it up, examining its contents. It was a bag of apples and from the feel of things, most of them were rotten. Ripping the bag open, Wes felt each one, tossing aside the ones that were beyond consumption. Finally he found two that were firm.

Holding one between his teeth and the other in his hand, Wes quickly vaulted from the dumpster and wiggled back into the brush at the back of the store.

"Thank you Jesus for this food, amen," he said, crunching into the apple.

Soft footfalls on the sidewalk had Wes going stone still, un-chewed apple sitting on his tongue. He swallowed the bite whole then slowly peered around the corner of the building as someone approached the pay phone at the end of the parking lot. The sound of the receiver being lifted and coins clinking echoed across the otherwise silent night. Wes' ears perked up as a man's voice spoke low into the phone. Although his words were spoken quietly, they carried clearly on the night air.

"Yeah, Sean, it's me. Look, I'm sorry to call so late. My mom's had the phone tied up all night. I finally came out to the pay phone. No, there's nobody around to see me," the man assured. "I've got some news that will make you happy. You heard? Uh huh. It's just a matter of time now. I'm positive. Wes Cooper is going to be put away for life. Everything is going to work out just like I planned."

At the sound of his name, Wes leaned farther around the corner of the building. The hazy glow of the street light fell on the shadowy figure in the hooded sweatshirt at the phone booth.

"You have to be more patient," the man continued.

Where had Wes heard that voice? It was vaguely familiar.

"The gas company jumped the gun sending that surveyor out. Wes is a very dangerous man, as this town's coming to find out." He paused and held the receiver away from his ear for a moment. "Calm down!" he commanded, bringing the handset back to his ear. "I'm not going to let anything happen. Are you kidding? I've been working at this for more than ten years, I'm not going to let it get ruined now. You've got plans, Sean, well, so have I. I've been working on my plans for all these years, I'm not about to let them fall through. Not when everything I've ever wanted is finally within my reach. That land is gonna be ours soon and then we'll be rich. You don't know everything about me, Sean. Wes Cooper may be dangerous, but so am I. So am I. You'd do best not to forget it."

The man slammed the receiver back into its cradle. Wes watched as he took a handkerchief from his pocket and wiped the phone off carefully before turning to go. The hood of his sweatshirt fell back slightly and the light from the street lamp shone down for a split second before the figure moved quickly away. Wes pulled back and pressed himself flat against the block wall of the grocery store, his heart thundering.

No wonder the voice had sounded vaguely familiar!

Mechanically he lifted the apple to his mouth and took a bite. He had to think. Now he knew who was trying to run him off his land, and he knew why. He just didn't know what he was going to do about it.

CHAPTER TWENTY SIX

Rhonda pried her eyes open and lay staring up at the ceiling. Someone had tied her stomach into at least five knots. She reached down and rubbed her aching belly through the quilt. For some reason she thought of Emma, of the baby growing inside her womb. Did she and Tyler lay in bed in the mornings with his hand on her stomach, quietly marveling at the life growing inside?

Tears pricked Rhonda's eyes. Yesterday morning she had been so full of hope, so full of peace.
What a difference a day made. The fear and anger she had been battling evaporated in the cool morning air as sorrow crept in. Why was happiness always being wrenched from her grasp?

She had left her bedroom window open all night and now the curtains billowed slightly in the morning breeze. A pair of cardinals called out to one another, their distinctive song echoing across the quiet farmyard. She heard it again. First one set of notes then an answering set not far behind. Rhonda pictured the pair of birds sitting out in the trees singing their love songs to one another. Even the birds had each other!

Rhonda shook herself before self-pity could gain a firm foothold. She slipped her feet over the side of the bed and sat up. She had to get to work. The thought brought a groan to her lips as she brushed back her hair. It took every ounce of discipline she had not to crawl back beneath the covers and pull the quilt over her head. The last thing on earth she wanted to do was face the people of Atlanta. The news would have spread like wildfire and by now they would all know about Wes Cooper.

"O Lord, help me," she whispered. "If ever there was a time when I needed your peace, it's now."

Rhonda's eyes fell to her nightstand and the Bible laying there. Pushing herself up from the bed, Rhonda snagged the Bible and went to stand at the window. The bird calls sang out once more and she smiled slightly as she flipped open her Bible. An envelope was stuck between the pages where it fell open. Rhonda's eyes fell to the page. Psalm 9. Wes' Psalm. The thought had her taking a shuddering breath. She read the words slowly, this time applying them to herself instead of Wes.

"And those who know Your name will put their trust in You; for You, Lord have not forsaken those who seek You," she read aloud. Pausing, Rhonda stared out at the quiet farmyard beyond her upstairs window. "Jesus, I know your name. I'm putting my trust in You. You have not forsaken me. Somehow, get me through this day."

Blake was waiting outside the Spot of Tea when Rhonda arrived. As soon as she was out of her truck, he was pulling her into his arms.

"Are you okay?" He asked, burying his face in her hair. "I was out of my mind with worry when I heard." He pulled back and framed Rhonda's face then touched her shoulders and arms, as if assuring himself she were in one piece.

"I'm fine," she began to answer.

Blake yanked her back against his chest, seemingly unaware of Rhonda's stiff posture. Part of her longed to take comfort in his embrace, but her heart reminded her that she had the Lord to see her through this ordeal. He would be enough. She could not continue to lead Blake on.

"Thank the good Lord for that," Blake breathed, holding her tightly. Finally he eased back some and looked into her face, as if he couldn't get enough of her. "I tried calling last night, but your mom said you had already gone to bed."

"Yeah, I'm sorry." Rhonda pulled away and headed for the door of the restaurant. "I know I probably should have called you but it was all too…it was all just so…I just…" She stopped, her shoulders drooping. "It was a hard night. I just wanted to go to sleep and forget it ever happened."

"I understand." Blake pulled her back into his arms, more gently this time. "I should have been there for you. When I think about it…" He squeezed his eyes shut. "If I get my hands on Wes, I'll kill him," he said between gritted teeth.

Rhonda repressed a shiver and backed out of

Blake's embrace. She reached for the door handle and yanked it open.

"Yeah, well, I think you'll have to fight Nate for that privilege."

Wes crawled from the hollow log where he had spent the night. The woods were coming awake with the rising of the sun. Stretching, Wes smiled as a pair of acrobatic black squirrels played monkey in the top branches of some aspen saplings. Their crashing through the trees made it sound like an army of deputies was moving through the forest, reminding Wes of his own precarious position. He rubbed his whiskered face, thinking of the conversation he had overheard the night before. The man had been planning his demise for years, but Wes was still unsure what he was going to do about it. All he knew was that he would never give up fighting for his land.

Stomach grumbling, Wes began making his way through the woods toward his farm. He was sure the place was probably under surveillance, but he had no other choice. He needed food and he needed to find a way to get in touch with his attorney. He needed someone on his side. If the place was only guarded by one deputy, it would be easy enough to overpower the man. After all, Wes thought grimly, he had been trained to kill. He had killed in the past and he could kill again if his life depended on it.

The thought left him cold. No, he couldn't, wouldn't kill ever again. He'd had enough of killing. Wes sat down beneath a white birch tree and leaned back against the trunk. Just last night he had vowed he was trusting the Lord. How quickly he had tossed that vow aside, ready to take matters into his own hands. Just as he had done yesterday at the pond, creating this whole mess.

Closing his eyes, Wes recalled the feel of Rhonda's slender form pulled back against him. He shuddered to think of the ordeal he had put her through. After all she had done for him. Wes opened his eyes and squinted up at the weak sun as overwhelming sadness enveloped him. Rhonda was probably looking up at the same sun and hating his guts for what he had done.

"Lord, I never meant to hurt her." Wes closed his eyes against the pain and prayed. "All she ever did was try to help me, even at the risk of her own safety. And I never meant to fall in love with her, either. Now she thinks I'm a cold-blooded killer."

A cool breeze passed over Wes, causing him to shiver as he jumped to his feet. Changing direction, he headed toward the Weaver farm. Somehow he had to see Rhonda. He had to convince her of the truth.

"I'm going to go feed the horses," Rhonda said, pushing herself up from the dinner table.

"Leave them be for now," her dad replied, looking up from his plate. "You've had a rough day. I'll take care of the horses when I'm done."

"No." Rhonda shook her head adamantly, causing curls to dance about her face. "I want to do it. Being around the horses helps me relax, and heaven knows I need all the help I can get right now."

The day had been an ordeal, that was for certain, Rhonda thought as she stepped into the mud room and pulled on her quilted jacket. The Spot of Tea had been abuzz all day with the talk of Wes Cooper, fugitive on the run. Emma, dear, thoughtful, tenderhearted Emma, had tried so hard all day to shield Rhonda from the worst of it. Rhonda was just thankful that only her mother and Emma knew the extent of Rhonda's involvement with Wes and how close she had come to making the biggest mistake of her life.

Pushing out the back door, Rhonda filled her lungs with the crisp northern Michigan air, hoping it would help clear her troubled mind. She headed toward the barn, thinking about Blake and how caring and considerate he had been of her. His distress over her ordeal at the hands of Wes had touched Rhonda's heart, but she knew it wasn't enough. God had shown her the error of her ways. She knew deep down that Blake was not the one for her, she just didn't know how she was going to break that news to him.

With a sigh, she pushed back the barn door on its well-oiled wheels. She flipped on the lights and went to the far end of the barn to open the gate. Sandy and Smokey trotted into the barn, heading straight for their stalls, their hoof beats echoing hollowly through the quiet barn.

Rhonda went about the familiar chore of filling the horses feed troughs with grain and their hay racks with hay. Unwinding the hose, she pulled it across the aisle and stuck it into Sandy's water bucket. She leaned against the stall door waiting for the bucket to fill, listening as Sandy ground the grain between her teeth. As always, the comforting evening ritual relaxed Rhonda's taunt nerves. No matter what happened in the world outside, she had her horses.

She put away the hose and returned to lean over Sandy's stall door. The buckskin mare turned so Rhonda could scratch her head.

"I wish I was a horse," Rhonda quietly confided. "Horses don't have to worry about all the craziness going on in the world. Don't have to worry about affairs of the heart or who's good or who's bad, who's right or who's wrong." Sandy nuzzled her hair in sympathy.

"Remember how I told you I wasn't going to fall in love with Wes Cooper? Well, I lied. And now he's on the run and will end up in prison. I had thought maybe... I had hoped... Oh, I guess it doesn't matter now." Rhonda ran her fingers through Sandy's black forelock. "I guess I had hoped so hard it blinded me to reality. That's why I'd like to be a horse. Horses never have to worry about stuff like that."

With one last pat on Sandy's neck, Rhonda pushed away from the stall and headed for the door. A dark object leapt from the rafters above her head. A scream tore from her throat, cut short by the hard hand that clamped firmly over her mouth as Rhonda stared, terrified, into the cold, grey eyes of Wes Cooper.

Wes saw the fear in Rhonda's blue eyes, then watched as they darted back and forth as if searching for something. He glanced to the right, seeing a pitchfork leaning against the side of the stall. She may have just confessed her love for him, but that wasn't about to prevent her from running him through if she could!

"Don't get any ideas, Rhonda," he whispered low. Her frightened gaze latched onto his once more. Slowly he raised a finger to his lips, motioning for her to be quiet. "I won't hurt you, I promise," he continued in a whisper. "But you have to promise me that if I take my hand away, you won't scream."

He stared deeply into the eyes he had come to love, sorry for the fear he saw there. It hurt knowing she was scared of him, even if it was with good reason. For years it had been his mission to strike fear in the hearts of others, but he had never wanted to strike it in the heart of the woman he had come to care deeply for.

"Promise me, Rhonda," he said again, shaking her slightly.

Tears trickled from her eyes and tracked slowly down her freckled cheeks. The sight of them dealt a blow to his heart.

"I swear I won't hurt you," he repeated, more gently this time. "I know what you're thinking, but it's not true. None of it. I did not kill Brian," he said emphatically.

Wes eased his hand away from Rhonda's mouth, expecting her scream to rend the still air.

"But it was your knife," she whispered hoarsely. Wes breathed a sigh of relief.

"Yes, it was my knife. But I didn't do it."

"Then why did you run? You…you held a gun to

my head!" she practically shrieked, striking out at him in sudden anger. Wes easily caught the small fist before it could land a blow. He pulled her hard against his chest to prevent any further struggle.

"I'm sorry," he whispered the apology, looking down into the stormy sea of her eyes. "It was just a reflex. I didn't plan to do it. If you hadn't given away that it was my knife, I would have gone in for questioning. I've been interrogated by a lot more intimidating figures than the Montmorency County Sheriff's Department. They never would have gotten anything out of me and they would have had to let me go. But once you gave it away that it was my knife, I knew I didn't stand a chance. If I had gone in, I never would have come back out. I had to run."

He raked the curls away from her temples then framed her face with his hands.

"But I would never hurt you Rhonda, you have to know that."

"How? How would I know? How do I know that you aren't lying like all the other times before?" Rhonda tried to ease back from his arms but Wes tightened his hold.

"What other times before? I've never lied to you." He saw the skepticism in her eyes and could practically read the thoughts that were running through her pretty head. "I did not murder my brother. Someone has set me up, I'm being framed."

He felt Rhonda begin to relax as his words sank in. "Then the things you told me about, they really happened, you didn't just make them all up?"

"No." He smiled down at her and pointed to his

battered face. "Did you honestly think I did this to myself?"

She looked down guiltily. "Well...I did sort of wonder."

Wes lifted her chin with a finger, forcing Rhonda to look at him once more.

"I haven't been lying to you. It's all true. Someone is after me and they want me dead, or at least in prison for life."

"You can't stay here," Rhonda said suddenly, fear returning to her eyes. "They have people out looking for you everywhere. They're watching your house and are probably watching this one, too. Nate is determined to catch you after the way you humiliated him, and what you did to me."

"Rhonda." Wes shook his head and chuckled at the irony of it all. "You forget who and what I am. The United States government paid a lot of money to insure I was trained in the art of not getting caught." He looked deeply into her eyes and smiled sadly. "Except by you. All the training in the world didn't keep me from being captured by you." Wes traced a finger down her cheek. "I had to see you. I knew what you would be thinking and I had to make you understand that I didn't kill Brian and explain why I did what I did. And I want you to be careful."

"Be careful of what?" Rhonda stared up at him, her eyes dazed.

"I know who's after my land. I saw him, heard him talking to someone about a plan he's been working on for ten years..."

Wes looked down into Rhonda's deep blue eyes

that were staring at him in wonder. Her lips were parted in surprise. Wes lost his train of thought and slowly lowered his head, his mouth settling softly over hers. Rhonda melted into his arms, her hands grasping the front of his t-shirt.

"You leave my sister alone!"

From the corner of his eye, Wes saw Becca launch herself at him.

"Daddy!" she cried out.

"Becca, no!" Rhonda said sternly, grabbing at her sister. "Hush up! It's okay, Wes wasn't hurting me!"

Wes finally got his arms wrapped around the bundle of fury, pulling her back against his chest. He could feel Becca trembling and hear her ragged breathing.

"Wes wasn't hurting me," Rhonda repeated softly, her warm gaze running between Wes and Becca.

"He wasn't?" Becca didn't sound convinced as she slanted a wary glance over her shoulder to stare up at Wes.

"No, I wasn't," Wes assured. "I love your sister, Becca. I won't ever hurt her." He loosened his hold and set Becca away from him. "Now I've got to get out of here before the sheriff shows up with guns blazing." He looked around the barn. "I don't suppose you have any food out here?"

"Food?" Rhonda questioned. "Not unless you want to eat some oats."

"Actually, that wouldn't be so bad." Wes nodded his head and watched as Rhonda lifted the lid on a barrel and brought a coffee can brimming with oats over to him. He scooped up a handful and stuffed it into his jeans pocket.

"There's some carrots and sugar cubes in the tack room," Becca added. She hurried to retrieve them, handing Wes the meager offering. He took them with a grateful smile.

"Thanks," Wes said. "If you need me, I'm hiding out by the old deer blind, just off the trail you ride the horses down. Be careful, both of you. Nothing is as it seems. No matter how it looks right now, nothing is as it seems."

He allowed his gaze to linger on Rhonda for just a moment more before heading from the barn and melting into the night.

CHAPTER TWENTY SEVEN

Wes hadn't killed Brian. He had finally kissed her. He *loved* her! Rhonda contemplated these amazing facts long into the night, her heart singing. But Becca had interrupted them before Rhonda could ask Wes who was after him. Who was she supposed to be careful of? He had warned that nothing was as it seemed, but what did that mean? And if Wes hadn't killed Brian, then who did? And how did his knife get in the pond?

Rhonda spent extra time in prayer the next morning, re-reading the Lord's words in Matthew 10:26. "Therefore do not fear them," Jesus had said. "For there is nothing covered that will not be revealed, and hidden that will not be known."

She needed to be patient, to wait upon the Lord's timing. Wes had declared his innocence and Rhonda had to believe him. She was trusting the Lord to be his vindicator. Whatever plot had been hatched from the shadows, eventually it would come to light. The truth would be shouted from the housetops.

It took all of Rhonda's strength not to shout the truth about Wes' innocence throughout the day as he continued to be the favorite topic of conversation at the Spot of Tea. Repeatedly, Rhonda had to clench her teeth to keep from defending Wes. She couldn't give away the fact that Wes had visited her. Rhonda knew she would immediately be arrested for aiding and abetting a fugitive. And it would look decidedly odd if the same woman he had held at gunpoint suddenly started proclaiming his innocence. So she bit her tongue, repeating to herself over and over again that God was in control.

"Vengeance is mine, I will repay, says the Lord," Rhonda muttered to herself as she prepared an order in the teashop kitchen.

"Calling down God's vengeance on Wes?"

Rhonda's head snapped around to see Blake lounging in the kitchen doorway, a small smile turning up one corner of his impish mouth.

"No." She shook her head in denial and turned her attention back to the order in front of her.

"Well, no one would blame you if you were," Blake said, sauntering across the kitchen. "Not after what he put you through. And after all that time when you were loving your neighbor as the Bible tells you to. I think God would understand you wanting to extract a little vengeance."

He came up behind Rhonda and laid his hands on her shoulders. Rhonda stiffened. How was she going to break up with Blake? She was going to have to tell him the truth, but not now. It was imperative she keep her feelings for Wes a secret until this whole mess was straightened out.

"Are you going to be home tonight?" Blake's voice was low, his breath warm against Rhonda's ear.

"Yes."

"Good." He gave her shoulders a squeeze. "I'll come by around nine. I've got a surprise for you."

Dropping a quick kiss on the top of her head, Blake turned and left the kitchen, leaving Rhonda staring after him perplexed.

"Oh, Blake," she whispered sadly to the now empty kitchen. "I'm afraid it's you who is going to end up surprised."

Rhonda glanced over at her bedside clock for the hundredth time, her stomach churning. It was nearly nine. Blake would be here any minute and she still hadn't found a way to tell him the truth. Resolutely, Rhonda flipped her Bible closed and tossed it down on the bed. She would just have to trust that God would give her the words when the time came. Getting up from the bed, Rhonda clattered down the stairs in search of Becca. Her parents had gone to Lewiston for dinner with her sister Val's family.

Rhonda found Becca in the family room lounging in an overstuffed chair, her feet dangling over the arm, her nose buried in a book.

"Blake's going to be here soon," Rhonda said. Becca laid the book upside down on her stomach and turned to look at Rhonda. "I...I may have to go out for awhile."

"Wes said he loves you." Becca looked at Rhonda with clear-eyed innocence. "Do you love him, too?"

"Yes," Rhonda admitted with a small smile.

"Then what about Blake?"

"I have to break it off with him. I'm planning to tell him tonight that I can't see him anymore."

"Oh." Becca scrunched up her nose in distaste. "That won't be fun."

"No, no, I don't think it's going to be any fun. But I have to be honest with him. It's only fair that he know the truth."

"Well, remember Wes said to be careful," Becca reminded, picking up her book. "He seemed to think there's danger lurking around out there."

"Maybe for Wes. He's the one on the run, not me." A knock sounded at the front door. "That's Blake. Pray for me." With a nervous wave of her fingers, Rhonda headed for the front door.

"Hey, sugar!" Blake greeted when Rhonda swung the front door open. The roiling in her stomach began once more and Rhonda took a deep breath.

O, Lord, have mercy! she silently pleaded. *Help me say the right thing.*

"It's a beautiful night," Blake declared as Rhonda stepped out on the porch. "I was thinking it's the perfect night for a walk. Come on."

Blake took her hand and headed down the driveway. Once out on the road, he leaned back his head and stared up at the sky.

"Look at those stars, will you. They're beautiful. Just like you, Rhonda. Have I told you lately how beautiful you are?" He stopped in the middle of the road, his intense brown eyes looking down at her.

"Blake..."

"I know I haven't told you that often enough." Blake framed her face with his hands. "But that's going to change. I realize now I could have lost you. Wes could have put a bullet through your head. I've wasted so much time, but no more."

"Wes wouldn't have shot me," Rhonda couldn't help but defend. The tumbling in her stomach increased with every word Blake spoke. "I...I don't believe he would have hurt me. He just used me to get away."

"It doesn't matter, that's all in the past." Blake took her hand once more and headed down the road at a brisk pace. "Soon Wes will be in prison and we won't have to worry about him anymore. Then we can both put the past behind us and look forward to a new day. Doesn't the Bible say something about that? Something about putting childish things away? Well, that's what I'm doing. I know I've been acting like a kid all this time, having fun, not wanting to settle down. But no more. I'm ready to grow up, Rhonda. I'm ready to give you everything you've ever wanted."

Rhonda slowed, realizing that Blake was leading her up the Cooper's driveway. The stone house shone pale in the moonlight, the dormer windows staring down at them like blind eyes.

"Blake, we shouldn't be here. The police, I don't

think they would like it." Rhonda hung back. Blake turned to smile at her.

"It's okay, baby," he said, tugging her hand. "This is all part of my surprise."

"I don't think I like this surprise," Rhonda began to argue.

"Of course you'll like this surprise. I just told you, I'm going to give you everything you've ever wanted."

They were at the house now and Blake triumphantly climbed the step to the porch. He turned to look down at her, his arms held open wide.

"All of this, it will all soon be mine, ours." Blake turned a slow circle. "You've always loved this house, you always said it was the house of your dreams. I'm going to give you your dream, baby. And on top of it all, we'll be rich."

"What are you talking about?" Rhonda asked, her brain reeling. She shook her head, trying to make sense of the scene before her. "This is Wes' house. How can you possibly say it will soon be yours?"

"I just told you, Wes is going to end up in prison for life. Imagine the legal bills he's going to rack up. You know how the justice system works, appeal after appeal. He'll go broke trying to pay for it all. And in the end, it won't matter because he's still going to spend the rest of his life in jail. He'll be forced to sell out, and I'm first in line to buy this farm."

"But you hate farming," Rhonda argued inanely, feeling sick at the thought of Wes spending one day behind bars. "You've told me time and again you would never break your back farming. And heaven knows you would never be rich."

Blake's laughter echoed through the night air.

"Silly, silly girl." He jumped from the porch and stood before Rhonda. "I would never farm this land. No, there's something much more valuable here than corn or potatoes."

"Gas," Rhonda whispered the word as the truth began to dawn.

"You already knew, huh?" Blake looked at her curiously. "Yep, this farm sits on one of the largest pockets of natural gas in Michigan history. A veritable gold mine. We'll both have what we've always wanted. You get the house you always wanted and I get you. And lots and lots of money."

"No." Rhonda shook her head and backed away, cold fear pounding with each beat of her heart. "I could never live here with you. It would be…" She swallowed hard. "It would be too awful. The memories and everything. I couldn't." Rhonda could feel the panic building. She had to keep her senses about her. She couldn't let on that she knew what Blake had done.

"Of course you can," Blake reasoned in an even voice. "We'll make new memories. Happy ones. Me, you and our babies. I thought you wanted lots of babies."

"I do, but Blake," her voice cracked and his eyes narrowed. "I can't marry you."

"Of course you can." Blake repeated, taking a menacing step toward her. "That's what all of this has been for. All my life, everything I've done, has all been leading up to this point. You led me to believe we had a future together. You love me."

"No." Rhonda shook her head again. "I don't want to hurt you, Blake. I care for you a great deal. You've been very good to me. I'm so sorry, but I don't love you. Not the way a woman should love her husband. It wouldn't be fair for me to marry you. You deserve a girl who will give you her whole heart. I hope you can forgive me for leading you on, I never meant to. But I know now that I could never be the wife you deserve. My heart," her voice caught. "My heart will always belong to someone else."

"Brian," the name came out in a low growl. "You can't still love Brian, he's been dead ten years!" Blake's voice rose an octave with each word.

"It's not Brian," Rhonda said quietly.

"Oh, I see now," Blake said, his voice going perfectly quiet and calm. He stepped closer to Rhonda and sneered down at her. "I've known it all along. It's Wes. The good for nothing, rotten murderer."

Rhonda didn't deny the charge. The glint in Blake's narrow eyes sent a chill clear through her bones.

"Wes isn't a murderer. He didn't kill Brian."

"No, no he didn't." Blake shook his head and with snake-like quickness reached out and grabbed Rhonda by the hair. "But now everyone will think he killed you!"

"What? Blake, what are you doing?" Rhonda cried as she was dragged past the house, her shoes sliding on the grass wet with dew. She searched around frantically. Where were the cops that should be guarding the house? Why wasn't anyone around to hear her cries for help?

Pain spiraled down from the top of her head, making tears prick her eyes. "Blake, you're hurting me," she whimpered.

The woods pressed close in around them as Blake pulled her on, heedless of her pleas to stop. Within moments, Rhonda found herself spun around by the hair. Moonlight glinted off the still surface of the pond.

"What are we doing here?" she asked, terror gripping her throat.

"Why, we've returned to the scene of the crime," Blake said triumphantly. "Act four, scene one." Roughly, he turned Rhonda to face him and she stared wide-eyed at the glittering dagger held before her face. "This time you get to be the victim. Wes will get blamed, of course. It's a shame, really. But ultimately, I'll still get most of what I wanted. Minus you, that is. Don't you understand?" His brown eyes suddenly turned pleading. "All of this, it's all been for you. I did it all for you!"

"Wes? Wes?"

Wes heard the broken sobs and the voice that was quietly calling his name in the dark.

"Wes? Are you here. Please, Lord Jesus, let Wes be here. Wes?" The voice called again.

Wes moved closer to the trail and heard the sniffling cry that ended on a quiet sob. A slender form fell, kneeling in the middle of the path. A curtain of hair fell forward, shielding the face.

"God, please help me find Wes!" the girl cried.

"Please held me help my sister."

"Becca?" Wes stepped from the shadows onto the moonlit trail. Becca's head snapped up and she leapt to her feet.

"Oh, thank God, Wes!" She threw herself into his arms and clung to his filthy t-shirt.

"What are you doing here?"

"You've got to help me! Blake has Rhonda, he's going to kill her!" Hysteria laced each word.

"Becca." Wes shook the girl roughly. "Calm down. You aren't making any sense. What happened?" Wes asked as the dread climbed up his spine.

"Blake came to the house. Rhonda told me she was going to break it off with him."

Wes nearly froze, remembering the curly-haired man at the phone booth a few nights before and the chilling words he had spoken into the phone.

"They went walking down the road and I...I followed. I remembered what you said, about nothing being as it seemed. Blake, he's never seemed to be what he acted like. There was just something about him." Becca shivered.

"So you followed them?" Wes prodded

"Yeah," Becca nodded her head. "I followed them to your place. I heard what Blake said. About giving Rhonda your house and about being rich. Rhonda told him." Becca gulped. "Rhonda told him she wouldn't marry him, that she didn't love him. He grabbed her by the hair and was dragging her toward the pond. I ran home, but Mom and Daddy aren't there. You have to help her, Wes!"

"Yes, of course I will," Wes stated, sounding

calm despite the slamming of his heart in his chest. "Run home and call the sheriff." Wes turned Becca around and gave her a nudge back up the trail. "Hurry now. You tell them what you told me. Ask for Nate, he'll listen to you. But don't tell him about talking to me. Just tell him about Blake. Oh, and Becca." The girl turned frightened eyes back to him. "Let Ranger loose. Now run!" Wes watched the teen sprint up the trail and disappear into the dark woods.

"Lord, help her hurry," Wes prayed as he turned and headed in the opposite direction. "Watch over her and Rhonda. Keep her safe until I can get there."

CHAPTER TWENTY EIGHT

On silent feet, Wes approached the clearing. The surface of the pond glittered like diamonds in the moonlight. Blake's blond head was clearly visible as he stood beneath the tall oak tree.

"Don't you understand?" Blake cried out. "All of this, it's all been for you. I did it all for you!"

"No, I don't understand," Wes heard the bewilderment in Rhonda's voice. "I don't understand any of this."

"Well, let me explain it all then." Blake was cool and collected as he stood before Rhonda. Wes caught sight of the glittering edge of a knife as Blake gestured around. "I told you before that I've loved you my whole life. Did you think I was joking? But first there was Brian. You could never see me because Brian was always in the way. So, I eliminated that problem."

"You killed Brian?" Rhonda screeched. "You killed Brian because of *me*?" Wes could hear the rage and grief building in Rhonda's voice. "How *could* you?"

"It was all terribly easy, really," Blake continued calmly. Wes felt the bile rise in his throat at the man's callous attitude. Had *he* ever been that cold about killing? The truth hit Wes smack in the heart. Yes, he had.

"I snuck into the house when everyone was gone." Wes brought his attention back to Blake's dissertation. "Brian had bragged to everyone at school about the knife Wes had gotten for his birthday. I took it. Then I waited until I caught Brian alone at the pond. I knew he was always sneaking off to get out of chores. I told Brian to break up with you. I poured my heart out to him and you know what he did? He laughed! Laughed hysterically. Told me he would never break up with you. That you were the only girl for him. That he would love you 'till the day he died." Blake shook his head as if mystified by the idea.

"I guess that was true enough, because he died that very day. It was all pathetically simple. I threw the knife in the pond, knowing that Wes would be blamed. To be honest, I expected them to find it way before now. I had no idea it would take ten years." Blake shook his head in disgust.

"You!" Rhonda threw herself at Blake in fury. He whirled around, brandishing the knife. Wes struggled to keep from shooting forward, his eyes glazing with a red haze of rage as he watched Blake yank

Rhonda's hair and place the tip of the knife at her throat. Breathing deeply, Wes removed the pistol from his belt and took aim as Blake continued his story.

"Now, now. Just calm yourself. You're the one who said you wanted to understand. I'm trying to make you see the extent of my love for you. I only killed Brian because I loved you so much. I had no idea you would be so besotted with grief that you couldn't even look at another guy. That whole escapade with the cop car? It was stupid, but I was only trying to get your attention. But then I realized I didn't have to worry because you never gave any other guy the time of day. So, I bided my time. Built up your confidence in me. And you have to admit, it was working. I had everything so well planned out."

Blake eased his grip on Rhonda's hair.

"The Coopers, that went exactly as planned. I couldn't believe how perfectly I pulled that off. But then Wes had to show back up." Blake sighed with disappointment. "I was counting on him getting killed in the war. Of course, there was no way I could go to Iraq and make sure he took one for his country. But I was so hoping he would. It would have saved me so much trouble."

"You killed Brian's parents?" Rhonda asked in stunned amazement. The white hot rage building in Wes nearly erupted.

"At first it was just you I wanted. I hadn't planned on the farm. Until I heard about the gas. I knew how much you loved this place, how you had always wanted to live here. I figured it would be easy enough to get. Take care of the parents then buy

Wes out. We would be set for life. I could give you everything you ever wanted and deserved. But Wes," Blake's voice filled with disgust. "Wes wouldn't sell. Stupid fool. Not even to save his own soul. I tried warning him off. I gave him plenty of time to get away. But you, in all my perfect planning over the years, the one thing I didn't figure on was you falling for Wes. Poor Brian. When you meet him in heaven tonight you're going to have a lot of explaining to do."

"No, Blake." Wes stepped from the trees, his pistol pointed straight at Blake's chest. "It's you who's going to have a lot of explaining to do to your Maker."

Rhonda's sharp intake of breath echoed through the clearing. Blake grabbed Rhonda and thrust her in front of him, holding the dagger to her throat.

"Go ahead and shoot, Wes," he taunted. "Kill her and save me the trouble. You were going to take the blame one way or another."

Wes stared into Rhonda's terrified eyes and tried to send her silent encouragement. Where were the cops? *Please God, let them get here soon!* He had to keep Blake talking, that was their only hope.

"I heard everything you said." Wes held the gun steady despite the roaring of blood in his ears. "You killed Brian and my parents. You're the one who's going to take the blame, Blake."

"Ha! And who will there be to tell? You? You honestly think they're going to believe you? I'll tell them I saw you kill her. I'll tell them I followed Rhonda down here, that I saw the two of you argue and that you put a knife through her chest just like

Help Me, Rhonda

you did your brother's. It will be easy enough to convince them."

"Will it, now?" The quiet, commanding voice spoke from behind Blake and he spun. Nate Sweeney stood there, gun drawn, along with Lydia Ebersol and Detective Epworth. Becca stood a few paces behind. "Go ahead, Blake. Convince me that it's not you holding a knife to Rhonda's throat right now."

Just then another form came barreling from the trees. Ranger, growling low, teeth bared, launched himself at Blake, his teeth sinking into the flesh of Blake's arm. The knife went flying. Rhonda lurched away from the ball of canine fury. Blake's scream curdled the night air as the dog toppled him to the ground.

"Get this dog off me!" he yelled. "This isn't what it looks like. I was just bluffing. I was just using Rhonda as bait, to get Wes out in the open. See, there he is!" He pointed at Wes with his free hand. "The fugitive you've been hunting for! Arrest him." He continued to try and wrestle out of Ranger's grip.

Wes moved forward and laid a hand on Ranger's collar.

"Let him go, boy," Wes commanded. The dog immediately obeyed.

"Arrest *him*!" Rhonda shrieked, pushing past Wes to point accusingly down at Blake. "He killed Brian! He admitted it. And he killed the Coopers and he was going to kill me! He killed Brian!" Dropping to her knees she pummeled Blake's chest with her fists as sobs wracked her. "He killed Brian!" she repeated over and over.

Lydia sprang forward, capturing Rhonda by the shoulders to pull her away. Rhonda's broken cries tore at Wes' heart.

"Blake Dalton, you're under arrest for the attempted murder of Rhonda Weaver," Detective Epworth intoned as he yanked Blake to his feet. Ranger gave a low growl. Wes placed a hand on the dog's head, watching as Blake was handcuffed and read his rights.

"And you." Nate turned steely blue eyes on Wes. "You and I have some unfinished business."

"I understand." Wes held out his gun, butt first. Nate quickly relieved him of the weapon. Wes turned and put his hands behind his back, waiting to be handcuffed.

"I don't think that will be necessary," Nate said gruffly. "But I do have to take you in and get this whole thing straightened out. Did you hear Blake confess to killing your brother and your parents?"

Wes nodded, swallowing the hard lump in his throat.

"Well then, we'll get your statement and Rhonda's too, and Becca's. Then there's the nasty little business of your alluding arrest. We'll see what a judge has to say about that."

Rhonda sat beside Wes in the back of the detective's car as they sped toward town. She stared unseeing out the window, heedless of the tears that continued to course down her cheeks. She felt Wes gently take her hand.

"You okay?" he asked quietly.

Help Me, Rhonda

She shook her head. Would she ever be okay again?

"It's not your fault."

"Brian's dead because of me!" Rhonda turned to look at Wes, his figure blurry beyond her tears. "Brian, your parents, everything that happened to you. It was all because of me."

"No," Wes said firmly. "It was all because of Blake. You had no way of knowing."

"But Brian's dead because he loved me," Rhonda wailed. Detective Epworth glanced into the rearview mirror, forcing Rhonda to get a grip on her emotions. Wes put a comforting arm around her and Rhonda melted against his chest.

"Brian's dead because there's evil in the world," Wes said against her hair. "And a very wise woman once told me that everything God allows into our lives, He uses it for good somehow. God has allowed all of these horrible things to touch our lives. It's up to us to allow Him to use it for His good."

"I feel so guilty," Rhonda sighed, pushing herself out of Wes' arms. "I never suspected Blake, never once. I had no idea so much evilness resided in his heart. How could I have not known?"

"Because you're good, untainted by all the horrible realities of the world beyond Atlanta. That's one of the things I love about you. I've seen enough of the big, bad world for both of us. Your innocent trust has helped take the bitter edge off my heart."

The confession made Rhonda's heart soar.

"Do you remember that first day we met after

you came home? You met me in the driveway with a gun." Rhonda didn't know why the memory made her smile.

"And you never even blinked, I was quite impressed."

"You have no idea how hard I was praying though." Rhonda chuckled and shook her head.

"And God answered. He does not forget the cry of the humble."

The detective pulled into the parking lot of the sheriff's department.

"It's a good thing, because I sure have done a lot of crying lately." Rhonda swiped a hand under her eyes as she got out of the car. " I hope this is the end of it."

Wes sat across the table from Nate as the deputy hastily filled out paperwork. The door opened and Wes turned his head to see Ken Morris walk in. The tall, bespectacled man had dark hair graying at the temples and carried a bulging briefcase. Nate's pen stopped scratching. He looked up as the attorney laid his briefcase on the table and clicked open the latches.

"Okay, the judge says you can go," Ken informed Wes with a tired smile as he removed a sheaf of papers from his briefcase. "I had to do a lot of talking to convince him you weren't a flight risk, after that stunt you pulled. But since we have several eyewitness accounts of Blake's confession, and with your exemplary military record, he finally capitulated and said you could be released on your own recognizance. You'll still need to go before him to clear up the matter of the weapons charge and alluding arrest. I assured him we'll be in court bright and early Monday morning."

Ken laid the necessary paperwork in front of Nate, who quickly scanned the documents.

"Alright, Cooper," Nate said, nodding his head. "It looks like you're free to go. But I'm sure we'll be meeting again." His intense blue eyes bored into Wes, who only smiled coolly in return.

"I'm sure we will, Sergeant," Wes agreed as he rose from the table. "But hopefully it will be on friendlier terms next time."

Nate rubbed at the shoulder that had been wrenched when Wes flipped him over onto his back.

"Guess that depends on which one of us is looking up from the ground," he returned with a small smile.

"Yeah, well." Wes had the decency to look sheepish for a moment. "Sorry about that. It wasn't anything personal. Just put it down to my military training. I hope you'll accept my heartfelt apology." Wes met Nate's stare head on. Several seconds ticked off the clock while the two men assessed one another. Finally, Nate gave a small nod.

"Apology accepted. Now get on out of here. I think Rhonda's still waiting out there for you." Nate gestured toward the door with his head.

Wes gladly reached for the door and pulled it open. He immediately saw Rhonda sitting in the small waiting area. She rose from the chair when Wes headed toward her.

"Well?" she asked, when he stopped a few feet

in front of her.

Wes thought about pulling her leg, making her think he was being held overnight. But when he looked into her worried blue eyes, he realized they both had had enough for one night. There would be time later for jokes.

"I'm free to go," he answered.

"Really?" Her smiled of relief brightened the drab room.

"Really. I have to see the judge on Monday. There's still a couple matters that have to be cleared up. But for now, Ken will drive us home." He hooked a thumb over his shoulder toward the lawyer who stood at the front desk. "Right now, all I care about is getting home, taking a shower and having something to eat."

"Carrots and sugar cubes?" Rhonda asked, stepping close and smiling up at Wes. He wrapped his arms around her and nuzzled her hair.

"Those carrots and sugar cubes saved my life, but if I never have to eat them again it would be fine with me. I am definitely glad that I'm *not* a horse! Maybe you could help me out with something a little more substantial?"

"Hmmm." Rhonda seemed to be giving it some thought. Then she smiled once more. "I think I may be able to help you out there. I think I know just what you need."

"I know just what I need, too," Wes declared, crushing Rhonda to him, mindless of his filthy clothes. "You. You're just what I need."

"You two ready to go home?" Ken asked,

approaching them. Wes and Rhonda stepped apart, their eyes glowing as they looked at one another.

"Yeah, we're ready," Wes answered with a nod. He took Rhonda's hand and headed for the exit. "Let's go home."

Help Me, Rhonda

EPILOGUE

Rhonda stood on the porch of A Stitch In Time, one hand resting upon her protruding belly as she waited to hear the Atlanta High School marching band coming down the street. She felt a tugging on her pant leg.

"Mommy, when will the soldiers come?"

Rhonda looked down into the freckled face of her three year old son.

"Soon, Brendan, soon." She heard the clashing of symbols, followed by the rest of the marching band. "I hear the band now, they'll be here any minute."

"Auntie Em, Auntie Em," Brendan called, spinning away from Rhonda. His auburn curls bounced as he ran to the end of the porch where Emma sat rocking baby Elijah. "Daddy's coming! Come on, Tiff'ny." He grabbed Emma and Tyler's five year old daughter by the hand. "Come see my daddy marching with the soldiers!"

Help Me, Rhonda

Rhonda's eyes misted with tears at Brendan's pride in his daddy. The two came to stand beside her.

"Can we go down on the sidewalk, Mommy? I want to see the soldiers."

"Sure, lets go down on the sidewalk. Is it okay if Tiffany goes with us?" Rhonda turned to Emma who gave assent with a nod and a smile. "Okay, guys, let's go. But stay on the sidewalk, you hear me? No running out in the street." She took each child firmly by the hand as the sound of music grew closer.

The trio joined Rhonda's parents on the sidewalk. David Weaver hefted Brendan into his arms as the band drew abreast of them, followed by the VFW and American Legion color guard. Rhonda bit her lip as she caught sight of Wes, still so handsome and trim in his uniform, even after being out of the service for nearly six years. It was sad, how few veterans were left to march in the Memorial Day parade. Their numbers seemed to grow smaller every year. But Wes was campaigning hard to get more of the Gulf War and Operation Iraqi Freedom veterans involved.

"Grandpa, put me down, I need to salute!" Brendan demanded. David hurried to oblige.

The flag drew up to them and Brendan solemnly put his little hand to his brow in salute as Rhonda placed a hand over her heart. Wes smiled at them as he marched past. Some of the more frail veterans rode in a convertible classic car behind the marchers and Brendan waved at them with enthusiasm.

"There's Uncle Nate!" Brendan cried, pointing to the sheriff's cruiser bringing up the rear. "Hi,

Uncle Nate!" he called. Nate returned the little boy's wave as he drove by.

When the parade had passed, Emma and Tyler and the baby joined them on the sidewalk and the small crowd crossed the road, walking to Briley Township Park where the wreath would be laid on the Thunder Bay River. Wes and the other veterans stood at parade rest as the short prayer was read, then the wreath was tossed onto the flowing waters of the river. They snapped to attention when the order was given and soon the shots of a 21 gun salute rang out across the water, reverberating through the trees along the shore. When the sound had died away, the haunting notes of a bugler playing taps broke the silence, followed by an echoing bugle on the opposite side of the river. Rhonda placed a hand over her heart and let the tears flow freely as the notes rang out clear and true, reminding her of all the men and women who had given their lives so that she could live free in the United States of America. Free to worship God, free to raise her children, free to live the rest of her life with the man she loved.

The last of the notes drifted away on the cool spring breeze.

"That song gets me every time," Penny admitted shakily from behind Rhonda's shoulder.

"Me too." Rhonda swiped at her cheeks with the heel of her hand.

"Daddy!" Brenda sprang forward and rushed into Wes' arms as soon as the assembly had been dismissed.

"Hey, buddy." Wes lifted his son and placed a kiss on his freckled cheek. He moved toward Rhonda and she was amazed at the way her heart held suspended in her chest, as if she had just gone over the top of a Ferris wheel. Even after five years! She thanked the Lord every time, for making every one of her dreams come true.

"Daddy, I told Tiff'ny that when I growed up, I'm going to be a soldier just like you and I'm going to march in a parade!"

"That's great, buddy, just great." Wes squeezed Brendan in a tight hug. "Nothing would make me and Mommy prouder, right Mommy?"

Wes held Brendan out and Rhonda gladly took the little boy into her arms.

"Right," she answered with a smile. "But can I have you a little while longer before you go off to the army?"

Brendan giggled. "I have to growed up a little bit first."

"Yep, you have to grow up a whole lot," Rhonda agreed. "Until then, how about you practice by being in the Lord's army?" She set Brendan on the ground and she and Wes each took one of his hands.

"Do I get to wear camouflage?"

"Sure," Wes answered. "You can wear whatever you want, Jesus doesn't mind. He's a good commanding officer, but it's not easy. You have to obey His orders. Do you know what His orders are?"

Brendan shook his head, looking up at his father with wide eyes.

"Jesus gave his commands in the Bible, so to be in His army you have to do things like listen to your mommy and share your toys with other children and most important of all, tell other people that Jesus loves them. Think you can do that?"

His little brows drew together in thought.

"It sounds awful hard."

Wes squatted down and looked Brendan straight in the eye.

"It is hard," he agreed. "But Mommy will help you and Daddy will help you, and Jesus will help you. Jesus is the best helper of all."

Wes stood and took Brendan's hand once more in his own as the three of them went to join Penny, Emma, Tyler, Tiffany and baby Eli on the sidewalk. Rhonda glanced at her husband and smiled as her heart overflowed with love.

*"God is our refuge and strength,
a very present help in trouble." Psalm 46:1*

THE END

Help Me, Rhonda

Dear Readers,

I want to thank each and every one of you for going on this "adventure" with me. The love, encouragement and support that I have received from so many of you is what really has kept me going during this entire writing process. I could not do this without all of you!

I know that many of you have fallen in love with Atlanta, and you feel that you have come to know Emma and Tyler, Penny and Nate, and Rhonda and Wes. I hope that they will live on in your hearts long after you have closed this book. So many of you have asked me, "what's next?" and I know you would love for the Northwoods Adventures to continue forever. But after much prayerful consideration, I have decided that too much of a good thing is a bad thing. And so, this adventure will end here.

But, this is not the end of my writing career! I have many, many more stories swirling around in my head, many more characters waiting to come to life. If you would like to receive advanced notification of the publication of my next project, e-mail me at amycorron@northwoodsnovels.com, and I will add you to my mailing list. Also, you can log onto my web site, www.northwoodsnovels.com, to see my calendar of events which lists my many book signings and speaking engagements. And you might even get a sneak peak at my next book!

I love hearing from readers, so please e-mail me with your comments or questions. Thank you all for taking this wonderful roller coaster ride with me! May God continue to bless and keep you all in His love and mercy and grace!

Sincerely,
Amy A. Corron